# The Escape

Compass Key, book five

Maggie Miller

*Second chances do exist.*

Five former sorority sisters, all in their 50's, undertake the adventure of a lifetime when a mysterious invite reunites them at an exclusive resort set on a private island.

Olivia was the quiet one. Her divorce from her alcoholic husband freed her in many ways but caused a rift with her daughter that seems impossible to heal.

Amanda was the perfect one. Widowed and desperately broke but hiding it, she needs a new start more than anyone can imagine.

Leigh Ann was the cheerleader. Her ongoing divorce is completely amicable, or so she'd like everyone to believe. The truth isn't quite as rosy.

Grace was the party girl. And she still is, much to the dismay of her husband, who's struggling to keep their restaurant afloat. Grace hopes her time away will give them both the space she thinks they need.

Katie was the brains. Now she's incredibly successful but hiding secrets that could change her life if they were to get out.

When their beloved house mother invites them on an all-expenses-paid vacation, then drops a huge surprise on them, the five friends face a major decision. Can they overcome their pasts in order to take advantage of the amazing future being offered?

Take the journey to Compass Key with them and find out.

# Chapter One

The early morning sun came through the blinds, waking Amanda. She blinked, realizing she'd forgotten to close them the night before, but she didn't mind. There were worse things to wake up to than a view of endless blue sky, swaying palm fronds, and abundant sunshine.

She smiled and got out of bed, then padded downstairs to the kitchen to make coffee. Something she could actually do now, thanks to Duke and his generosity.

Yesterday afternoon, he'd taken her grocery shopping, which had allowed her to stock her new kitchen with all of the essentials, coffee being at the top of that list.

She would pay him back very soon. For all of it. She'd kept the receipt.

One of her first goals was to open a local bank

account and get checks. That would happen as soon as she got paid. And she had some free time.

Which would happen soon, so long as everything else was still on track with the resort. The paid part, not the free time.

She was meeting with all of the girls at Iris's house for breakfast this morning. Olivia was going to give them an update on the embezzlement case.

Olivia, Vera, and Eddie had gone to the police station yesterday to report the crime, share the evidence Olivia had uncovered, and get the investigation underway. Amanda hoped the situation could be resolved quickly and easily but stealing nine million dollars was no small thing. It might take a while to sort out. If it *could* be sorted out.

At the very least, it seemed to Amanda that Freda Switzer, the accountant, and possibly Chef Glenn, her boyfriend, would have charges filed against them. Maybe they'd even end up going to jail.

Amanda got the creamer out, then leaned against the counter. That's exactly what would have happened to her late husband, Brian, if he hadn't driven his car into a tree to escape the allegations against him. But his death hadn't solved anything for her. It had only made things worse.

Thankfully, Iris and her generous offer of ownership of one-fifth of the island and the resort meant

Amanda was getting a much-needed second chance. An escape from the dismal reality of her old life.

The coffee maker dripped the last few drops into her cup. She added a little sugar and a splash of creamer, then took it back upstairs to shower and get ready for the day.

She turned on the shower to let the water heat. What an interesting day it was going to be, too.

There'd been a flurry of activity the day before yesterday that had culminated with Iris's return from the hospital, then going right into Olivia's bombshell announcement to the group that she'd discovered the embezzlement.

Because of that, Iris had asked the five friends to stay longer on the island than they'd originally intended. She'd wanted them to stay so badly that she'd offered to help them hire moving companies to go to their homes, pack their things up, and transport it all here, eliminating any need for them to leave the island and do it themselves.

After some discussion, Leigh Ann and Katie had decided to officially accept Iris's offer to become part-owners in the resort, which meant all five of them were in.

Grace had promised to make sure her trained-chef husband, David, was ready to take over the resort's restaurant full-time due to the likelihood that the current head chef, Glenn, was about to become permanently unavailable.

That was another reason Iris had asked them all to stay, too. She'd told them she wanted them around to help her and the resort get through the investigation and the turmoil it would undoubtedly cause.

Amanda understood completely. She'd gone through much of her late husband's troubles alone, not wanting to bring further grief or embarrassment to herself or her children.

She didn't need Iris's offer of moving help, however, as she'd already asked her sister to do that for her. Of course, she didn't have an entire house to worry about. Her life had been pared down to a large handful of boxes in the last couple of years, in part because of her husband's death but mostly because of the tsunami of bills and debt he'd left her with.

The house had been sold right away, and she'd been forced to move in with her mother, causing Amanda to whittle her things down to the bare minimum.

Her mother, not so affectionately known as Militant Marge, hadn't wanted a lot of boxes cluttering up her garage, so Amanda had gotten rid of even more things. She'd sold off some of her clothing, shoes, and purses. Digitized most of her paper mementos. Given away odds and ends.

She stepped out of the shower, and wrapped

herself in a towel. She'd be getting rid of even more possessions when those remaining boxes showed up.

Winter clothes, for one thing. She could see keeping a few outfits, along with a coat, hat, gloves, and a pair of boots, should she ever need to travel north again. But there was no point in storing an excess of sweaters, warm tights, turtlenecks, wool pants, or any of the things that had been her staples during the cold months.

Maybe she should call Denise to see if her sister wanted any of her clothing. Not a bad idea. It would save them both some work and Amanda some money, because again, once she got paid, she'd be paying her sister back for the cost of shipping those boxes.

Amanda finished her makeup and glanced at the time. The call would have to wait until after breakfast.

She dressed simply in khaki walking shorts and a flowered silk shell with her white sandals. She put her jewelry on, grabbed her phone and the bungalow key, then carried her cup down with her.

That went in the sink. She turned the coffee pot off and was out the door. The walk didn't take long. Iris's house was basically around the corner from the staff bungalows. But as she walked, Amanda went through her to-do list for the day.

She needed to work on signage for the celebrity wedding that was now only three days away, on Sunday. Nothing too fancy, but wedding signs were all the rage and she thought that a sign on the beach indicating the Parker-Campbell Wedding might be nice. Maybe one in the Treasure Pavilion, too.

Years ago, she'd taken a series of calligraphy classes, but she wasn't sure how much of that skill she'd retained. She planned to test it out today if she could find a chalkboard and some chalk.

Those had to exist around here somewhere. Chalkboard signs were popular all over. And practical, too, since they could be used over and over again.

Maybe Grace had seen one in the storage room during her search for the decorative arch and dance floor—which reminded Amanda she needed to have a look at that dance floor and make sure it was in usable shape. It would probably have to be cleaned. Amanda could do that today, too.

She also needed to check in with Mindy, the florist, and make sure that was all going smoothly. Her husband, a retired photographer, had agreed to come out of retirement to do the photos. That was a real boon, since Amanda had been unable to find anyone else to do it.

Plus, Amanda wanted to confirm details with the officiant, and have a chat with Duke's sister, Jamie, about her playlist for the reception.

Amanda exhaled. She would never normally have taken on such a short-notice affair, but the groom, J. Henry Parker, was one of Hollywood's hottest directors at the moment, and he and his girlfriend, plus some of their family and friends, were scheduled to arrive at Mother's Resort early Sunday afternoon for a week-long stay.

That stay was actually going to be their honeymoon, since upon arrival, J. Henry wanted to surprise his fiancée, supermodel Miranda Campbell, with this secret wedding.

Amanda wasn't about to turn down the chance to bring some additional business to the resort while also carving out a niche for herself. What good were her skills as a wedding planner if she couldn't put them to use here?

Making such a high-profile guest happy was a big bonus, too.

Iris's house was up ahead. One of her cats, Calico Jack, lounged on the landing of the newly built ramp up to the first floor.

Amanda smiled at him as she went up. "You found a good spot to sun in, huh?"

He rolled over onto his back, stretching a paw up toward her. She gave his chest a quick scratch, then finished her walk to the front door.

Vera answered her knock. "Come on in."

"Thanks." Delicious aromas were coming from the kitchen. Bacon, mostly. Amanda entered and saw Leigh Ann, Olivia, and Iris already at the table having coffee. Vera went back to the kitchen.

"Morning." She joined them, putting her hand on the empty chair on the other side of Leigh Ann. "This all right?"

"Absolutely," Leigh Ann said. "How's life in a staff bungalow?"

Amanda smiled. "It's glorious. I love it. I can't wait to have you all as neighbors." She pulled the chair out and sat, looking at Iris. "How are *you* doing?"

"I'm fine, thank you." Iris was recovering from the surgery to repair the hip she'd broken in a fall down the steps to the second floor. She made a face. "Nick is coming by after breakfast for my first round of physical therapy at home. I am not looking forward to that."

Amanda nodded. "I'm sure you're not."

More knocking at the door. Leigh Ann hopped up. "I'll get it, Vera."

She ran to the door and let Katie and Grace in.

"Morning, girls," Katie called out.

"Morning," they all said back.

"It smells so good in here," Grace said. She sat by Amanda. "Anything new on the wedding front?"

"Nothing yet," she answered. "Any chance you saw a chalkboard in that storage room when you were looking for the extra chairs?"

"Hmm." Grace's eyes narrowed. "Not that I remember, but once I found the chairs, the arch, and the dance floor, I stopped looking. You want me to check again?"

"I don't mind having a look. Or helping."

Grace nodded. "Then let's go over after breakfast."

"Okay."

Leigh Ann had gone into the kitchen to give Vera a hand and now the two women were bringing food to the table. Vera carried a big casserole dish of quiche. "Bacon, onion, and sundried tomato quiche with cheddar and chives."

Amanda's mouth watered. She saw a lot of happy faces around her, too.

Leigh Ann had two large serving bowls, both with big spoons sticking out of them. One was filled with home fries and the other with fruit salad.

"This looks incredible," Amanda said. But then, all she'd had for breakfast the day before was a granola bar, and that was only because Duke had brought it and a cup of coffee to her. He'd brought her a banana, too, which she'd eaten as an afternoon snack.

"Hang on," Vera said. "I've got coconut muffins, too."

Grace groaned. "And here I'd actually lost a couple pounds. So much for that."

They all laughed. Iris was practically beaming, clearly thrilled to have them all at her table.

Amanda understood. These women were more than just friends. They were family. "You know, Iris, we should do this once a month. If we can. All of us together like this. Wouldn't that be nice?"

Iris nodded. "I would love that. But only if Vera is up to it."

Grace shook her head. "Vera doesn't have to do the cooking. If you don't mind us in your kitchen, we can all pitch in."

Amanda lifted her cup of coffee. "I'm in."

They all raised their drinks in a toast to the idea.

Vera came over with the basket of muffins. "I'm all for help in the kitchen, but does this pitching in include cleaning up, too?"

Olivia laughed. "Good question."

The food got passed around and dished up, and when they all had full plates, Iris spoke. "Now that we're settled in and everyone has their food, why don't you give everyone an update on how things went at the police department yesterday, Olivia?"

"I'm dying to hear," Amanda said.

Olivia nodded. "I'd be happy to." She took a sip of water, then looked around at everyone, her face taking on a much more serious expression. "According to Detective Murphy, it's very possible that arrests could be made today."

Amanda hadn't been expecting that and from the looks on the faces around her, neither had anyone else.

# Chapter Two

Grace sucked in a breath at that news, her mind instantly working. "Really?" If one of those arrests was Chef Glenn and it happened at the resort, that would definitely get people talking. And not in a good way. David would undoubtedly get a lot of questions from the kitchen staff.

Anyone who saw it, or heard about it, would want to know what was going on. Rumors and gossip would spread like wildfire, she imagined.

Olivia nodded. "Really. Detective Murphy didn't want to get too specific, but his goal is to get access to Freda and Glenn's bank records today."

"He's getting warrants," Amanda said.

Olivia nodded. "Must be. He said once that happens, they'll compare Freda and Glenn's accounts with my forensic analysis and if either one shows the police what they're looking for, they'll be able to move forward."

Grace hoped that happened. "Fingers crossed Freda's account shows an excess of nine million dollars and that she hasn't spent it all."

"That won't necessarily matter," Olivia said. "I mean, if she's spent it. They're going to look at any major purchases over the last six years, too." She smiled. "I don't mean to brag, but Detective Murphy was very impressed with the audit I did. He said that kind of solid evidence will speed up this process immensely."

Iris patted Olivia's arm. "Good girl. I'm so grateful to you for that." Then she looked at Grace. "Did you get a chance to speak to your husband about taking over as full-time head chef?"

Grace nodded. That had been an interesting conversation. "I did and David is basically doing Chef Glenn's job now, so he's good to go. He was less shocked than I expected him to be when I told him what we suspected was going on." Her eyes narrowed. "According to David, Chef Glenn has mentioned more than once how he plans to retire to Ecuador. I looked it up and Ecuador does have an extradition treaty with the U.S., so even if he does go there, the police can get him and Freda back."

Olivia snorted. "We might have an extradition treaty with Ecuador, but that doesn't mean they'll honor it. I know this from an article I read in *CPA Monthly* last year. There are quite a few countries like that."

Katie's brows went up. "There's a magazine for CPAs?"

Grace laughed as Olivia answered, "Yes, and I'm sure all of you would find it extremely boring." Then she looked at Iris. "But that info about Ecuador seems like something that should be passed on to Detective Murphy."

"I agree," Iris said.

"I'll take care of it," Olivia said.

Iris looked around the table again. "Prepare yourselves, ladies. If there are arrests made today or anytime this week, even if they don't happen here at the resort, word will travel. There will be questions and speculation. Mother's is very much like a small town in that respect."

Grace sighed. "I was just thinking about that. How do you want us to handle that? What should we say?"

Iris thought a moment, then shifted her gaze to Katie. "Can you work with me to prepare a statement from the resort that can explain things to employees and also let them know how to answer any questions they might get from guests? Something semi-vague, but upbeat."

"Sure," Katie said. "I am the Communications Director, after all."

"Thank you. I'd like to do that right after breakfast." Iris smiled. "Now, on to happier news. Amanda, how are the plans for the wedding coming?"

"Really well," Amanda answered. "We're on track to making it happen. I almost can't believe that, since we had such a short amount of time to work with, but everyone here has been willing to help or make suggestions, and that's what's made it possible."

"Do you hope to do more weddings here?" Iris asked.

Amanda nodded and looked at Grace. "With Grace and David's help with the food part of the receptions, I absolutely do. Compass Key is such a romantic getaway. Why wouldn't people want to get married here? Although it would be nice if I had a little more notice for future events."

From the kitchen, Vera snorted in amusement.

"You know," Iris said. "Once upon a time, Arthur and I talked about adding on a traditional hotel building that could provide a small number of standard rooms and another restaurant. Possibly another pool area. Something like that could be very handy if Compass Key becomes a wedding destination."

"I like that idea," Grace said. "But wouldn't that take away some of the exclusivity of this place?"

Iris nodded. "That was one of the reasons we never did it. Mother's is special in part because it only allows for a limited number of guests at a time."

"Also," Katie added, "you get the clientele you do because those who can afford it know that coming here means being left alone. Too many guests and you'd lose some of that."

"I agree," Iris said. "It's a slippery slope."

Leigh Ann gestured with her fork. "So you're saying there's still room to build here?"

"Oh, yes," Iris said. "You'd be surprised how much. On both sides of the island, too."

Grace glanced around the table. She could practically see wheels turning in her friends' heads. She smiled. "Look at all of the dreaming going on."

They laughed, Iris with them. She nodded. "It's something to think about it, isn't it? I'll see if I can dig up those surveys in the next few days so you can have a look for yourselves."

"That would be great," Olivia said. "Iris, I have a question for you."

Iris looked at her. "Yes?"

"Now that you're back here and feeling better, and you have that ramp out there, have you finally given up on the notion that you're leaving us?"

"Good question," Grace said. "One that had better have a good answer."

Iris smiled. "You girls really want me to stay."

Vera spoke up. "We all do."

Grace nodded. "She's right. And while you have to want to stay, obviously, there's more to it than that. We *need* you to stay. There's so much you can teach us about this place and how to run it the way it should be run. No one else can do that."

"They can't," Amanda said. "Because they didn't build it. Who else is going to keep us mindful of how Arthur would have wanted things done?"

Leigh Ann nodded. "That's a great point."

"Stay, Iris." Katie's eyes shone with sincerity. "Think about how much the cats would miss you. And how much you'd miss them."

"Duke, Jack, and Grant didn't build that ramp because they wanted you to leave," Leigh Ann added.

Iris nodded. "I suppose they didn't." She took a breath. "So long as my recovery goes well, I'd be happy to stay."

Grace smiled and clapped her hands. "Now *that* is worth celebrating. I didn't want to say anything, but David felt bad that you were leaving. He's barely had a chance to get to know you. He'll be so happy that he'll be able to cook for you some more."

Iris looked a little weepy. "You girls are so wonderful. I can't imagine leaving you at this point. But you realize, I've given you everything. I'll have to pay you rent to stay!"

"Not a chance," Olivia said. "I hereby motion that Iris be allowed to live rent-free in her own home for as long as she wants."

"I second that," Grace said.

Vera brought a fresh pot of coffee over. "Here, here."

Grace looked at Olivia. "She's got to have an income, too."

Olivia nodded. "I promise we'll get it all worked out."

"Oh, that's too much," Iris said. "I don't need an income. I have plenty in my personal account with what Arthur left me. And you girls need to focus on running this place and recovering from Freda's theft. Trust me, there are many things that haven't been done that need to be."

"I'm sure," Leigh Ann said. "I know for the first couple of years in the studio, any big things that needed doing got set aside until the money was there. Considering you've lost millions over the last few years, it's understandable some things would have been put off."

Grace looked at Iris. "What are the most pressing, do you think?"

Iris pinned a chunk of potato with her fork. "The biggest one is the main building. It needs to be reroofed and repainted. The staff pool needs to be drained and refinished. There are other repairs, too. Another thing is, there are at least a dozen long-term employees who haven't gotten raises in the last few years because of all this, but they should have."

Olivia nodded. "I promise we'll get all of that done.

I've already looked at the possibility of raising the rates for guests."

Grace spoke up. "And David will find ways to save money in the kitchen, if need be. He's a genius with food costs."

Amanda wiped her mouth. "The resort will definitely make some money off this wedding and, hopefully, we'll have more of them in the future."

Contentment filled Iris's gaze. "There's hard work ahead of us, I know that, but it does my heart good to know you'll all be here with me. Together, we'll get through this." She smiled at all of them. "What else has been going on? There's more to your lives than just this place. Leigh Ann, how are things with your divorce? Katie, what about you and Owen? Still going strong? Olivia, are you and Jenny still on good terms? Amanda, any word from your mother? Grace, you and David seem back on track, yes?"

Everyone looked at each other to see who would answer first.

# Chapter Three

Katie took the lead by raising her hand. "I have news, but it's not about me and Owen, although things between us are wonderful." She also had news she couldn't share just yet. News she knew would make Olivia – and her daughter, Jenny – very happy.

"That's marvelous," Iris said. "What other news do you have?"

"Well, as you know, *Star Watch* revealed some very personal information about my past recently."

"Terrible thing," Iris said. "They should be sued."

Katie laughed. "They were. Or at least they were threatened with it, thanks to Owen. They backed off pretty quickly and, thanks to his attorneys, we settled out of court for two and a half million dollars."

Shocked silence greeted her.

Then she was met with laughter and applause. She nodded at them all. "Isn't it amazing? Granted, some of that will go to pay his attorneys, because I'm not letting him foot that bill while I make out like a bandit, but it's still a nice payday."

She looked at Iris. "I'm happy to put that money toward any repairs that need doing. I really am. I don't need it to live on. With the new movie deal especially, I'm in a good place financially."

"I won't hear of it," Iris said. "That's your money."

"Um..." Katie raised her brows. "Now that I'm part-owner, I don't think you can stop me from investing in the resort."

Olivia snorted. "She's right, Iris. You can't stop her."

Iris rolled her eyes. "I've created monsters. Wonderful, beautiful monsters."

Katie chuckled. "I do have some more news." She took a breath, her nerves kicking in for no good reason. "I talked to my son."

Forks went down. Vera came out from the kitchen and stood next to Iris. But no one said anything for what seemed like several minutes.

"It went well," Katie said. "Really well."

A collective exhale could be heard.

Iris put her hand to her mouth. "Oh, Katie. That must have been the best experience."

Katie nodded. "It was something I wasn't sure would ever happen. He's such a nice person. Kind and understanding. Smart. Funny."

"How could he be anything less?" Olivia asked. "He's your son."

Katie smiled and fought back tears. "We're going to meet sometime this summer. No date yet, but he teaches school, so his summers are open."

"That's awesome," Leigh Ann said. "I can't even imagine what that was like for you. I'm so happy."

"Me, too," Grace said. "Wow."

"Wow is right," Amanda added. "Who would have guessed that something good would have come from all of that paparazzi nonsense?"

Katie shook her head. "Not me, but to be honest, they're the ones who lost. I got money and my son. I basically hit the invasion-of-privacy lottery."

They all laughed some more.

"Oh!" Katie realized she'd forgotten one piece of information. "And get this—I'm a grandma. He's got one little girl and a baby on the way."

Iris squeezed her hands together. "Please bring them here. I want to meet them. It's been ages since I've held a baby."

"I hadn't thought about that," Katie admitted. Would Joshua be interested in coming to her? Asking him to travel with kids might be too much. But Mother's was a pretty sweet carrot to dangle. And if she paid their way... "I can talk to him about it, see what he says, but no promises."

"Of course," Iris said. "But how exciting for you either way."

Katie nodded. "You can say that again."

"How's Sophie doing with being here?" Grace asked.

"Really well." Katie shook her head. "Better than I thought she would. But then, she's gone all moony-eyed over Gage, Owen's security guy. He's gone a little moony-eyed over Sophie, too. I think that's helped. But according to her, she's fine with moving out of Brooklyn, something I *never* thought she'd say."

Katie looked around. "I suppose you all know by now that Sophie and I are a package deal, which means she'll be moving here with me."

"The more the merrier," Iris said. "Although a staff bungalow might not be enough room for you."

"I haven't seen one yet," Katie said. "But I think we'll be all right in there. Our place in Brooklyn isn't exactly huge."

"There is another option," Iris said. "And I'll put this out there for all of you to consider, so that you can decide among yourselves, but the second floor of this house is available. As you know, Nick is staying on the third floor. I'm dearly hoping he'll decide to stay past my recovery. I realize now I should have brought that up with all of you, but I like having him around."

"Of course you do." Katie had a sudden, fierce understanding of Iris's need to keep Nick close. "He's

Arthur's son. You must see Arthur in him. That has to be a comfort to you, knowing Arthur lives on in Nick."

"It is," Iris said. "But besides that, I thought it would be nice to have a doctor on the island. Peter does a tremendous job of filling both roles as a paramedic and a massage therapist, but Nick is a very capable young man."

Olivia nodded. "We've definitely seen that. I have no problem with him staying on. Especially if he's contributing to making things better and looking after you."

Katie agreed with that. With Iris staying, Vera couldn't be expected to be her housekeeper, cook, *and* nursemaid. Having Nick on hand would be invaluable. "Anyone opposed to Nick staying?"

Leigh Ann, Amanda, and Grace all shook their heads.

"Then it's settled," Katie said. "Nick can keep on living in the third floor suite for as long as he likes."

"You're all so kind," Iris said. "But the fact remains that the second floor of this house is unoccupied. It's got three bedrooms, two baths, and an open-floor kitchen, dining, living room area, much like this floor. You should all go up and have a look. If one of you were to move in there, it would mean having another staff bungalow available for employees."

Amanda held her hands up. "I'm sure it's lovely, but

I'm not moving. I adore my bungalow. It's perfect for me."

Leigh Ann nodded. "I'm thinking the bungalow will be just fine for me, too. I don't need much space."

Olivia smiled. "If you think you're going to talk me out of living next door to Eddie, you haven't been paying attention."

Grace grinned at Olivia. "I wouldn't even try." Then she looked at Iris. "David comes home pretty late from the restaurant. I'm not sure you'd want someone wandering around above you at midnight every night. A bungalow would suit us just fine."

They all looked at Katie. She'd never considered there might be somewhere besides the staff quarters to live in. "I'll have a look at it. I wouldn't mind having more space, since Sophie will be with me. And Fabio, my cat."

Iris lit up. "I forgot about your cat. Maybe he'd like to get to know my babies."

"He might," Katie said. "I know he'd love the big porches. And having that third bedroom would mean I'd have a dedicated office space. That's kind of a big thing for me."

Iris nodded. "The smallest of the bedrooms is already situated as an office. Arthur used it that way."

Katie checked the expressions around her. She really didn't want to step on anyone's toes, even though they'd all just given reasons why the second floor wasn't for them. "No one would mind?"

They all shook their heads.

"All right. I'll check it out after we're done here." She looked at Iris. "And after we get that statement drafted."

"Invite your sister over if you want, so she can have a look at it, too," Iris said.

"I will," Katie said. What would Sophie think? She didn't know Iris the way Katie did. Would it be weird for her to live above the woman? And below Nick? Of course, life in Brooklyn meant close neighbors. Maybe Sophie wouldn't care.

Then again, maybe Sophie wouldn't want to leave Owen's guest cottage. Not as long as Gage was at Owen's estate.

But Katie was done with her news, so she looked at Leigh Ann. "What about you? How's the divorce going?"

# Chapter Four

Leigh Ann blew out a long, slow, frustrated breath. "It's not. Even using the adultery angle isn't helping. I wish I could tell you differently, but Marty refuses to agree to my terms and sign the paperwork. He honestly thinks he's going to talk me into giving up my demands. He's so stubborn. I'd strangle him except that wouldn't help."

Amanda had a grape stuck on the end of her fork. She gestured with it. "Not a bad Plan B, though. Maybe you could just strangle his girlfriend."

Olivia shook her head. "I can't believe she's not pushing him harder to get this divorce over and the wedding underway. Especially with what we know about her."

Vera hovered nearby, a curious expression on her face. "What do you know about her?"

Leigh Ann looked over. "Katie overheard them talking, and apparently, Candi is pregnant, which is why she wants to do this wedding so quickly."

Vera's eyes widened. "You're kidding."

Katie nodded. "I heard it with my own ears. I was in the pool near them while they had the whole conversation."

Iris sighed, then clucked her tongue. "I'm so sorry that man continues to be a thorn in your side, Leigh Ann. The good news is he and his girlfriend must be leaving soon. Maybe he'll do it when he gets home."

"Maybe," Leigh Ann said. "But I was really hoping to get this thing settled already and get that big payout from him." She explained about her plan to hold the note on the studio for her instructors. "I'm not sure how fast I can make that happen now. Or *if* I can make that happen. I'm so frustrated!"

"I bet," Grace said. "I wish we could come up with a plan to help you."

Amanda's eyes narrowed and she smiled. "Maybe we can."

"What are you thinking?" Leigh Ann asked. She was game for anything.

The gleam in Amanda's eyes spoke volumes. "With all of this wedding planning I've been doing and how I hope to do more of them here at the resort in the future, maybe we should start advertising a little."

"Go on," Leigh Ann said.

Amanda glanced at Iris. "If you wouldn't mind, I

was thinking I could create a flyer to distribute to the guest bungalows announcing our new wedding services. I don't necessarily expect to get any immediate business out of it but for Candi, it might be a reminder of what she's hoping for."

Iris nodded. "I like it."

Amanda looked at Katie. "Will you help me? I know you already have work on your plate with the embezzlement statement, but—"

"I'm in," Katie said. "I love the idea. I think we could push it further, though."

"Meaning?" Olivia asked.

"Meaning that any time any of us is near Candi, we talk about the wedding. About the flowers, the food, how beautiful the bride will be, anything that might help stir up her wedding fever. Without giving away the actual identities of the bride and groom, of course."

Olivia smiled. "Oh, that's good."

"I agree," Leigh Ann said. "That's brilliant. It's like psychological warfare. We'll get her so wound up about getting married that it'll be all she can think about, and she'll drive Marty mad with it."

Iris rubbed her hands together. "It's a little devious, but so clever. Anything you need me to do, you just tell me."

Leigh Ann nodded. "Thank you. You guys are the best." She wasn't entirely sure the idea would work, but she was willing to try just about anything.

"You know," Grace said. "You could just talk to her yourself. Woman to woman."

Leigh Ann wasn't so sure about that. "And say what?"

Grace shrugged. "Tell her you understand what she's going through. Become her friend. Or at least make her think you're her friend. If she likes you, she'll sympathize with you. She might really get on Marty's case to wrap this thing up."

"Or," Iris said. "If you really want to play games, you could plant the seed that his refusal to sign the divorce papers means he has no intention of marrying her. Or tell her that he tried to get you back."

Leigh Ann laughed. "Iris, I had no idea you could be so ruthless."

Iris smiled. "When it comes to protecting those I love, I am more than capable of showing my claws."

Behind her, Vera nodded. "You girls have no idea what Iris has been through. Being married to a man like Arthur made her the target of a lot of jealousy."

Iris waved Vera's words away. "That was a long time ago. And some things are better left in the past."

Leigh Ann was interested, but if Iris didn't want to talk about it, she understood. "Even without hearing those stories, we know how strong Iris is. After all, she had to deal with all of us when we were in college."

Grace laughed. "Now there are some stories."

Amanda shook her head. "I'm almost afraid of

some of those. I know I was a handful in those days. So full of myself."

Leigh Ann glanced at her friend. "You weren't always. Just because you and Olivia didn't get along back then didn't mean you weren't a good friend to me." Plus, Leigh Ann had understood how much pressure Amanda's mother had put on her.

"Thank you," Amanda said. "But I'm very glad Olivia and I have moved past that."

"So am I," Olivia said.

"We all are," Leigh Ann said.

"What are your plans for the day?" Iris asked Leigh Ann.

"I was hoping to have a look around at the bungalow that might be mine, then maybe see Grant at the studio, and at some point, I'd love to get a tour of the spa, since that's one of the areas you'd like me to manage."

Iris nodded. "Very good. And you're right, I would like you to manage the spa. I think there's a lot more that can be done there. It's one of the places that hasn't been upgraded in a while due to finances, so please, look at it with that in mind."

"I will," Leigh Ann said.

"Has Grant taken the painting to the studio yet? His big party is tomorrow night, isn't it?"

Leigh Ann nodded in answer to Iris's question. "It is tomorrow, but I don't think he's taken the painting to the gallery yet, unless he did it without me realizing it. Are you coming to the party?"

Iris shook her head. "I would love to, but I think that might be a bit much for me. But I'll be there in spirit, I promise."

"What about going in your wheelchair?" Amanda asked.

Iris's face clouded over. "I do not want to be seen in public like that."

"I understand," Leigh Ann said. "And it's okay. You shouldn't do too much until you're a little more recovered." A new thought occurred to her. "I know you're doing physical therapy with Nick, but I'd be happy to give you some private yoga lessons that would help build your balance and core strength, along with increasing your flexibility."

Iris shook her head. "That's so sweet of you, but I don't think I could do yoga."

"I promise you that you could. There are all kinds of yoga and what I would recommend for you would all be very gentle. Some of it would be done from a chair. It could really help you. I'd be happy to run it past Nick, if you want his approval. This is what I do, Iris. It isn't just about getting people bikini-ready. It's about working with all ages to improve their quality of life."

Vera came over to refill coffee cups. "I'll do it with

you, Iris. Sounds interesting. We could all use a little more strength and flexibility."

Leigh Ann nodded. "She's right. As we get older, strength, flexibility, and balance are how we protect ourselves from the way aging attacks the body."

Iris seemed to be considering it. "Talk to Nick about it. If he thinks it's worthwhile, I'll give it a try."

Leigh Ann smiled. "I will." She knew she could talk Nick into it. He was open-minded and progressive. And then she'd have a way to personally help Iris, something she'd been wanting to do for a while now.

That opportunity, combined with the new push to get Marty to sign off on the divorce papers, had Leigh Ann feeling pretty good. Not to mention, she was going to spend some time with Grant today.

Something she imagined would happen even more once she lived here.

Life on Compass Key was going to be all right.

# Chapter Five

Olivia helped Vera clean up after breakfast, carrying some dishes into the kitchen. Grace and Amanda brought in the platters of leftover food, too.

"You girls don't need to do that," Vera said.

"We don't mind," Olivia said.

"We don't," Amanda agreed. "Not after you prepared all of this."

Vera took the dishes from Olivia and put them into the dishwasher. "But you all have work to do."

Iris turned slightly in her chair. "Plus, I have something for all of you."

"What's that?" Olivia asked. She couldn't imagine Iris giving them anything else after all she'd done for them.

"Vera?" Iris looked at her housekeeper.

Vera nodded. "Be right back." She went into another area of the house, coming back with a stack of turquoise shirts. "Here you go. Mother's Resort staff shirts. We tried to guess the right sizes for everyone."

"The only thing I ask," Iris said, "is that you don't wear them just yet. I need to make an announcement to all of the employees about what's going on, so they know who all of you are. I was hoping to do that announcement in person, but with the shape I'm in, I'm just going to send out an email to all resort employees instead."

Olivia went over to find her size. She loved the color of the shirts. Even more, she loved what they represented. "Iris?"

"Yes?"

"I think you should hold off on that email a little bit longer. Get it ready, but don't send it just yet. Chef Glenn knows that David's here to replace him, and Glenn's been leaning toward retirement for a while, so David's arrival makes sense. However, if Glenn finds out you're turning the whole place over to a new crew of people, he could get spooked. Freda, too."

Grace nodded. "That's a good point. The last thing we want is for him or Freda to think their activities might be under scrutiny by new management."

Iris's brows lifted. "I hadn't thought about that, but you're both right. I'll hold off on the announcement, then. At least until we see what happens with the investigation."

Olivia agreed. "The shirts should stay here until then, too."

Katie and Leigh Ann were nodding.

Then Grace spoke up. "But the employees have to know something's up. With the way Amanda and I have been helping out and working on the wedding stuff, plus Leigh Ann teaching sunrise yoga, there has to be some speculation."

Iris sipped her water. "Some of them know, obviously. Eddie, Duke, Carissa at the front desk, Peter, Rico at the marina. The rest of them haven't been told anything, but I agree, there must be some speculation. As soon as the police act, I'll send out the email."

"Okay," Olivia said. "That'll be our plan. And I'm going to call Detective Murphy this morning and tell him that Ecuador might be a potential escape plan for Glenn and Freda."

She really hoped the police figured this out before they ran. She desperately wanted Iris to get her money back. Or at least as much of it as possible.

"Anything else we can help with?" Katie asked.

Olivia shook her head. "Not that I can think of. But I'll let you know."

Katie finished her coffee, then took the cup into the kitchen. "Iris, if it's all right with you, I'll go have a look at the second floor."

"Fine with me," Iris said. "You can sign your paperwork when you get back down. Although we still need to work on that statement."

"Then let's do those both first."

But a knock at the door stopped anyone from going anywhere.

Olivia went over and answered it. Nick was standing outside. She gave him a nod. "Good morning."

"Morning," he answered, but there was no real cheerfulness in his eyes.

"Come in, Nick," Iris called out. "Would you like a cup of coffee? We've just finished breakfast."

"No, I'm all right. I'm not here for physical therapy yet. I just needed to speak to you."

"Go ahead," Iris said. "What is it?"

He sighed. "I'm sorry to say, but we have a problem."

Iris put her hands on her walker but stayed in her chair. "What is it?"

He rubbed the bridge of his nose. "It's my fault. I thought she'd be happy for me."

Olivia was getting a bad feeling about this. "Is this about your mother?"

Nick sighed and glanced over at Olivia. "Yes." He refocused his attention on Iris. "I finally talked to her this morning to tell her where I was and what was going on with me. The conversation started out really good. She was calm and in a good mood, and I decided to share more specifics with her. Namely, that I'd come here."

"And?" Iris asked.

"And it went all right. Until I told her about the money Arthur left me and how I got it by signing off on any claim to this place."

Iris nodded, as if she'd anticipated this. "She didn't like that, did she?"

"No."

Olivia felt for Nick. He looked miserable. Like a puppy that had been kicked. "What was her reaction?" Olivia asked quietly.

He stared at the floor for a moment before answering. "She said she was going to sue Iris for harassment, alienation of affection, and anything else she can think of. Plus, she said something about suing Arthur's estate on my behalf, because clearly I should have gotten my fair share and not just a couple million dollars."

He groaned and ran his hand through his hair. "I feel terrible. I never should have said anything to her."

Iris pulled herself up and made her way toward him. "You did nothing wrong, Nick. Talking to your mother shouldn't end in threats. This is on her. I'll talk to my attorney right away and make him aware of her intentions, but this could very well be a bluff on her part."

Nick shook his head. "I wish that were true, but I think she really intends to sue. There's nothing she loves more than money. And she sees this place as a giant bank account. She always has."

Iris nodded. "I know that's true. Well, whatever happens, we'll deal with it."

He frowned. "I appreciate your attitude, but I still feel bad about this."

"Don't." Iris stood her ground. "She would have found out sooner or later."

Olivia smiled sympathetically at Nick.

Iris patted the pockets of her caftan, then sighed. "I've left my phone on the table. Can someone get it for me?"

Olivia grabbed it and brought it over. "Here you go."

"Thank you." Iris looked at Nick. "I'm going to call my attorney right now and let him know I need to speak to him. After that, we can start the physical therapy."

He nodded, still looking rather forlorn.

Then Iris looked at Olivia. "You tell me what Detective Murphy says after you talk to him, all right?"

Olivia nodded. "I will." She also knew that was her cue to get moving. For all of them, really, but the girls seemed to understand that, as they were moving toward the door already, except for Katie, who was digging a pen out of her bag. Olivia gave Nick's arm a quick squeeze. "It'll all work out, you'll see."

"I hope so."

She turned toward Vera. "The quiche was delicious. Everything was. Thank you for cooking for us."

Vera gave her a nod. "You're welcome."

"Iris, I'll talk to you soon." Olivia waved her goodbye as she opened the front door.

Iris, on the phone, waved back, then put it to her shoulder. "Make sure you get your bungalow keys from Vera."

Olivia stopped in her tracks as Vera ran them over to her.

"Here you go," Vera said. "I meant to give them to you earlier but got a little distracted."

"Understood," Olivia said. She left with Leigh Ann, Amanda, and Grace following.

Amanda shook her head as they hit the path at the end of the ramp. "Iris really doesn't need a lawsuit right now."

"I was thinking the same thing," Grace said.

Olivia sighed. "I don't like it, either, but she has a good attorney. I'm sure he'll know what to do."

At least, Olivia hoped he would. They had enough going on with the embezzlement without dealing with a money-grabbing lawsuit, too.

# Chapter Six

Amanda said goodbye to the girls at the fork in the path and went on to her bungalow. Once back inside, she sat down with her phone and notebook to make her calls.

But before she could dial Mindy's number, her phone rang.

She stared at the caller ID in shock. She picked it up and answered. "Hello, Mother."

"I hope you understand what a grave disappointment you are."

Not the greeting Amanda had expected, but with Militant Marge, she never really knew what was coming. Amanda wasn't sure how to respond to her mother. "I didn't think you were talking to me anymore."

"I'm not, but this matter needs to be discussed."

Amanda had no idea what she was talking about. "What matter is that?"

"You are sending your sister to retrieve your things from my house. Do you believe that's appropriate?"

"I do. She's willing to do it and then you don't have to see me again. I thought you'd be happy about that." Amanda knew she'd never understand her mother, which was why she'd stopped trying.

"You're a coward, Amanda. I don't know why that should surprise me, but it does. Perhaps that's something you got from your father, because I didn't raise you to act that way."

Militant Marge was angling for a fight. Amanda understood that much. But she wasn't going to give in. She kept her tone civil and as light as possible. Being in her new home helped a lot. It was a great reminder that her life was now completely her own. "Is there anything else I can help you with?"

"Do not dismiss me. We need to discuss this, Amanda."

"I'm at work right now, so why don't we make an appointment to have this talk later?"

"At work? Where are you working?"

Amanda took a breath. Staying civil was getting harder. "As I told you, I work at the resort now."

Her mother snorted air through her nostrils. "As what?"

"I'm the Hospitality Director."

"What do you know about hospitality?"

The muscles in Amanda's jaw tightened. She

really didn't need this, but apparently her mother couldn't let go, despite her claims that she and Amanda were done. "I know everything you taught me."

Let her argue that one.

"Hmph. Running a home and running a *resort* are two very different things." Margaret said the word "resort" like it was something that shouldn't be uttered in polite company.

"Making people feel welcome is a universal skill," Amanda said. She'd learned how to do that from her mother, just as she'd also learned from her how to make people feel *un*welcome. Something Miltant Marge excelled at when she so desired. Amanda supposed for the first skill, she should thank her mother. Although she knew Margaret wouldn't take it in the spirit intended.

Margaret seemed to run out of steam a bit. "Perhaps." She took a moment, like she was gathering her thoughts for Round Two. "Are you still dating that *man*?"

"Yes, Duke and I are still dating." Amanda smiled. "In fact, I live one bungalow away from him now. We had dinner together the other night. And then he very kindly brought me breakfast."

"Because you slept with him?"

The smile stayed on Amanda's face. "Not yet, but if that's what you want..."

"You know very well I do not approve of such behavior."

"The thing is, Mom, I'm an adult. It doesn't matter if you approve of my behavior or not. I can do what I like. That's the beauty of being an adult. Now, I really do have to go, because this wedding isn't going to plan itself—"

"You're getting married?" The last word was almost a shriek.

Amanda grimaced and pulled the phone away from her ear for a second. "No, I'm planning a..." She listened. The phone had already gone dead. She sighed and ended the call on her end. "Great. Now she thinks I'm getting married to Duke."

She tipped her head back and groaned but a few moments later, she laughed. What else could she do?

She supposed she ought to call her mother back and explain, but when she tried, her mother's phone went straight to voicemail.

Amanda groaned a second time and dialed a different number, this time for her sister. But Denise's number went to voicemail, too.

Margaret was probably filling Denise in on Amanda's latest disappointing behavior. Or her imaginary impending nuptials.

Amanda rolled her eyes and left her sister a message. "Hi, Denise. I have a feeling you're talking to Mom right now. I think she thinks Duke and I are getting married. We're not. I said something about a wedding I'm planning, and she didn't let me explain before hanging up. That wedding is for someone else. Anyway, I'd love to chat when you get a chance. Thanks. Talk soon."

Amanda put her phone down and went to get herself a glass of water. Her mother continued to be unbelievable in every possible way. Amanda didn't think that would ever change. And it was sad.

They *could* have a relationship, if they worked at it and made compromises and were willing to be truthful about the state of things, but having a relationship seemed less important to her mother than being right. Or whatever she thought she was being.

Amanda took her water back to the coffee table and called Mindy, the florist.

"Island Blooms, how can I help you?"

"Mindy? This is Amanda from Mother's."

"Hi, Amanda. How's it going?"

"Good. I was about to ask you the same thing. Flowers all ordered? No snafus?"

"Flowers are not only all ordered, but the first shipment is due to arrive this afternoon. My daughter and I will be working on the arrangements starting tonight."

Amanda exhaled in relief. "That's fantastic. Great news. If anything comes up, please let me know."

"I will. But be assured that we're on track."

"Just what I wanted to hear. Thanks. Have a good day."

"You, too."

Amanda called the officiant next, who confirmed he was set for the Sunday date. He was a lovely middle-aged man named John Paul Heffernan. He'd offered to dress accordingly for the occasion, too, giving her the option of a seersucker suit or a Hawaiian shirt. She'd gone with the seersucker suit, figuring it was better to have the officiant overdressed as opposed to under-dressed.

She checked her phone, noted that J. Henry had yet to get back to her about his menu selections for the reception, and was about to text Grace to say she'd be ready to meet her at the storage room in twenty minutes or so, when Denise called back.

"Hi there," Amanda said. "I take it you got my voicemail?"

"I saw that you'd called, but I haven't listened to it yet. I just got off the phone with Mom, but I bet you knew that."

"I had a feeling. That's why I called you. Let me guess—she thinks I'm marrying Duke?"

Denise laughed. "You nailed it. And, boy, is she losing her mind. I'm pretty sure she's cutting you out of the will."

Amanda wasn't surprised by that. "To be honest, it's more shocking she hasn't already done that."

“I tried to tell her that she was wrong. She is, right?”

Amanda smiled. “She is. Duke and I are not getting married. What *is* happening is that I’m planning a wedding for some incoming guests and happened to mention that the wedding wasn’t going to plan itself, which she took to mean my wedding to Duke.”

“Ah. I see. Why didn’t you explain what you meant?”

“Because she freaked out and hung up before I could do that.”

“Sounds like Mom. But hey, that’s great that you’re getting back into the wedding business.”

Amanda nodded. “I’m pretty happy about it, too. Officially, I am the new Hospitality Director, so I’ll be doing more than weddings, but it’s really nice to be able to put those skills to use again. And while I can’t tell you who I’m doing all this for just yet, I will say that you’ll be impressed when I am able to share that information.”

“Hmm. Top secret stuff, huh?”

“Something like that. Trying to ensure the guests’ privacy.”

“So they’re well-known?”

“They are.”

“Like Hollywood famous or sports famous?”

“Denise, you’re not going to get it out of me with

Twenty Questions." Amanda laughed. "But points for trying."

"Do I know who they are?"

Amanda shook her head. "Probably. And that's the last question I'm answering."

Denise laughed. "All right, but will you send me a picture?"

"Maybe. I don't want to violate anyone's confidence in me. But I'll at least tell you about it after it happens."

"Fair enough." Denise paused. "You okay with Mom cutting you out of the will? You sounded pretty cavalier but that had to hurt a little."

Amanda shrugged. "I think I've had so many small hurts from her over the years that they've started to roll off of me. Plus, my life here is really shaping up. I've moved into my new bungalow and it's so beautiful. The views from my front porch are postcard perfect."

"Well, send me some pictures."

"I will. I promise."

"Great. By the way, I should have your stuff on the way to you in about a week. I talked to the POD company and they're meeting me there on Monday."

"Do you think Mom will try to stop you?"

"I don't know. It's certainly a possibility, but it's nothing you have to worry about. I can handle her."

"I hate to put you in that position. I really do."

"What's she going to do? Cut me out of the will, too?" Denise laughed, but that laugh faded. "I guess she could, but if she does, she does. I can't control her actions."

"That's a true statement. I really appreciate all you're doing for me."

"I know you do. And I also know you'd do the same for me."

"You're right," Amanda said. "I would. And listen, now that I'm getting settled into my new place, you should really think about coming to visit in a month or so. I have a guest room and you'd have your own bathroom."

"Sounds nice. I'd love some sun and sand."

"That reminds me," Amanda said. "You should go through my clothing and take any of the winter items you want. Or at least weed out anything that looks really worn or out of date. No point in sending that stuff down here when I will only just end up getting rid of a lot of it."

"That's kind of you to offer, but I'd feel bad taking your clothes without you there to be able to decide what you want to keep for yourself."

"You mean because I have so little already?"

"I wasn't going to say that. But that does play into it. I know how much you've already given up."

Amanda smiled. She felt like her relationship with Denise was already getting better. "Take the ivory cashmere sweater and pants set, and the wool houndstooth dress. You know the ones I mean?"

"I do," Denise said. "Aren't those St. John? You could get some money for those if you sold them."

"Take them if you want them. I'm serious, Denise. At least I can do that for you for helping me out this way."

"If you're sure."

"I am. Just like I'm sure you need to visit me here."

"I will, I promise. And not just because I want to meet your new fiancé."

Amanda laughed out loud. "Right. Okay, I'd better get back to work. Thanks again, sis."

"You're welcome. Love you."

Those were such sweet words. Words she hadn't heard from anyone often enough in her life. It was time for that to change.

Amanda smiled. "I love you, too."

# Chapter Seven

Grace sat in the bedroom chair while David got ready for the day. Steam wafted out of the open bathroom door, the remnants of his shower.

He leaned his head out, his face slathered in shaving cream. "Any news from J. Henry yet on the menu?"

"Not yet, but I'll ask Amanda when I meet up with her. We're trying to find a chalkboard to use for wedding signage."

He disappeared back into the bathroom. "Let me know what you find out about the menu. I don't want to get caught short."

"I will. By the way, I'm going to pick out our bungalow later. Unless you want to have a say in that?"

"Whatever you decide on is fine with me." He leaned out for a second again, smiling. "Just make sure it has a nice view."

She laughed. They liked to talk about how every spot on the island had a good view. “I will, promise.”

“Then I’m good.”

She took a breath. “So, listen.”

Over the sound of water running in the sink, he answered her. “I am.”

“There might be some arrests made today.”

The water turned off. “Really?”

“Yep. If anyone says anything about it, don’t comment. At least not in a way that implies you know anything.”

“I won’t. But wow. I didn’t realize it was going to happen so soon.”

“Me either, but the sooner they can wrap this up and hopefully get Iris’s money back, the better.”

“Some of that is your money, you know.” The muted sound of his razor scraping over his face paused. “One-fifth of it anyway.”

She hadn’t thought about it that way. “I suppose it is. Hard to think of it that way, though. One-fifth of it is ours, not mine.”

The water came back on for a moment, then he looked out again. Spots of shaving cream still dotted his face. “Maybe on paper, but not in my head. This all happened because of you and your connection to Iris. I had nothing to do with it.”

She smiled. “You realize that would make me your boss.”

He waggled his eyebrows at her. "I've never slept with my boss before."

She laughed. "Settle down."

He used a towel to wipe the rest of the foam off of his face, his expression turning more serious. "We haven't talked about it for a while, but how are you doing?"

She knew what he meant. Her drinking. She nodded. "I'm doing really well. I get tempted sometimes, but I really think changing my environment has helped."

"Even though alcohol is a big part of being at a resort like this? People drink on vacation."

"They do, but the thing is, *I'm* not on vacation. Not anymore. Now I'm at work. And that mindset has helped. So have the girls. They've been so supportive." She lifted her booted foot. "And as soon as this stupid thing comes off, I'm going to get serious about putting my health first. There's a whole fitness club here that I could be using. Not to mention swimming, kayaking, paddleboarding, walking, all of that stuff."

"I love that. I should do it, too." He came out of the bathroom and patted his stomach. "And not just because I'm surrounded by food all day. If we're going to live in paradise, we should be healthy enough to enjoy it."

"Exactly. And there's no winter here where you can hide behind bulky clothes and big coats."

"That's for sure." He pulled on his chef's uniform of loose pants, a plain white T-shirt, then his chef's coat over that. The coat had "The Palms" embroidered on the chest over his heart.

As he put his clogs on, she got up and grabbed her purse. "I'll walk with you. I have to meet Amanda over at the storage room anyway."

They left together. He pulled the door shut behind them. "Let me know what bungalow you pick out."

"Yep."

As they walked, a couple approached from the other direction. They smiled as they saw David's chef coat and the wife pointed to it. "You were the chef last night at the restaurant, weren't you? I think you came by our table."

David nodded. "That was me."

"That grouper last night was amazing."

"Thank you." David grinned as the couple went by, then he leaned toward Grace. "That's never happened before."

"Oh, come on. People tell you how much they love your food all the time."

"No, I mean being recognized like that."

A crazy idea popped into Grace's head. She grabbed David's arm. "You know what?"

"What?"

"You should do a Mother's Resort cookbook. Think about it—your own cookbook that would also promote the resort. Plus, we could sell copies in the resort's boutique. There's no way it wouldn't sell. It would make a great gift for people to take home with them. Or a souvenir. You could autograph copies and everything."

His brows lifted. "I love the idea, but do you think people would actually want it?"

"Are you kidding? People love your food. And they love this place. Of course they'd want it."

"I'm willing to try, but I don't know the first thing about publishing a cookbook. Or even where to start, outside of gathering recipes."

"Doesn't matter," Grace said. "There are two people on the island who know all about that stuff. Katie and her sister, Sophie. And if it's all right with you, I'm going to talk to them about it today. Iris, too."

He nodded, smiling. "My own cookbook, huh? You know that's always been a dream of mine."

She hooked her arm through his. "I know. And it's about time that dream came true."

After kissing David goodbye outside of the restaurant, Grace texted Amanda that she was in the main building and ready to meet her in front of the boutique.

Amanda showed up a few minutes later in shorts and a T-shirt. "Hey."

"Hey. You look ready to work."

"I am. I figured if I'm going to dig around in the storage room, I should be prepared to get dirty."

"Good assumption." Grace put her hands on her hips. "You know, that whole room should really be gone through and reorganized. If there's stuff in there that's broken or unusable, we should get rid of it."

"I agree. We should put that on our to-do list." Amanda glanced toward the restaurant. "Is David already at work?"

"He is. Any news from you-know-who about the menu selections?"

Amanda frowned. "No. And he should have gotten back to me on that." She pulled out her phone. "Let me send him a text and remind him."

"Thanks. David's waiting on those."

Amanda typed her message, then tapped Send. "I told him it's urgent."

"Good." Grace rubbed her hands together. "Ready to see the storage room?"

Amanda laughed. "Yes, but I don't think I'm as excited about it as you are."

Grace grinned. "I'm excited about the idea of cleaning it out. Come on, it's through here."

Grace led Amanda down the hall to the storage room. She unlocked the door and turned on the lights.

Amanda looked around. "There's a lot more stuff in here than I imagined."

Grace nodded. "There is. We have our work cut out for us."

"A chalkboard should be easy enough to find." Although Amanda didn't seem like she knew where to start. "I need to check out the dance floor, too. See what kind of shape it's in. I'm sure it'll need to be cleaned."

"No doubt about that," Grace said. "Everything in here does." She led Amanda back to where the dance floor pieces were stacked. "Here it is."

"Have you looked at every piece?"

Grace shook her head. "Nope."

Amanda straightened. "Are you willing to help me? I know it's a lot of work, but I need to make sure it's usable."

"That's what I'm here for."

They got to work, moving every single piece of the dance floor, checking each one for damage. As they worked, Grace brought up her cookbook idea to see what Amanda thought of it. "To me, it seems like something that would benefit the island and David, obviously, but would also make a nice souvenir."

"I love the idea," Amanda said. She wiped a bead of sweat off of her brow. "In fact, if David's willing, I think we should try to get him some interviews, too."

Grace straightened as she set the last piece of the flooring aside. "Interviews?"

Amanda nodded. "You know, local newspapers,

Florida-based magazines, even local news programs that might want a chef to come on and cook. Think about how cool it would be if we could turn David into a minor celebrity. Having a chef like that at the resort's restaurant would be amazing."

Grace nodded. "It would be."

Amanda straightened. "Hey, would he be willing to give some cooking demonstrations? Now that I'm the Hospitality Director, I've been trying to think of ways to engage the guests a little more. More things like Grant's watercolor class." She went back to rummaging under another tarp.

Grace didn't want to answer for David. "I'll have to ask him." But she loved the idea of turning David into a celebrity chef. Was that really possible? She didn't want to get her hopes up too high, but the thought was pretty exciting.

"Hey," Amanda said. She pulled a locked wooden box out of a pile of odds and ends. "What's this?"

Grace came over to look at it. "I have no idea. Pirate treasure?"

Amanda gave the box a gentle shake. Something moved inside. Slid, maybe.

She looked at Grace. "I don't know about pirate booty, but there's definitely something in here. It's got some weight. Not enough to be a treasure trove of gold coins or anything like that, but it's not a box full of feathers, either."

Grace nodded. "I'd love to know what, but I think we should take it to Iris. It's her property, after all."

Amanda nodded. "Good idea."

But that didn't stop Grace from wondering what the box might contain.

# Chapter Eight

After Katie and Iris roughed out a draft of the statement to the resort's employees, and Katie signed her ownership papers, she headed upstairs to check out the second level.

Now she stood in the living room of the second floor. The layout was very similar to the first level, although decorated more simply. It had the same big, spacious kitchen open to the dining room and living room area, but instead of the big round table that seated six downstairs, this table only seated four.

Still plenty of room for Jenny to come over and meet with them once in a while, if that all worked out. Or for Owen and Gage to join Katie and Sophie for dinner.

Smiling at that thought, she stood in the kitchen, trying to picture herself making breakfast here, or fixing lunch, or getting dinner ready. It was easy to do.

The kitchen was a good space with a lot of counter area and a nice wide, deep sink. She turned the water on and off, watching it splash against the stainless steel.

Even with the lights off, the big open room was plenty bright. That was great. She loved natural light.

She went through to the bedrooms and bathrooms, finding the office right away. The masculine space smelled of a man's cologne and leather-bound books. She smiled, knowing this had been Arthur's space. What an honor it would be to write in here.

She could picture it, too. The desk was set so that it took full advantage of the incredible view.

Nothing like that in Brooklyn, that was for sure. Her office there was the size of a small walk-in closet, and her desk was pushed up against the wall, a configuration she hated, to be honest.

She went on to the bedrooms. Both were about the same size, with similar bathrooms and walk-in closets.

The space was great. The views were downright gorgeous. And Katie had no problem imagining herself here. Or Fabio. He'd love the porches, which were all screened. Could Sophie see herself here, though? Katie didn't want to make that decision for her sister.

She took a few pictures and sent them to Sophie with a text message. *What do you think? Could you live here? This is the second floor of Iris's house. Completely self-contained with its own entrance. Bigger than the bungalows, since there's two of us. Three, if you count Fabs.*

While she waited for Sophie to answer, Katie went back to the office and sat at the desk. She smoothed her hands across the wood top, the years of work that had been done here evident in the small scars and blemishes.

This home had something their place in Brooklyn didn't. A feeling of history that made sense to Katie. One she cherished. And she loved that about the space.

Her phone buzzed. She took it out and checked the screen.

*It's beautiful. Are you saying that's available to us? Wouldn't that make the other women jealous? I don't want to step on any toes.*

Katie answered, *They've all turned it down and are okay with us taking it, since there's two of us and we have Fabio. Means having neighbors upstairs and down.*

*That doesn't bother me*, Sophie replied. *Looks great to me. I'm in if you are. Send me a few more pics?*

Katie smiled. *Will do. You can come over and see it.*

*I will, at some point, but I already love it.*

*Then I'm going to tell Iris we'll take it.*

She snapped photos of the bedrooms and bathrooms, plus the closets, then went out and took a picture of the living room and kitchen and sent them all to Sophie. *Pretty nice, huh?*

*So nice. Wow.*

Still smiling, Katie opened one of the sliders and walked out onto the side porch. There was a rattan sofa and a side chair along with two end tables and a coffee table. She sent pics of that to Sophie as well.

Then she stared out at the view and the broad expanse of crystal blue water. Palm fronds shushed against each other as a breeze blew across them. What a change this would be for Fabio. The most fresh air he got in Brooklyn was an open window in the cooler months.

Sophie texted back. *I call that porch as my new office. lol #escapefromNY*

Katie laughed. *Maybe we'll both work out here.*

She wondered if changing her surroundings would change the stories she wrote. At the moment, they were all set in the city, but she'd already talked to Sophie about a new series set on an island very much like this.

Would her readers like those books as much? She had no idea, but it was possible that changing her life this way could affect her career. And not in a good way.

Then again, if it did, she had the resort to fall back on.

Moving here was a risk. She knew that. But it felt like a risk worth taking. She took a deep breath of the clean, sweet island air, then went back inside and downstairs, using the outside stairs this time, just to get a feel for them.

She knocked on Iris's front door.

Vera let her in. "What did you think?"

Katie smiled. "It's beautiful. I sent Sophie some pictures and she loves it, too. We'll take it."

Vera's eyes lit up. "That's great."

"Ow!"

Katie and Vera both looked toward the side porch where the cry had come from.

Vera pressed her lips together to keep from laughing. "Iris isn't a fan of her physical therapy, but Nick's not a quitter, bless his heart." She glanced at Katie again. "She'll be done in a few minutes."

"I'm happy to sit and wait."

"You want something to drink?"

Katie shook her head. "No, I'm fine. Thanks." She took a seat on the couch and surfed through her social media to see what Sophie had put up today. Looked like she was using some of Jenny's new graphics.

They were great. So sharp and professional and catchy. She read through some of the comments, smiling at how positive they were.

Someone knocked at the door.

Katie leaned forward to see through the window to the front porch. "It's Grace and Amanda," she told Vera. "I'll let them in."

She got up and opened the door. "Hey, guys. What's up?"

Amanda held up a locked wooden box. "We found

this in the storage room and figured we'd better bring it over."

Katie nodded. "Iris is finishing her physical therapy. I'm waiting for her myself."

Grace had an unsure look on her face. "Did you check out the second floor?"

"I did," Katie said. "And I love it. I sent Sophie pics and she feels the same way. That's why I'm waiting for Iris. To tell her we're going to take it."

"That's great," Amanda said. "Of course, once you marry Owen, you'll be living over there."

Katie snorted. "Hey, let's not start that rumor. You never know who might be listening." Although she couldn't help but smile.

Grace pursed her lips and looked at Amanda. "And when you marry Duke? Which bungalow will you end up in?"

Amanda's cheeks brightened to a shade of pink Katie hadn't seen before. "Duke and I are *not* getting married."

Katie laughed. "You never know."

Amanda shook her head. "Trust me. Things aren't that way between us. I adore him. I really do. But I think this is just a...not a fling, exactly, but it doesn't seem that serious to him."

Katie crossed her arms. It was hard to read Amanda's face. "How do you feel about that?"

"I feel fine with it. I like the way things are between us." Amanda lifted her chin. "They're easy and casual. There's nothing wrong with that."

"That's good," Katie said. And yet she couldn't help but think her friend wasn't exactly telling the truth.

# Chapter Nine

Iris hurt. There was no other way to describe it. She knew the therapy was good for her. She knew it was necessary. But pain was still pain. She sat in her chair on the side porch, wiping her forehead and catching her breath.

"I know it's hard," Nick said. He was crouched beside her. "I'm sorry about that. But it will get easier. And you will get stronger."

"I know," Iris said.

"The yoga you mentioned will help, too."

She just nodded. It wasn't the boy's fault she hurt, and she didn't want to take her frustrations out on him. After all, she was trying to get him to stay. She punctuated her next words with a kind look. "I just wish that easier part would come sooner."

He nodded, his gaze full of sympathy. "You want some pain medication?"

She shook her head. "No, I'm fine. I don't want to get addicted to that stuff."

He smiled. "I understand, but it's still early days. You only just had surgery. If you want some pain medication, it's perfectly understandable. Now, if you still want it in two weeks, we're going to have a talk."

She looked up at him and smiled. "All right. I'll have some. But only because you suggested it."

"That's my girl." He winked at her. "I'll send Vera back with them and, for now, I'll get out of your hair. See you tomorrow?"

She nodded. "Tomorrow. And thank you."

"You're welcome."

He left, and she exhaled, dropping her smile. She really didn't want to get hooked on the pain pills, but at the same time, she was happy to take them. Happy to get some relief.

Vera came out with two large white pills and a glass of water. "You okay? Nick said you were hurting."

"I am. Physical therapy is actually medieval torture, but they don't call it that because then no one would show up."

Vera's smile was sympathetic. "I'm sure it's miserable. But maybe this will cheer you up—Katie, Grace, and Amanda would like to speak to you."

"I'm all sweaty. I should take a shower first."

Vera shook her head. "I don't think they care about that one bit. And they really want to see you now."

"All right," Iris said. "Send them out. Wait. Where are the cats?"

"Probably at the marina. Eddie had an early fishing trip this morning. You know how they like scraps."

Iris laughed. "I do. And Eddie spoils them."

Vera nodded. "They definitely have him wrapped around their paws. You sit and relax. You can have your shower after you see the girls."

"All right."

A few moments later, the three women came out onto the porch. Amanda carried an old wooden box. "Hi, Iris. How are you doing?"

Iris smiled. "I'm all right. Feeling better since I talked to my attorney, who believes that he can easily get a dismissal of any lawsuit Nick's mother might bring as malicious prosecution."

"That's great news," Grace said.

"It is," Iris agreed. That tidbit had given her the strength to get through physical therapy. "What is that you have with you?"

Amanda set the box on the coffee table. "Grace and I found it while looking in one of the storage rooms."

The girls all took a seat on the couch. Iris furrowed her brow as she studied the box. "What's in it?"

"We have no idea," Grace said. "It's locked and we didn't try to get into it. But there is definitely something in there. We brought it here because we figured it belongs to you. You should be the one to open it."

Katie smiled. "This is the kind of thing I'd write into a book."

Grace nodded, clearly amused. "But in an Iris Devereaux book the box would contain millions worth of diamonds, or very naughty love letters."

"Or both," Katie said.

Amanda looked at Katie. "Okay, I need to read one of your books."

Iris laughed. "You can borrow one from me. I have them all."

Grace pointed at the box. "Any chance you might have the key to that thing?"

Iris shook her head. "No. It's not mine. I've never seen it before."

"But it's on your property," Katie said. "That makes it yours."

Vera came outside. "Would you girls like a drink?"

Amanda nodded. "I'd love some water."

"Me, too," Grace said. "Vera, have you ever seen this box before?"

Vera took a few steps forward to get a better look. She put her hands on her hips. "I'm not sure." She glanced at Iris. "Didn't Arthur keep a box like that on his bookshelves? Not saying it's the same one. Just that it reminds me of that one."

"If it was similar," Katie said, "do you think there'd still be a key around here that would fit it?"

Vera shrugged. "I'm not sure, but we do have a

bunch of keys in that little fish-shaped bowl. That came from his office. It used to sit on his desk."

"Would you get it, please?" Iris asked.

"Sure. I'll bring it with the waters."

Iris looked at the girls, completely caught up in the mystery, but not ready to get too excited about it herself. "You know there's very little chance there are any diamonds in there. Or anything of value. That storage room is a dumping ground."

Katie laughed. "So you're going with sexy letters then?"

Iris giggled. "Now, those would be interesting."

Vera returned shortly with two bottles of cold water in one hand, and a cobalt blue ceramic bowl in the shape of a fish. She gave the bottles to Amanda and Grace, and the bowl to Iris.

But Iris shook her head. "You try those keys, Vera. Your eyes are better than mine."

"All right." Vera took the bowl back and knelt down in front of the box. The lock was medium-sized and there was a bit of rust on the box's metal hinges. She dug through the keys in the bowl looking for the ones that were about the right size.

Iris watched as Vera worked, trying key after key and setting aside the ones that didn't do anything. She glanced at the girls. "I'm not sure we're going to get it open."

"We could always get a crowbar," Grace said. She

looked at Amanda. "Or Duke. I bet he could get it open."

Amanda nodded. "I'm sure he could."

"Hang on," Vera said. The key she had in the lock turned a quarter of the way. Then stopped. She shook her head. "Nope. False alarm. Sorry."

Iris was surprised that she'd felt a zing of excitement. "Keep trying."

"I am," Vera said. "But we're running out of keys."

Iris sipped her water. "Maybe we should get Duke."

Vera let out a little whoop. "I got it!"

"Well, open the lid," Iris said.

Vera did, causing the hinges to creak softly in protest. Then she gasped. "Iris. Look."

Inside was a large, flat box wrapped in colorful paper, tied with ribbon, with a sealed envelope on top. Iris's name was written on it.

Her heart clenched. "That's Arthur's handwriting." She looked at the women around her. "Is this some kind of joke? Some kind of trick?"

"I swear it's not," Amanda said. "We honestly just found that box in the storage room, like we said."

Vera rocked back on her heels. "You know Arthur loved his surprises. Maybe he was hiding this from you in the storage room because he thought you'd find it otherwise. He must have done it right before he got sick. And then...time ran out."

Iris put her hand to her mouth. This was too much. "If that's true..."

"You should open it," Katie said. "Obviously, he meant for you to have it."

Grace nodded. "I agree. And I think it's wonderful."

Iris put her glasses on, then held her hands out.

Vera took the envelope and box out and gave them to Iris.

She held them for a moment. Had Arthur really meant this for her? The envelope did have her name on it in his handwriting.

"Start with the card," Amanda said. "Maybe that will give you a clue."

"Good idea." Iris carefully opened the envelope, knowing she would save every scrap of wrapping, ribbon, and paper that was part of this. The card had a beautiful bouquet of roses on the front, accented with glitter.

Inside was a note in Arthur's handwriting. She read it out loud, doing her best not to turn into a complete mess.

*"To my dearest girl,*

*"If you find this before I can give it to you, then you're in trouble for snooping. I do think I've found a hiding place you won't uncover this time, however."*

She looked at the girls. "He's right. I used to find his gifts for me all the time."

They laughed as she went back to the note.

*"Our anniversary is coming up. So is Christmas and Valentine's Day and your birthday and all the other special days I'm going to miss. I know that, because I just found out today how sick I am."*

Iris's throat clogged with emotion. She shook her head, unable to go on. She handed the card to Vera. "Read the rest to me."

With tears in her eyes, Vera took the card, nodding.

*"Whatever happens to me, I want you to know that you have been the greatest love of my life. I hope this trinket brings you some joy until we can be together again. All my love, Arthur."*

Vera sniffed hard. "That man was such a romantic."

Tears blurred Iris's vision as she carefully pulled the ribbon off the box, then undid the yellowed tape holding the wrapping paper. It wasn't hard to remove, due to the time it had been in storage.

Under the wrapping paper was a white box of hard, pressed paper. She took the lid off of that and revealed a black velvet box inside. But the velvet box fit so snuggly inside the paper one that she couldn't get it out. "Help me, Vera."

Vera wrestled the velvet box free.

Iris took hold of the top and opened it. Her jaw unhinged and the air left her lungs. Inside, on a cushion of more velvet, hung on a chain of gleaming platinum, sat a robin's egg-sized, pear-shaped diamond, haloed by smaller diamonds that would still be considered large, had they been solitaires.

She'd never seen a diamond that big in person. The women around her had fallen silent, clearly as awed as she was. She picked up the cushion and the diamond pendant together and realized there was a folded piece of paper underneath.

Another note from Arthur? She clutched the diamond in one hand and reached for the note with the other.

# Chapter Ten

Leigh Ann walked into Grant's island studio, eager to see him and spend time with him. It felt like it had been days, which in a way it had, since he'd been busy helping build the ramp at Iris's house. "Hi there."

His face lit up as soon as he saw her. He was in the middle of wrapping *The Queen of the Eagle Rays* painting in bubble wrap but stopped to greet her with a kiss. "Hello, beautiful. How are you?"

She grinned, a natural reaction to kissing him. "I'm good. And I have some news."

His brows lifted. "Your divorce is final?"

She rolled her eyes. "Sadly, no, that's not it. But I think my news is almost as good. Maybe better."

"Better?"

She nodded, excited to share. "I'm moving to Compass Key."

His mouth opened, then curved into a smile. "Yes! That is *fantastic* news."

"I thought you'd approve."

"I more than approve. I'd sponsor the move if you needed me to."

She laughed. "Iris beat you to that."

"I guess she did." He picked Leigh Ann up and twirled her around once, making her squeal like a schoolgirl. "That made my whole day. My whole week."

She was still laughing as her feet touched the floor again. "I'm very glad. Do you need help with anything?"

"Nope." He let her go. "I just need to finish wrapping the painting, then we're ready to move it. Thank you for helping me."

"I'm happy to do it. And excited to see your gallery."

He got the rest of the bubble wrap on, securing it with packing tape. After that, he added a layer of thick brown paper, securing it the same way. Then he used twine to connect two handles to the painting on the back. When he was done, he nodded at her. "Grab a side and make sure you can lift it without any issues."

"I'm sure I can. It's not that heavy."

"It's not heavy at all," Grant said. "But it is big and that makes it unwieldy. I just want you to get a feel for it."

She understood. This was his baby. He needed to be sure she could carry it comfortably. She took hold of the edges of the wrapped canvas with both hands and picked it up. "Yep. It's fine."

"Okay, great. We're going to take it to the boat, and then I'll need you to hold it while I drive. Which will be very slowly, I assure you. A canvas this big is like a sail. It can catch the wind like you wouldn't believe. That's why I put the handles on it, to give you something more substantial to hold on to."

She nodded. "Got it." Under no circumstances would she let go, even if that meant she went into the water with it. Which she was really hoping would *not* happen. "How would you do this if I wasn't here to help you?"

"I'd have to bring one of the gallery assistants over."

"I see." She grinned. "So I'm free labor then?"

"Exactly." He gave her a wink. "Actually, I was going to take you to lunch afterwards."

"Aw. Thanks."

They carried the painting outside, set it down for a moment so he could lock up the studio, then they went on to his boat in the marina. He let her get aboard first, then used the handles to carry the painting on. He laid one edge as flat as possible, but the canvas was so large that it leaned over Leigh Ann, meaning the handles were really her only way of keeping a good grip on it.

She could see, however, that a big gust of wind would mean a fight to keep the canvas in the boat.

"What do you think?" Grant asked. "Feel secure?"

"It does," she said. "You think this twine is strong enough? Against a gust of wind?"

He nodded. "It should be. I doubled it up, which is how I've always done it. But like I said, I'm going to go slow. And, thankfully, there's not too much wind today, so we should be fine. If at *any* time you need help, just yell for me."

"I will." She smiled at him. "This isn't getting away from me without a fight. I promise."

He nodded in appreciation. "I know it's in good hands. But it's also just a painting. If you're in danger, let go."

"I'll be fine." Still, it was sweet that he cared.

He started the boat and maneuvered them away from the marina. She expected him to pick up a little speed, but that never seemed to happen.

"You could go a *little* faster," Leigh Ann said. The breeze was light. Even so, she could occasionally feel it beneath the canvas. Nothing she couldn't control, though.

He glanced back at her. "I don't want to push my luck."

"You're the captain."

The trip to his house took easily twice as long as usual and she was glad when they finally arrived.

She'd been gripping the handles so tightly that her hands ached. Probably overkill, but she hadn't wanted anything to happen to the painting.

Grant took the canvas off the boat first so that Leigh Ann had free passage. He leaned the painting against the dock railing and gave her a hand. "Thank you so much for that. Now we just need to load it into my truck and get it to the gallery. Then we can grab lunch."

She nodded. "I want to look around the gallery first."

"I'll give you the grand tour, which won't take long."

She helped him carry the painting around the side of the house, then waited while he secured it in the bed of his truck with tiedowns.

The ride to the gallery wasn't quite as slow as the boat trip, but she got the sense that he was still taking it easy.

The gallery was in a small shopping center that looked fairly new. There was also a hair salon and spa, a little French bistro, a jewelry store, a law office, a dentist's office, and an interior decorating store. Grant's gallery sat at one end, like an anchor store.

They drove past all of the shops and around to the back, where a set of steel double doors had already been opened.

"Nice little area," Leigh Ann said as she got out.

He nodded. "Thanks."

"Is it new? Or newly redone?"

"Newly redone. Well, not that newly. It's been six years now. Trust me, it needed it. And I didn't want the gallery to seem out of place."

She squinted at him. "You make it sound like you had something to do with the remodel."

He unhooked one of the tiedowns and nodded. "I did. The shopping center got remodeled because when I bought it, it was pretty rundown and out of date."

"You own this place?"

"I do. Impressed?"

"Maybe." She took another look at it. She was totally impressed.

"Duke's dad, Jack, did the remodel."

"Nice." She couldn't wait to see inside the gallery. In the front window, one of his paintings had been on display, so she hadn't even caught a true glimpse of the interior.

A young woman came outside. She had long dark hair and wore a tropical sundress. "Hello, Mr. Shoemaker."

"Hi, Cheyanne. This is my beautiful muse, Leigh Ann."

Leigh Ann had to smile at that introduction. "Hi, Cheyanne. Nice to meet you."

Cheyanne smiled back. "Nice to meet you! Mr.

Shoemaker mentioned he'd finally found some worthwhile inspiration. I can't wait to see the new painting."

Leigh Ann helped Grant carry the painting inside into what turned out to be a back room area, as she'd suspected it would be. A young man was working at a long table preparing prints to be shipped.

He took out one of his earbuds. "Hello."

"Hi," Leigh Ann said.

Grant gave the young man a nod. "Nesto, this is Leigh Ann, my muse."

Nesto smiled. "Good to meet you."

Grant set the painting down. "Cheyanne manages the front of the gallery while Nesto handles the backend stuff. Shipping, packaging, inventory."

Leigh Ann looked around while Grant spoke to Cheyanne, who stood between the door to the room they were in and the rest of the gallery. "Give me a couple minutes to get it unwrapped and set up and I'll call you back to see it."

She nodded. "Okay."

Cheyanne left. Nesto had both earbuds in again and was back at work.

Leigh Ann looked at Grant. "Are you nervous to show the painting to everyone?"

"No, I'm not." He started to carefully unwrap it. "I know there will be some who won't like it, but those people are not my audience. And at tomorrow night's party, everyone who's coming is a friend or previous client."

"No critics?"

"There will be a few from the press, but I don't worry too much about them. One of them will stay five minutes, then write something about how I exploit the tourist trade by allowing them to believe my paintings are more than just an overwrought money grab."

Leigh Ann looked at him, horrified. "What?"

He shrugged. "Marlene Fortescue. She's given all of my paintings bad reviews since she came on to me and I turned her down about three or four years ago. She's so predictable that it's just funny now. But there will be others, like Jim Martinelli, who will praise the work and announce it my best ever."

Grant smiled. "The universe has a way of balancing itself out."

"I guess." She chewed at the inside of her cheek.

He dropped the brown paper wrapping in his hands and came over to her. "You're worried that Marlene will say something untoward about you."

"The thought had occurred to me."

His eyes narrowed. "She might. Will that upset you terribly?"

Leigh Ann thought about that. "I'd hope not. But my ego has only recently regained some confidence so...I'm not sure."

He took her hands in his. "Please don't let her

get to you." He lifted Leigh Ann's hands to his mouth to kiss them. "Marlene will undoubtedly be jealous of you. You're beautiful, younger than her, and I'm about to publicly declare you as my muse."

"I'll try," Leigh Ann said.

"She's probably also going to figure out pretty quick that I'm in love with you."

Leigh Ann smiled shyly, thankful Nesto was lost in his work and music on the other side of the painting. "You are?"

He nodded. "Beyond all shadow of a doubt. And now that you're moving here, I'm not afraid to say it. I hope that doesn't frighten you, but you must realize by now that I'm a man who feels things deeply."

She nodded. "I do realize that."

He kissed her, a soft press of his mouth to hers. "You don't need to say it back until you feel it. I understand you still have a lot going on."

She took a breath. She kind of *did* feel it. But she wasn't sure she could say that to Grant when there was no clear end to her divorce in sight.

"Come on," he said. "Help me get the rest of this wrapping off so Cheyanne and Nesto can see the painting and we can go to lunch."

"Okay." She felt bad not expressing her feelings for him, though. He was pretty advanced emotionally, at least compared to a guy like Marty, so maybe Grant really did understand she wasn't there yet. Or didn't feel like she *should* be there.

It was all so complicated.

But she felt like she had to say something. She stopped pulling paper off of the canvas. "Grant?"

"Hmm?" He had a ball of packing tape in one hand.

"I like you very, very much. More every day. But with this divorce dragging on...it's making me feel like I can't really say what I want to say. Does that make sense?"

He nodded as he started to work on the layer of bubble wrap. "Of course it does. That divorce is keeping you tied to your old life and until it's final, you won't really be able to step fully into your new one."

She stared at him, marveling at how he always got it. She really did love him. And she was going to tell him that just as soon as Marty signed those papers.

Maybe it really was time for Leigh Ann to have that talk with Candi.

# Chapter Eleven

Olivia hadn't bothered Jenny with chitchat, as her daughter had been working at her computer, headphones on, a sure sign that she was deeply engaged in something.

Instead, Olivia had started packing up her things. About halfway through doing that, Jenny walked into the bedroom.

"What are you doing? Packing?"

Olivia nodded. "I got the keys to my bungalow today, so I figured I'd start getting things together to move in there."

Jenny smiled. "Can we go see it?"

Olivia put the shorts in her hands down on the bed. "I suppose we should. I haven't actually seen it. I just know it's the one next door to Eddie's.

Jenny wiggled her brows. "Isn't that convenient?"

Olivia laughed. "Hush. Come on, let's go have a look."

"Then maybe we can get some lunch? I'm starving. All this work I've been doing really builds up an appetite."

"Sure."

Together they walked over to the staff area.

"Hey," Jenny said. "This is really nice."

"What did you think it was going to be?" Olivia asked. "A couple of tents and a firepit?"

Jenny laughed. "Not quite that but not this fancy, either. I mean, you have your own pool and hot tub and a whole area to hang out in. Very cool."

"It is," Olivia agreed.

They walked around to the row of bungalows where Eddie's was, going to the front side. She pointed. "That's Eddie's, so I think the one next to it is mine. I guess we'll know if the key works."

They went up the steps to the front porch. Jenny turned to look at the water. "Great view."

"Isn't it? I can already see myself having my coffee out here." Olivia slid the key into the lock. It turned. "This is it. Let's see what it looks like."

She pushed the door open, and they went in.

"Air needs to get cranked on," Jenny said.

Olivia nodded. "It's a little warm in here. We'll do that before we leave." She walked in through the small foyer. Just like at Eddie's, there was a set of steps in front of them that led upstairs.

She went into the living room. "I can work with this."

"Mom." Jenny's lip curled. "That sofa is ugly."

Olivia sighed. The plaid fabric looked more like it belonged in a den than in a condo situated on a tropical island. "Yeah, it's not great, is it. But if it's comfortable, I can get a slipcover and that plaid won't matter."

Jenny went over and sat on it, bouncing up and down a little. "It's not bad." She glanced at the chair next to it, a tan leather recliner. "At least the chair is in decent shape."

"It seems to be."

Jenny stood and stared down at the rug.

"The carpet is fine," Olivia said. "It might not be exciting, but it doesn't need to be." The sand-colored nubby carpet seemed very durable. And easy to put an area rug over, if Olivia wanted to go that route.

Jenny nodded. "Exactly." She rubbed her hands together. "So which bedroom would be mine?"

Olivia laughed. "Making plans, are you?"

"You bet," Jenny said.

"The downstairs one. Let's have a look."

Together they went past the kitchen, which was lovely with its tan granite and white cabinets, and into the first bedroom.

It had the same carpet. A twin bed was pushed against the wall to make room for a small desk with a matching chair. No nightstand, but there was a dresser on the wall opposite the desk.

"Only a single?" Jenny shook her head. "I guess Nick won't be sleeping over."

"Jenny!" Olivia shot a look at her daughter.

Jenny winked. "I need to see the bathroom."

"We already passed that door."

They went back out, looked at the bathroom, found the pantry, washer and dryer, and then went upstairs.

"Oooh," Jenny said. "This is nice. You have your own sitting room up here."

Olivia hitched her mouth to one side, considering the ratty loveseat and old coffee table that currently occupied the space. "I will probably get rid of that stuff and set up an office out here."

"Won't you have an office already?"

Olivia shook her head. "I don't think so, because right now, accounting is handled off the island, not here. Which means I'd have to set something up."

"Oh. Well, this gives you the space to do that. You'll just have to get a desk."

"If I can't find one cheaply, I can work at the dining table downstairs."

"True. But if I'm here, I might have to work there, too. Although I can work on the couch and use the coffee table. Like I'm doing now."

Olivia peered at her daughter. "You seem to be

making plans to be here. Is there something you haven't told me?"

Jenny grinned. "Nothing concrete yet, but Owen and Katie have petitioned my firm on my behalf with the request that I be allowed to open a satellite office here. To serve them better, of course. In fact, Owen sweetened the deal by offering to give me the OM coin account if my firm agrees."

Olivia's jaw dropped. "Why didn't you say something sooner?"

"Well, like I said, it's not a done deal yet. I wasn't going to give you the news until it was confirmed but seeing this place...I had to share."

Olivia hugged Jenny. "I'm so happy. I'm sure you are, too. I really hope your firm agrees." She let her daughter go. "Have you told Nick?"

Jenny gave a quick shake of her head. "No, and I don't plan to until I know for sure. It would just be miserable if I told him and then it didn't happen."

"I understand that." Olivia clasped her hands in front of her, thrilled at the news and praying that it came to be. "We would be all right here together, don't you think?"

Jenny smiled at her mom. "Are you having second thoughts?"

"No! Not even a little bit. I was just thinking about both of us working here at the same time."

"I swear, Mom, I will not get in your way. I promise.

I'll be quiet and keep my headphones on and you won't even know I'm here."

Olivia smiled and pulled her daughter into her arms again, hugging her hard. "Oh, honey, I'm not worried about that. I'd be happy to know you're here. I just don't want us to get on each other's nerves."

As they broke away from each other, Jenny shook her head. "We won't, Mom. I am completely aware of what you're doing for me by letting me stay here. I will be totally respectful of your space."

Jenny's smile turned sly. "Besides, I know you and Eddie will want alone time."

Olivia gave her daughter a smirk. "I am very capable of going to his place for alone time. Which doesn't mean what you think it does."

Jenny held her hands up. "You're a grown woman and you're both consenting adults. What you do in your free time is completely up to you."

Olivia rolled her eyes. "I'm going to look at my bedroom and bathroom now, if you don't mind."

She went through to the bedroom, which was nicer than she'd expected but still a little masculine. The simple slatted oak headboard at least matched the nightstands and dresser. Above the bed was a generic print of a sailboat.

"You don't love it, do you?"

Olivia wrinkled her nose. "It's fine, but it's not very pretty."

"You could always paint the furniture. I'd help you. That's what I did in my apartment. I bought stuff from secondhand shops and painted it. It's not hard. I bet Eddie would help."

Olivia thought about that. "That would help. I could probably paint the walls. This blue is a little murky."

"It is. What would you do instead?"

Olivia remembered a picture she'd seen in a decorating magazine. "White walls with aqua-blue furniture."

"Really?" Jenny smiled. "That's pretty bold. I like it." She nodded. "Let's do it. Let's do all the stuff you want to do to make this place feel like home for you. I'm serious. We'll go hit some thrift shops or whatever they have around here. I bet we find some great things. I'll pay you rent in sweat equity."

"You sound like Eddie with the thrift shops. He said the ones here are loaded with amazing items, since there are so many people moving in and out." Olivia got an idea. "What would you think about bringing Eddie with us? I happen to know he'd like to get a few things for his place as well."

"I'd love that, Mom. I know he makes you happy. And he's a really good guy. If I tease you about him too much, just say so. But I only do it because I like him. And I like you guys together."

"You do?"

Jenny nodded. "This might sound odd, but it makes me feel better about how awful I was to you for so many years to see you happy now. I know it doesn't make up for those years, but it feels like it balances some of that. Is that weird?"

"No. Not weird. I'm happy for you and Nick, too." Olivia was especially happy that Jenny might be staying on Compass Key.

After so many years of being estranged, this new relationship was something she couldn't get enough of. Having her daughter nearby meant they'd be able to keep working on that relationship and strengthening it.

"Thanks," Jenny said. She tipped her head. "We should probably do a quick inventory of the place, see what's here and what's not in terms of things needed to actually live here, then we can go grab some lunch before we pack up the bungalow. After that, I'll help you haul that stuff over here. What do you think?"

"I think you've grown into a remarkable young woman and I'm proud to call you my daughter."

Jenny looked pleased. "Thanks, Mom. Getting to know you like I have this past week has been amazing. You're pretty remarkable yourself."

Olivia smiled. How could she not?

# Chapter Twelve

"This is a great salad," Amanda said as she took another bite of the lunch Vera had made for all of them.

Grace and Katie nodded in agreement.

"Vera makes the best salads," Iris said.

Amanda smiled. Iris hadn't wanted them to leave, so she'd bribed them with lunch. Not that it had taken much of a bribe. And the salad was delicious, with lots of mixed greens, chopped veggies, grilled chicken, dried cranberries, and slivered almonds. Vera had made a quick vinaigrette to go with it. Plus, there were leftover coconut muffins from breakfast.

Vera had joined them, as well, something all three younger women had insisted on. It was silly for her not to. She was as much a part of their new community as Iris was.

The other guest at the gathering was the diamond, which currently sat in its box next to Iris's plate. Her gaze continually drifted back to it throughout the meal.

They *all* kept looking at it. And just like Amanda, they were probably all wondering about the second note underneath the diamond. Iris had yet to read it. After she'd found it, she'd said she couldn't. That she was too overwhelmed.

That's when Vera had helped Iris off to her room to shower—after making the girls promise to stay for lunch.

Of course, while waiting on Iris to return, they'd done nothing but discuss and inspect the diamond, which she'd left with them. It was easily the most interesting thing that had happened since Iris had announced she was turning the island and the resort over to them.

Amanda had seen some amazing diamonds in her time. Her own engagement ring, sold long ago to go toward paying Brian's debt, had been a little over three carats. But this diamond? It had to be twenty-five or thirty carats. Maybe more. It was enormous.

When Iris had rejoined them, Vera had gone to work getting the salad together. They'd tried to help, but the most she'd let them do was set the table.

Lunch, so far, had been pretty quiet, with occasional drifts of small talk.

Amanda couldn't take it anymore. It felt like they were dancing around the obvious and she wasn't sure why. "Iris, when are you going to read that other note? We're all dying to know what it says."

Iris smiled. "I am, too. But I'm a little afraid to find out."

"Why?" Grace asked.

Iris shook her head. "I'm not sure. Maybe because it's the last note I'm ever going to get from Arthur. That makes it bittersweet."

Katie nodded. "I get that. You want to read it, but as soon as you do that, you'll never get to read it for the first time ever again. Or something like that. Is that about right?"

Iris nodded. "Yes, that's exactly right." She laughed softly. "We women are such odd creatures, aren't we? So sentimental." She sighed. "It gets worse as you get older, girls. Trust me. The safe cushion around your dearest memories gets thinner, meaning you feel them with greater intensity."

She set her fork down and picked up the diamond in its box, then removed the cushion and pulled out the note underneath. She lifted her glasses, which were dangling off a chain around her neck, and put them on.

She unfolded the note and began to read.

*"My darling Iris. I hope you like your bauble. I've officially had the name of this magnificent diamond changed to the Escape Diamond. The reason for that is twofold. One, should you ever need it, selling this stone will provide you*

*with all the money you need to go anywhere your heart desires."*

She looked at the girls. "I could never sell this." Then she went back to the note.

*"The second reason is that I hope you are able to look at this diamond and escape to a place where you remember that you are as precious to me as this stone is rare."*

Tears welled in Iris's eyes. She wiped at them, then went on.

*"The Escape Diamond is well covered by our insurance, so there is no reason for you not to wear it and enjoy it. My only regret is that I couldn't find a diamond as beautiful as you are."*

Amanda felt a little teary herself. "That's so sweet."

Iris nodded, seemingly out of words. Or perhaps just lost in a memory.

Grace sniffed. "What a love story." She poked Katie with her elbow. "You should really write their story."

"I might have to with this kind of ending," Katie said. "It's better than anything I could have come up with."

Iris folded the note and tucked it back into the box, then lifted the diamond pendant off of its cushion. She held it out toward Vera. "Help me?"

With a quick nod, Vera was on her feet, pendant in hand. She fastened the chain around Iris's neck. "There you go."

Iris adjusted it, then looked at them. "What do you think?"

Vera blinked. "I think we're going to need more security around this place."

That made them all laugh.

Katie chimed in next. "You look like you robbed Elizabeth Taylor."

Grace snorted. "You do look like a movie star."

Amanda nodded. "It's stunning. As are you."

Iris grinned, clearly pleased. "I need to see it."

Vera was up again. "I'll get your hand mirror."

Iris leaned in. "Do you think it's okay for me to actually wear this? After all, Arthur wanted me to."

Amanda had her doubts about the safety of such a thing, but she didn't want to tell Iris what to do, either. Not when Arthur had wanted this for her. "Maybe you could wear it, but not tell people it's real."

Grace shrugged. "Who's going to steal it? We're on a private island filled with celebrities." She glanced at Iris. "You do have security here, right?"

"Of course," Iris said. "There are cameras in the common areas, and at the marina. Also, at night, our waters are patrolled by the police to make sure we're safe. We pay a monthly fee for that service. Although Owen pays part of that, since they cover the whole island, which includes his end."

Amanda's brows rose. "Good to know."

Iris shook her head. "You can't run a business like this without your guests having peace of mind."

Katie seemed to consider all the factors. "If you want to wear the diamond, wear it. Arthur said in the note it's insured. I'd say just maybe call the insurance company to confirm that the policy is up to date, then go forth with confidence."

Vera returned, holding the hand mirror out. "Here you go. Can you see yourself?"

Iris looked into it, shifting the glass slightly. "Oh my. That is a *very* large diamond. It looks bigger on than it did in the box." She laughed, a little giddy as she continued to stare at it. "I don't know if people would believe it's real."

"On you?" Grace said. "They'd believe it. But, man, I'm sure glad Amanda found that box before anyone else did."

Iris gasped. "So am I! Amanda, you sweet girl. I owe you."

Amanda shook her head. "You owe me nothing. My reward is being able to play a part in this chapter of your story with Arthur. Really. That's all the reward I need." She meant it, too. She hoped Iris understood that.

"Well said." Katie smiled. "What do you think, Iris? Would you be interested in turning yours and Arthur's story into a book? A little something we could sell in the boutique to interested guests? We could sell it online, pretty easily as well. I know all about how to do that."

"Maybe," Iris said. "I'll think about it." Her hand went to the diamond. "I suppose a man like Arthur really deserves to have his story told, doesn't he?"

Amanda nodded. "He does. The book could be a reminder to other women that good men do exist, and real love is still out there."

Iris smiled, looking teary-eyed again. "That's so kind of you to say. But I think you've found a pretty good man, too."

Amanda laughed softly. "Yes, I have, that's true. But you and Arthur, that's a different sort of thing altogether."

Iris frowned. "How? You don't think you and Duke could be just as good?"

That was a complicated question for Amanda to answer, but everyone was looking at her, waiting for her to do just that. "I don't know. Possibly. I don't think it's that serious for either one of us."

Iris's brows bent. "Is that what you want? For it not to be serious?"

Amanda shook her head. "I'm not sure what I want. But I like what we have right now very much." Whatever that was. A comfortable friendship? A casual romance? She pushed a sliver of almond around her plate with her fork. "After what I went through with Brian..."

"The heart takes time to heal," Katie said.

Amanda nodded. "It does."

Was she healed? Sometimes she thought so. Sometimes she wasn't sure. But she dearly loved spending time with Duke. Maybe it would be all right if things got more serious.

But did he feel that way?

# Chapter Thirteen

With lunch over, Grace, Amanda, and Katie headed out. Katie was going back to her bungalow but Grace and Amanda still had a chalkboard to find.

Grace used the walk to talk about her cookbook idea with Katie. "I love the idea of writing Iris and Arthur's story and selling it in the boutique, but I had an idea for another book."

"Oh?" Katie didn't look particularly interested, but Grace wasn't surprised. People probably told her their book ideas all the time.

"I was thinking David could do a cookbook for the restaurant. *The Palms Cookbook* or *Mother's Resort Cookbook*. Something like that. I think people would love that as a souvenir, and it could be a tool to promote the resort."

Katie slowed and looked at Grace. "That's actually a fantastic idea. But cookbooks aren't easy. Lots of trial and error to get those recipes right. Plus, you need a great photographer to make the photos sing. Do you think he'd be interested in doing something like that?"

Grace nodded. "He would be. Totally. We've already talked about it."

"You know," Katie said. "A book like that wouldn't just be a promotional tool for the resort. It would give David some additional credentials. Not that he needs them. I'm not saying that. Just that a chef with a cookbook carries a little more weight. Am I making sense?"

Grace laughed. "Yes, and not only do I understand but I agree. In fact, Amanda suggested we try to get him some interviews with the local press."

Amanda nodded. "I did. Establishing him that way, giving him a little celebrity, would boost his reputation as well as the resort's. And with all of this embezzlement business going on, that might be a way to heal that wound."

Katie stared ahead, appearing to Grace like she was deep in thought. "I wonder if I could get Maxine to represent this. Maybe this could be bigger than we think. Chefs are hot. And a chef at a private celebrity resort like this?" She went silent for a moment, nodding like she was agreeing with her own thoughts. "I'm going to talk to my agent about this. See if she thinks it could be a viable product for the traditional market."

"Really?" Grace blinked. She'd never imagined the

cookbook would be more than something they'd produce themselves and sell in the boutique. "Thanks."

"Happy to do it," Katie said. She stopped in front of her bungalow. "This is me. I'm going to get packed and move over to Iris's. Then I'm going to work on getting Sophie and Fabio moved in, too. Will I see you guys at dinner?"

Grace looked at Amanda, who shrugged. "I'll be there," she said. "You don't seem sure, Amanda."

"I'm not," she answered. "I'm not a guest here anymore, so I don't feel like I should be eating in the restaurant."

"Iris eats there," Grace said.

"But she's the owner."

Grace smiled. "So are you. You signed the papers, didn't you?"

"Yes. But it feels different." Amanda shook her head. "I bought groceries, so I'll probably eat at my place."

"Or with Duke?" Katie said. "Don't worry, we get it." She nodded at Grace. "I'm sure Sophie and I will be there, because we don't have groceries."

"Okay, I'll see you then."

"Cool." Katie went up the steps to her door. "I hope you guys find that chalkboard."

"Me, too," Amanda said.

Grace started walking again, Amanda keeping pace

beside her. "If we don't find a chalkboard, what will you do?"

Amanda hesitated. "Maybe try to buy one. Although I'm not sure where I'd find one in town. That might be a hard thing to come by."

"What about hitting the local hardware store for some chalkboard paint and a piece of plywood? We could get Duke to cut it to whatever size we needed, then we could paint it and maybe decorate the edge with rope or shells or something like that."

Amanda smiled. "I don't know why I didn't think of that. You're full of all kinds of good ideas today."

"Yeah?" Grace grinned. "Being sober has really cleared my brain."

Amanda put her arm around Grace's shoulders. "I'm so glad to hear that. You look clearer in a lot of ways. Your eyes, your skin, your whole self seems happier."

"Thanks." She hugged Amanda back. "Your support has meant the world to me. And a big part of the change in me is David and me getting back on track. Things are so good between us right now. So good."

"That's fantastic. I'm so happy for you."

"You know," Grace said. "Whatever you decide about Duke, you have my support. Don't let anyone talk you into doing something you're not ready for. If you want to keep things casual with him, then keep it that way. If you want more, then tell him. You deserve to have the kind of life you want."

Amanda glanced at Grace, nodding. "Thank you," she said quietly. "I appreciate that. The truth is, I'm not really sure what I want."

"That's okay, too. You and Duke are going to the gallery party tomorrow night together, right?"

Amanda nodded. "We are. At least, I think we are. I'd better confirm that with him tonight."

They reached the storage room, Grace unlocked it, then they got back to work looking through everything in search of the elusive chalkboard. Forty-five minutes later, they were still minus one chalkboard.

Grace put her hands on her hips. "Well, we looked. No more diamonds and no chalkboard, either. I guess you're going to have to talk to Duke."

Amanda pushed a strand of hair out of her eyes. "I'm going to do that right now. I'm not sure if he's free, but if he is, it would be nice to get that done today. What are you going to do?"

Grace looked down at herself. "Probably shower. Then go have a look at our new bungalow. Although it would be nice to do laundry."

"The staff bungalows have a stacked washer-and-dryer unit. You could definitely do laundry there."

"That would be great. David's been getting his chef clothes cleaned by Housekeeping every day. He only has two sets." But Grace imagined that would change soon. "Maybe I'll take a basket of clothes with me." She sighed. "Never mind. I don't have any laundry soap."

She groaned. "You know, in some ways, living here is going to require me to be a lot more organized. If you forget something at the store, it's not like you can just run back out and get it."

"No," Amanda agreed. "But with all of us living so close, we have great neighbors to rely on. Stop by my bungalow and I'll give you some laundry pods so you can do your wash."

"Thank you. That would be great." Grace's phone vibrated in her pocket. She pulled it out and checked the screen. A text from David.

*Glenn was just taken out of the kitchen in handcuffs.*

Grace whistled. "Holy cow."

"What?" Amanda asked.

Grace looked up. "David said Chef Glenn was just taken out of the kitchen in handcuffs."

Amanda stared back at her. "I guess Iris had better send that email out to the employees after all."

Grace nodded and started dialing. "You text the girls and tell them. I'll let Iris know."

# Chapter Fourteen

Katie looked at the message from Amanda in disbelief. If Glenn had been arrested, that had to mean Freda was, too. Didn't it? She wasn't sure. She supposed they'd find out soon enough.

Her phone rang while she was still looking at the text. Iris.

"Hello."

"Hello, honey. Chef Glenn was just arrested. Did you hear?"

"I did. Amanda texted us all. I guess we need to send that email to the employees, huh?"

"I believe we should."

"I'll be right over so we can finalize the draft and get it out."

"Thank you."

Katie hung up, zipped her suitcase, laptop case, and carryon bag, then took one final look around to make sure she had everything. Satisfied, she headed back to Iris's.

Within ten minutes of sitting down at the computer, Katie had the email proofed and sent. She looked over at Iris. "All done. Have you heard from the police?"

Iris looked unsettled. "Not yet. But Olivia texted to say she was contacting them."

"Good. I'd like to know if Freda was picked up, too."

"So would I." Iris smiled, although the expression was tight and didn't quite reach her eyes. The diamond sparkled around her neck. "Thank you for your help with this."

"You're welcome. But it's my job now. You don't have to thank me."

That made Iris smile a little wider. "I'm so glad you girls are here. Are you taking your things upstairs?"

"I am. And then I'm going over to Owen's to help bring Sophie and Fabio over."

"Wonderful. Now, if you'll excuse me, I'm going to have a nap. It's been a long day already and it's barely afternoon."

"I don't blame you." Katie tipped her chin at the diamond. "I bet that rock gives you all kinds of sweet dreams."

"Oh, I like that idea." Iris took hold of her walker and stood.

Katie logged off the computer and followed her out

of the room. Katie had left her bags near the steps that led to the second floor. She grabbed the handles and hauled them up. She didn't plan on using the interior stairs much.

In fact, she wanted to get a baby gate to block the stairs so that Fabio didn't decide Anne Bonny and Mary Read were his new girlfriends. She really hoped that there wouldn't be any friction between her cat and Iris's crew, but she knew it was a possibility.

Fabio was used to being the only child. He might get a little jealous knowing there were three new roommates only a flight of stairs away.

She headed toward one of the bedrooms to start unpacking, then realized Sophie might want that room. Katie sent her sister a quick text. *I'm at our new house but I don't want to pick a bedroom without you. Which one do you want? Maybe you should come over here.*

Sophie answered shortly. *Is there a big difference between the two? Better view? Bigger closet? Nicer bathroom?*

Katie had a look to compare. The two bedrooms were on opposite sides of the house with the smaller office bedroom between them.

The closets were almost identical. The bathrooms were pretty close, too, although the one to the right of the office had a door that made it accessible to the rest of the house as well as the bedroom.

She explained that to Sophie, sending some more

pictures. Then she took pictures of the two different views and sent them along with a single-word question. *Well?*

Sophie took a little longer to answer this time. *I'll take the bathroom with the shared door. I don't mind. And I'm neater than you.*

Katie rolled her eyes, but she couldn't argue that. Sophie *was* actually neater. *You got it. I'm unpacking, then I'm going to come over and help you with Fabio.*

She really hoped he liked it here. There was already a scratching post in the office, as well as a carpeted cat house in the living room by the windows that looked onto the side porch, and a litter box in the laundry room. It was turnkey ready for his little fuzzy butt.

In fact, it was turnkey ready for her and Sophie, too, which meant they were going to have to get rid of a lot of their stuff. Or put some of it into storage, which didn't really make much sense.

To her, that was wasted money.

She looked at the bedroom that was going to be hers. It was nicely decorated and very similar to the bungalow she'd just come from, with the dark wood and rattan pieces combined with tropical fabrics and bright pops of color.

Pretty different from their place in Brooklyn, which was a much more eclectic mix of things they'd picked up over the years.

She took her laptop into the office and got it set up on the desk, plugging it in to charge. She smiled thinking about the books she'd be writing here. It remained to be seen how this new environment would change those stories, but she believed her readers would still like them.

She had to believe that. Because if they didn't, she'd have to work that out pretty fast. That got her thinking about Maxine, her agent.

She sat down at the desk, turned on her laptop, then drafted an email to Maxine. She needed to know things were changing in Katie's life. Katie also wanted to run the cookbook idea by her.

Writing that email took longer than Katie anticipated, but she had a lot to say and a lot to explain. Hopefully, Maxine would have some insights. Katie hit Send, then went back to the bedroom.

She put her suitcase on the bed and got to work unpacking. As she hung up the last sundress, her phone let her know she had a new text.

She got a happy jolt when she saw who it was from.

Owen. *How's it going? I understand you're moving in?*

*I am. We're now officially neighbors.*

*And yet you're still too far away.*

She smiled. *It's too bad I can't walk to your place from here. Seems like I should be able to do that.*

His response was three lightbulbs.

She shook her head, unsure what that meant. That

he'd had an idea? If so, what was it? She texted back. *What does that mean?*

*You'll see. No pun intended.*

That man. *Okay. I'd like to come over and get Sophie and Fabio soon. Can you send Gage?*

*I could. Or I could come get you.*

*Even better.* She signed it with a heart emoji.

*Fifteen minutes?*

*See you then.* She tucked her phone into her back pocket, then checked herself out in the bathroom mirror, making sure she looked all right. Her hair was a little crazy. She ran a brush through it, then pulled it into a ponytail and put on a ball cap.

She was going to be on a boat. Anything else wouldn't last five seconds. She grabbed the key to the house, although she had no intention of locking the door, and headed down the outside steps.

As she walked, she stared off toward the water. It was too bad there was no dock on this side of the island. It would be a lot more convenient for the staff and Iris. In fact, maybe it could be a dock that only served the staff and owners.

Katie didn't know what building such a thing would entail, but she immediately decided it was worth looking into. Owen might know. And with her newfound settlement money, maybe she could build it herself. So long as Iris and the rest of the girls were in favor of it.

Of course, having a dock would be great, but not as useful as it could be unless she also had a boat. Which she didn't. Easy enough to rectify, but she didn't know how to drive a boat. Captain a boat? She wasn't sure what the proper vernacular was.

Again, Owen would know.

Then she thought about it a little more. Maybe she didn't need a boat. Maybe there was something smaller she could get. Like a jet ski. But something not that noisy, because those things were like water motorcycles.

She was early to the marina by a few minutes, but Owen's boat was already pulling in at the end. He waved and she waved back, picking up speed to meet him.

"Your Uber, ma'am."

She grinned and took the hand he held out, jumping on board. "Early, too. You must be angling for a bigger tip."

"I am and I'd like that tip now." He pulled her in and kissed her. "How's your day going?"

"Crazy busy. But good." She patted his cheek. So handsome. "I have some questions for you."

"Uh-oh. What have I done now?"

She laughed and shook her head as he got them back out onto the water. "Nothing. I'm doing some fact-finding."

"Okay. What would you like to know?"

"You know where Iris's house is? Would it be a major undertaking to build a dock near there? On that side of the island? I was thinking it would be a lot more convenient for all of us and the rest of the employees if there was a dock just for us on that side."

He nodded. "It would be a lot more convenient, and if I remember correctly, Arthur had plans to do that at one time." He sighed. "I think it was right before he got sick and because of that, it all got put on hold."

That was good news, Katie thought. It meant there might be existing plans. "Any idea what a thing like that might cost?"

"Not sure what the current cost would be exactly. You'd have to get a contractor to rebid the job. But my guess? A couple hundred thousand dollars. Depending on how many slips you want, that sort of thing."

She seemed to think that over. "I could afford that. With my settlement money."

He nodded. "You could. Are you really considering it?"

"I am. I want to do it. So long as no one else is opposed to it."

He smiled. "Is that so I can get to you faster?"

She smiled, too. "Yes. But it benefits everyone."

"Very generous of you. Any other questions I can answer?"

"Yes. What kind of small boat could I get that

would be easy to drive? Like the boat equivalent of a bicycle."

He laughed. "Well, that would be a paddleboat and I wouldn't suggest that out here, not even for these calm waters. If you want something for going back and forth to the mainland and coming to my place, I'd suggest something like a small pontoon."

"That still seems like a pretty big boat."

He steered them around the curve of the island. "It is, but think of it this way—what if you go to the mainland for groceries or some other shopping and it starts to rain? With a canopied pontoon, you'd have some coverage."

She hadn't considered that. "Good point. Could I learn to drive a thing like that?" She knew Eddie had been teaching Olivia, but Katie didn't even have a car.

"You could. I could teach you. Or Gage could. Or you could take lessons. It would be easy for someone as smart as you to get a boat license."

She smirked. "You're giving me a lot of credit and I appreciate that, but you should know I don't even own a car. I haven't driven in years. My driver's license is only current because I need it for identification."

"I understand," he said. "When you live in an area with that much public transportation, why would you need a car?"

"Right. Not to mention the cost of parking and insurance," she added. She hooked her arm through his, her mind made up. "I'm going to build a dock and buy a boat with my *Star Watch* money."

"Some of your *Star Watch* money?" Owen raised his brows. "You're still going to have a lot left over."

"True," she said. "I might use the rest to put a new roof on the resort's main building. But don't tell Iris that."

# Chapter Fifteen

Leigh Ann kissed Grant goodbye at the dock, thanked him for the ride home, and told him she'd see him tomorrow at the party. She couldn't wait.

She had a few nerves about how the painting would be received. Or at least how her presence in the painting would be received. She wanted people to like it, because she didn't want Grant to think he'd made a mistake by using her as his model.

That wasn't a productive line of thinking, though, because there was nothing she could do about it now. Instead, as she walked back to her bungalow, she once again thought about how much she'd enjoyed her day with him. His gallery was a spectacular space and so beautifully done with dark, mottled sea green walls that made you feel like you were standing on the bottom of the ocean floor. Or maybe a better description of his gallery was that it reminded her of being at one of the nation's aquariums, with their cool, dark spaces and expanses of glass that allowed you glimpses of captivating underwater worlds.

His paintings were those expanses of glass. They were windows into a fantastical underwater world.

Leigh Ann could have spent another hour there, just looking at his work, finding new elements with each examination.

No wonder Cheyanne enjoyed her job so much.

Of course, Cheyanne had been abundantly complimentary toward Grant's new painting, as had Nesto, but Cheyanne had been effusive. Which was about what Leigh Ann had expected from the young woman. She clearly loved her job and loved Grant's work.

She might even love Grant himself a little, Leigh Ann thought. The way Cheyanne had looked at Grant had made her seem very much like a young woman with a crush, but Leigh Ann wasn't jealous.

Grant had confessed as much to Leigh Ann over lunch, that he suspected Cheyanne's affections for him, but also that he'd been introducing her to every single, eligible male he could find.

That had made Leigh Ann laugh.

As she walked the path toward the main building, she went inside and decided to have another look around the boutique for a little scarf or shawl to wear with the new dress. One thing she'd learned at the gallery today was that they kept the air cranked.

It had been downright chilly in there. She definitely wanted something to throw over her shoulders and the little white cardigan that she'd brought would totally ruin the look of that dress.

The boutique had a few other women in it but was still pretty quiet. Maybe the soft music helped maintain that serene vibe. Leigh Ann went to the rack of scarves she'd seen earlier by the dressing room entrance and looked through them for one that would work. She really should have brought her pashmina with her, but she'd thought it would be too dressy.

As she was browsing, a young woman came out of one of the dressing rooms with a handful of clothes. She stopped suddenly, a movement that made Leigh Ann glance over.

Candi.

"Hi," Candi said softly. There was fear in her eyes. What did she think Leigh Ann was going to do? Hit her? Yell at her? Cause a scene?

None of that was Leigh Ann's style, nor would it get her anywhere. Instead, she smiled. "Hi. Doing some shopping?"

"Um, yeah." Candi glanced at the things dangling over her arm. "You, too, huh?"

Leigh Ann nodded. "Yep."

Candi stayed there but looked very much like she wanted to bolt.

"You don't have to be afraid of me," Leigh Ann said. "I'm not your enemy. No matter what Marty's told you."

Candi smiled weakly. "That's nice to know."

Leigh Ann found a shawl that would work, a fine weave of silky white with a subtle thread of gold worked through it. Perfect. She took it off the rack and turned toward Candi. "I want the divorce over with as much as you do. Probably more."

Candi just blinked and chewed on her bottom lip.

Leigh Ann took a step toward her. To Candi's credit, she didn't flinch. "If you don't mind me asking, what has Marty told you about why he won't sign the papers?"

Candi exhaled. "He keeps saying he doesn't want to give you the money you're asking for."

Leigh Ann nodded. "Do you know why I want that money?"

Candi shrugged. "Because it's money?"

Leigh Ann laughed softly. "That seems like a good enough reason, but it's not the main one. I want that money because I'm trying to make a new life for myself, ensure my kids get something, and because he humiliated me with his years and years of cheating."

Candi's eyes got slightly bigger. Did she think Marty wasn't a serial cheater? That was, after all, how Marty had come to be with Candi. She couldn't really be blind to that fact, could she? "That seems fair."

"I think so, too," Leigh Ann said. "After all, he's got

*gobs* of money." She smiled. "In fact, you should buy all of that stuff and charge it to the room. He won't mind. I bet it looked great on you."

Candi warmed to that idea. "Yeah? Maybe I should."

Leigh Ann nodded as a brand-new idea came into her head. One that might get her into trouble, but she was past caring. "You know what else you should do? You should come to the big party at the Shoemaker Gallery in town tomorrow night. Seven o'clock. Everyone's going to be there."

"Grant who?"

"Grant Shoemaker. He's a world-famous artist and he's exhibiting one of his new paintings. The new one's already sold but he's got others. Wouldn't that be a great souvenir to decorate your house with? Then every time you look at it you can remember your wonderful vacation here."

Candi nodded. "That would be good! And I love a party. Where did you say it was?"

Leigh Ann pulled one of the gallery's business cards from her pocket. She'd grabbed a few on her way out, thinking it would be nice to have them on hand. How right she'd been. "Here you go. Seven p.m. And you'll get to meet Grant in person."

Candi took the card. "Thanks. That sounds like fun." She smiled and looked at Leigh Ann. "You're a lot nicer than Marty's led me to believe."

Leigh Ann almost laughed. "That's so kind of you to say. You have a good night."

"You, too."

Leigh Ann took the scarf to the register, almost vibrating with mischievous energy. She had no idea what she'd just set in motion, but she hoped that Marty would show up, see how happy she was, and realize that she would be just fine waiting him out. So fine that there was no point in him delaying the signing any longer.

He needed to understand that she had moved on. And he needed to do the same.

That would be a fabulous outcome.

But it wouldn't hurt if he saw her at the center of Grant's painting and realized that another man, a very successful man, had found value in her.

Because Leigh Ann would be lying if she said the wounds from Marty's casual, careless treatment of her were gone. They weren't.

But Marty getting a little comeuppance would go a long way toward healing them.

# Chapter Sixteen

Olivia flopped down on the bed in her new bedroom. It was really good to be in her own bungalow, even if it did need some tweaking. She stared up at the ceiling. She should turn the fan on, but she was too exhausted from hauling their stuff over and unpacking. And everything else that had gone on. What a day it had been. And it wasn't over yet. She still needed to shower and meet the girls for dinner. Jenny was in the shower right now, getting ready to meet Nick.

Olivia really hoped Jenny's firm gave her the thumbs-up to move. That would be amazing.

Her phone buzzed. She rolled to the side so she could pull it out of her back pocket. It was Eddie. She smiled as she read his text.

*How's it going?*

*Good*, she answered. *I'm officially moved in next door.*

*Yeah? That's great!! Want to come over for dinner?*

*I can't. Already promised the girls I'd meet them.*

*No worries. Text me later if you want to hit the hot tub.*

*Will do. How was your day?*

*Good. Busy. Crazy day, huh?*

*For sure. At least Freda and Glenn aren't getting away with it.*

*Nope. Great timing, too, considering Iris's new sparkler.*

Olivia frowned. *What does that mean?*

*Maybe it's not my news to tell. You should talk to her.*

*I will. Hey, I may need some help getting this place in order. Painting some furniture, hitting some thrift shops, stuff like that.*

*I'm all yours. Plus, you still owe me some throw pillows.*

She smiled. *I remember. Any chance for tomorrow?*

*If we go early. I have an afternoon snorkel trip. Nine okay?*

*Perfect. TY*

*No problem.*

She got up, put her phone back in her pocket, then went downstairs to find a pen and paper. If she was going into town, she needed to make a list so that she didn't forget anything.

From the hardware store, she needed paint for the furniture and walls, and robe hooks for both bathrooms.

From the thrift store, she wanted to look for a desk and chair for the loft area upstairs, some nice art, throw pillows for Eddie, a slipcover for the sofa if she could find one, any cute accessories that would give the place some character, a lamp for next to her bed, and a small area rug for in front of it.

And then, if there was time, she could really use a trip to the grocery store. The fridge and the cupboards were bare, as was to be expected. But she and Jenny had to eat.

Jenny came out of the bathroom, wrapped in a towel. "Hey. What are you working on there?"

"Eddie's taking me into town in the morning so I can get some stuff for here. I'm trying to make a list of all the things we need."

"That's going to be a long list," Jenny said.

"I know." Olivia read through what she had so far. "What else can you think of?"

"Have you gone through all of the kitchen stuff? Based on the fact that it looks like a man lived here last, I bet the kitchen is woefully underequipped."

"Good point," Olivia said. "But you know, my kitchen in Ohio is completely stocked. I hate to buy things I already have. I know it'll be a while before that stuff gets here, but I need to make do as best as I can."

Jenny nodded. "Makes sense. And at least there's a coffee maker."

"That would be top of the list if there wasn't one." Olivia smiled. "Which reminds me, I hope to get to the grocery store, too."

"That's going to be a ton of shopping to get done. You sure you can manage all that? Plus, we have the gallery party tomorrow night."

"I know. Another busy day. I'll do what I can. And I still have more accounting work I need to do. With Freda out of the picture, I need to get up to speed on payroll."

Jenny grimaced. "Mom, you're going to be swamped."

"It's okay. I'll manage. This place is livable. It doesn't all have to be done at once."

"I'm happy to help in whatever way I can. My work right now only takes me a couple hours a day, although that will change if I get the OM coin job."

Olivia really hoped that happened, because that would mean Jenny was staying. "When do you think you'll know?"

Jenny shrugged. "I hope by tomorrow. I'm supposed to fly out the day after."

Olivia nodded. "Fingers crossed. I'd better go get my shower or I'm going to be late."

"Yeah, and I need to get dressed." Jenny headed toward the bedroom. "Water's good and hot and the pressure is great."

"I'm glad to hear that." Olivia took her list back upstairs, realizing she still had no clue what Eddie had meant about Iris's "sparkler," but there was no time to call now.

She raced through her shower, towel-drying her hair as she got out. With little thought to her outfit, she grabbed the least wrinkled sundress and threw it on with her white sandals. She finished drying her hair, added a little tinted moisturizer, mascara, and lip gloss, then her jewelry.

The walk to The Palms would take longer from here, which meant she was probably going to be a few minutes late, but it couldn't be helped.

She started downstairs, purse in hand.

Jenny was already at the door. "Are you leaving? We can walk together partway."

"I am." Olivia came the rest of the way down the steps. "Hey! Do you have a key?"

Jenny shook her head. "No. Do you think you'll be out late?"

"Probably not, but I might hit the hot tub later." And they only had one key, something else she'd need to take care of at the hardware store. "I'll leave it under the mat."

"Okay."

She followed Jenny out, locked the door, then tucked the key beneath the welcome mat. "What are you and Nick doing for dinner? Are you coming to the restaurant?"

"No. He's borrowing one of the pontoons and we're going to a place in town."

"Nice."

As they approached the fork in the path that split toward either Iris's or the guest bungalows, Katie and Sophie came through the trees. They stopped to wait for Olivia and Jenny. "Hi, girls," Katie said. "Right on time."

"Yeah," Olivia said. "Right on time to be late together."

Sophie snorted. "It's my fault. I got caught up in rearranging some stuff in the kitchen."

Olivia shook her head. "My only excuse is that it's been a long day."

"Yeah, it has been," Katie agreed.

Jenny pointed toward the house. "I'm meeting Nick. You guys enjoy your dinner."

"Thanks," Katie said. "Well, we'd better get moving or Leigh Ann and Grace will think we stood them up."

"Is Amanda not coming?" Olivia asked as they started walking.

"Wait," a voice called out behind her.

They turned to see Amanda almost running toward them.

"I didn't think you were coming," Katie said.

"Changed my mind," Amanda answered. She slowed as she joined them. "I figured we might not have too many more chances to eat together like this, since we'll all be in our own places, and I didn't want to miss out."

She smiled and brushed a little hair off her face.

"I'm glad you came," Olivia said. "Now we can all get caught up on how everything's going. Which reminds me—Eddie said something I didn't quite understand and when I asked him about it, he said to ask Iris, which I will, but do any of you know what he would have meant by her new 'sparkler'?"

Katie and Amanda started laughing.

"Boy," Katie said. "Do we ever. But it's really Amanda's story to tell. She found it."

"I only found the box," Amanda said.

Katie shrugged. "I suppose it's really Iris's story, then."

Olivia held her hands up. "Will one of you please tell me what you're talking about? The curiosity is killing me."

Amanda nodded, still smiling. "Grace and I went to look for a chalkboard in the storage room today and after digging around a bit, I uncovered an old, locked wooden box. We took it to Iris, figuring it was her property. Vera found a key for it in some of Arthur's old stuff. And in that box was a wrapped present and card for Iris from Arthur."

"That's amazing," Olivia said.

Katie nodded. "Apparently, he'd hid it in the storage room because Iris was a snooper."

"I could see that," Olivia said. "We never could get anything past her as a house mother."

"True." Amanda cleared her throat softly. "But you're never going to guess what was in that box."

"Just tell me. I can't stand it."

Amanda glanced at Katie, then back at Olivia. "Only the biggest diamond you've ever seen."

"What?" Olivia grabbed Amanda's arm.

She nodded and made a teardrop shape with her thumb and forefinger. "That big. Big enough that it has its own name. The Escape Diamond. It's surrounded by more diamonds, all on a platinum chain. Along with a card and a note from Arthur telling her all kinds of sweet, romantic things."

"But specifically," Katie added, "that he wanted her to wear it. So she put it on. Wait until you see it."

Olivia's hand went to her throat. "I can't imagine. I might have to stop by Iris's on the way home from dinner so I can see it for myself. Wow. Giant diamonds, arrests, moving...today really has been a crazy day."

She laughed. "And here I thought life on Compass Key was going to be so laidback."

That made them all chuckle.

"It'll calm down," Amanda said. "Although we do still have a gallery party and a wedding to get through."

"Not to mention the rest of this embezzlement business," Olivia added. "I really hope they find Iris's money. Otherwise, we might have to tighten our belts to get some of those things on her list taken care of. We can't let the resort fall into disrepair."

Amanda nodded. "I agree."

"We should wait to talk about that," Katie started. "Just until we're all together at dinner. Then we can make some decisions as a group."

"You're right," Olivia said. Although to her, it sounded like Katie had something else on her mind.

# Chapter Seventeen

Sitting down to dinner with the girls felt a little surreal and slightly bittersweet. Amanda wondered if any of the rest of them were feeling the same way. Their lives had all changed. The carefree days of visiting Mother's were behind them. They were owners of this place now.

Being on the island was different because of it. Just like eating at The Palms was different. She, at least, was acutely aware of the people around her. The *paying* guests.

She wanted to know if they were having a good time. She wanted to eavesdrop on their conversations and find out what they loved about Mother's. And what they didn't.

Of course, she wasn't about to do that.

There was too much for her to catch up on with the women around the table.

After drinks had been ordered, Katie smiled

brightly at everyone. "I have an idea. It's not going to cost the resort any money, but I believe it will be very beneficial for all of us who live and work on the island."

"Tell us," Amanda said.

Leigh Ann nodded. "Yes, what is it?"

Katie held her smile a moment longer, ever the queen of suspense. "A second, smaller marina. Straight out from where Iris's house is, on that side of the island."

Olivia, in true form, seemed to be calculating figures in her head. "I like the idea but there's no way that wouldn't cost us money."

Grace snorted. "I don't need to do math to agree with Olivia on that one. How do you figure it'll be free?"

"It won't be free," Katie said. "I would pay for it out of my *Star Watch* settlement."

"I don't know," Amanda said. "It seems unfair for you to pay for something that everyone would use."

"But it wouldn't be for everyone. Just for staff and owners who live on the island. It would be more convenient for them to keep their personal watercraft there, since the staff quarters are right there, too. Plus, it would open up more spots at the main marina for guests. I'm not talking about a duplicate of that one. Something smaller. Just eight or ten slips. Just enough for staff and owners, like I said."

"Still," Leigh Ann said. "That's going to be very expensive."

Katie shrugged. "I have more than two million dollars in found money. And I would really like a dock on the other side of the island."

Grace suddenly grinned. "So you can get to Owen faster."

"And Gage," Sophie said quietly.

"It would be more convenient," Amanda said. "From the staff bungalows, it takes almost fifteen minutes to walk to the marina. That's a long way when you're carrying groceries or packages. Having a dock two minutes away would be really nice. But it's still too much for one person to pay for."

Katie frowned, clearly frustrated they weren't cheering her idea. "But the alternative is no dock, because there isn't money in the budget for one. Not when this place needs a new roof. And whatever else needs to be done."

Amanda nodded but looked at Olivia. "How would it work? Katie investing her money like that?"

"It would all be recorded and considered as part of her share, which would—"

"No," Katie said. "I don't want it to be considered part of my share. I want to just do it and have it be part of the resort and that's it. Just like the roof for this place, which I fully intend to pay for as well."

Olivia made a face. "I don't know about that."

"Listen to me." Katie's expression became very stern. "I want to contribute, and this is how I can do that. Being Communications Director sounds great, but it's not going to be a lot of work. Not enough that I should draw the kinds of salaries you guys will be. But none of that matters, because I have my writing. Which I am still going to be focusing on. So let me do this."

Leigh Ann laughed. "So you're going to be doing less work but paying for more? You see the flaw in that argument?"

"I don't care," Katie said. "I've thought about it and it's what I want to do." She looked around the table at them. "All in favor of the new dock, raise your hand."

Katie put her hand up. Then, with a shrug, Grace did, too. Amanda knew she shouldn't, but her hand went into the air. Leigh Ann's followed.

Olivia laced her fingers together. "I can't just agree to this. I need to look at the numbers. I'm not saying no, Katie, but I need to at least research what a second marina will do to our insurance and upkeep costs. Then I'll make a decision."

Katie smiled. "Okay. That's fair." She reached for her water. "I don't know if it helps in that decision, but according to Owen, Arthur had plans to put a second dock there years ago. They were even drawn up. But then he got sick, and it all got pushed aside."

"So Iris probably wouldn't be against it," Amanda

said.

"No," Katie answered. "And you know, it would definitely make her life easier."

Olivia laughed. "Okay, enough with the hard sell. I just really need to see what the insurance increase would be. I'll research it tomorrow, I promise."

"Thanks."

After a brief lull in the conversation, Leigh Ann spoke up. "I ran into Candi this afternoon."

That got everyone's attention.

Amanda was instantly curious. "How did that go?"

Leigh Ann nodded. "It went...all right. Although I may have done something dumb."

"Such as?" Grace asked.

Leigh Ann sipped the glass of white wine she'd gotten. "I invited her and Marty to Grant's gallery party."

"Get out," Grace said.

Olivia seemed surprised. "Do you think they'll come?"

Katie's brows knit in obvious skepticism. "A better question might be, 'Why.'"

Leigh Ann shrugged. "I know it's petty and basic, but I really want Marty to see Grant's painting of me. I want him to understand that another man, an incredibly successful man, thinks enough of me to do that."

"I get it," Amanda said. "And I completely relate to that feeling. Sometimes, I wish Brian could see me now and know that I survived despite the hell he put me through." She smiled to soften her words. "Sorry. I didn't mean to get so dark."

"It's okay," Leigh Ann said. "Between him and your mom, a little darkness on your part is understandable."

Amanda shot a look of thanks at her friend. "I'd still like to put all of that behind me. I want to focus on my future. Not my past."

"You'll get there," Grace said. "We all will. And I know I've said it before, but I'm so glad we're doing this together."

"So am I," Amanda said. "Now, tell us what David's cooking tonight that we absolutely must order."

Grace laughed. "Oh, he's doing a Thai-inspired seafood noodle dish this evening that you don't want to miss. I'm getting it."

Their server, Stephen, had just approached the table. "I was just coming to tell you about our specials this evening."

"Go ahead," Amanda said. "It sounds fantastic, but I want to hear the whole thing."

"I tried it and it's so good," Stephen said. "Here's the full description as Chef gave it to us. Our special tonight is glass noodles in a rich seafood broth flavored with lemongrass and ginger. The noodles are topped with shrimp, scallops, and calamari, along with bamboo shoots and bean sprouts. It does have some heat, but the chilis can be omitted if desired."

"I'm in," Amanda said. "Chilis and all."

Leigh Ann nodded. "Same. A little heat never bothered me."

"Wonderful," Stephen said. "But I should tell you we also have a pan-fried red snapper with a lemon-dill sauce, fresh asparagus, and an orzo risotto."

Katie groaned. "How are we supposed to pick between those two?"

Sophie nudged her. "You get one, I'll get the other and we'll share."

Katie nodded. "Done."

Amanda loved their interaction. It made her miss Denise, even though they'd never had that kind of relationship. Already, though, things had begun to change for the better between them. She wanted that to continue.

She only wished their mother wasn't the common enemy that brought them together.

Amanda sipped her water. She also wanted to know where things were going with Duke. It was hard not to wonder after the girls had brought it up.

Could there be more between them than the casual relationship they had now? Or was she seeing something that wasn't there? Indulging in wishful thinking? She didn't know. Mostly because she wasn't sure a more permanent relationship was actually what she wanted.

# Chapter Eighteen

Jenny held Nick's hand as they walked into the restaurant, a cute little place called Red Fish. It was a mix of rustic and elegant, with rough wood planks on the walls alongside white tablecloths and candles in cut-glass holders. Fish made of metal, wood, stained glass, paper, and other mediums decorated the walls.

Most were, unsurprisingly, red.

A few people stood near the entrance, but Nick went straight to the hostess stand. "Hi. Reservation for two under the name Oscott?"

The young woman working there nodded, picked up two menus, and said, "Right this way, Mr. Oscott."

She took them to their table, which was by a window that looked over the water. Nick held Jenny's chair for her, then took his own seat. The hostess gave them their menus, told them to enjoy their meal, and left.

Jenny looked out the window. The spot where they'd docked wasn't too far away. With permission, Nick had borrowed one of the resort's pontoons. The little marina was shared by Red Fish and the much rowdier Froggy's next door. Music from Froggy's drifted over, although it was too muted for her to tell if it was rock or country or some mix of the two. She looked at Nick. "How did you know about this place?"

"Iris told me about it. She said she and Arthur used to come here. Arthur used to play cards with the man who owned it, although Iris said he'd passed on and the restaurant is in his kids' hands now.

Jenny nodded. "I like it. It's kind of like a fancy shack."

He laughed. "That's a great description. I'm glad you like it. I figured we should get off the island once before you have to go home."

She looked up from her menu. "Does that mean you're not going to the gallery party with me tomorrow night?"

"No, I am. I just meant we should get off the island by ourselves."

"Oh." She smiled. She really wanted to tell him she might be staying, but if that didn't happen, it would be so disappointing for both of them. She didn't want to be the person who built his hopes up, only to dash them. That wasn't how she wanted Nick to remember her.

She nodded. "I'm glad we did this. Glad you had this idea."

Nick reached across the table and took her hand. There was sadness and longing in his eyes, and she knew what he was going to say before he said it. "In case you haven't figured it out already, I'm in love with you."

Her mouth fell open. That wasn't at all what she'd thought he was going to say. Her heart pounded at his confession, but only because she'd been feeling the same things. She nodded. "I'm in love with you, too."

He laughed and shook his head. "I know, my timing is terrible, but when else was I going to tell you? Tomorrow night, while we're surrounded by people? The day after, when I kiss you goodbye for the last time?"

"It won't be the last time. We'll find a way to see each other." But she knew what he meant. It probably could be the last time for a long while.

Smile gone, he swallowed and gave a shallow nod. "I wanted to do it when it was just us. And we still had a little time left."

She exhaled, unsure how to respond. She held tight to his hand, finding strength in that contact. "I'm glad you did. You're the greatest guy I've ever met. I'm not exaggerating, either. Not a single guy that I've been out with in my life holds a candle to you. I don't want to leave. I really don't. More than anything, I want to see where we might go."

His smile came back. "So do I."

They looked into each other's eyes for a few long moments, no words needed. Jenny knew he understood her. Just like she understood him.

Their waiter walked past the table for a second time.

Nick's smile expanded. "We should probably order before they kick us out for loitering."

She nodded, laughing. "Good idea."

After a quick perusal of the menu, she chose the shrimp and chicken skewers over farro risotto, while he had the filet mignon topped with crab.

They talked about nothing of any import until the food came, then as they got into the meal, Jenny asked a hard question. "Have you talked to your mom again? Since she threatened to sue?"

He shook his head. "No. But I probably should. Just to see if I can talk her down."

"But it's easier not to talk to her, isn't it."

He sighed. "Yes. You know all about that, don't you? Which is why you have every right to push me to do it."

She smiled. "I don't want to push you to do anything you don't want to do, but if it could help..."

"I get it. But I'm not sure it would help. I keep thinking that if I hadn't talked to her in the first place, none of this would be happening."

"You don't know that."

"No, I don't. You're right." He sliced a bite of steak and crab, then put it on her plate. "You should really try this. It's amazing."

She narrowed her eyes at him. "Using food to change the subject, huh?"

He laughed. "Maybe. But she's such a hard subject."

"So was my mom for me. But look where we are now." What a difference a couple of difficult, but honest, conversations had made. Jenny's only regret was that those conversations hadn't happened sooner. And that she'd been so blinded by her father's lies.

"I couldn't be happier that you two have put all of that behind you. But there's a big difference between your mom and my mom."

"What's that?" She tried the bite he'd given her. The steak was melt-in-her-mouth tender, and the crab was succulent and sweet. Red Fish was a gem.

"My mother isn't a good person. I hate to say that, but it's the truth. She's selfish and puts her own interests front and center. Your mom, on the other hand, is literally amazing. Kind and caring and as nice as a person could be. The kind of mom I wish I'd had."

She didn't know what to say, because from everything he'd told her about his mother, he was right. She sounded mean and vindictive and out for her own best interests. The lawsuit seemed proof positive of that.

His brows lifted. "If I thought I could talk my mother down, I would attempt it. But I'm mostly just worried I'll make things worse."

Jenny sighed, feeling for him. "I wish I had some great advice for you. Some kind of solution that would fix all of this."

"It's okay. Just being here with you is all I need."

She put a shrimp and a forkful of risotto on his plate, using it to change the subject herself. "How's Iris doing with the physical therapy?"

"All right. She's stubborn. And it's not easy. The work is painful and tiring. But she didn't quit on me, either, so that's good." He forked up the food Jenny had just given him. "I wish she was my mother."

Jenny nodded, understanding. "Of course, if she was, I don't think you and I would be here right now."

He looked at her, silent for a moment as he appeared to be figuring out the logic of that. He nodded. "Good point." He lifted his glass of water. "Here's to fate knowing better."

She toasted him with her water. "To fate."

They finished up their dinner and their server returned to check on them and see if they wanted dessert. The young man, named Skylar, took their empty plates while he filled them in on what was available. "We have espresso chocolate torte, coconut flan, and key lime pie."

Nick looked at her. Jenny shook her head. "I'm good. Dinner filled me up."

"Okay." He gave Skylar a nod. "Just the check."

Jenny leaned in. "I had a thought."

He mimicked her body language, leaning in as well. "And what was that?"

"We could walk over and check out Froggy's."

He grinned. "Feeling adventurous, huh?"

She nodded. "Why not? We're here."

"I'm game." He paid the bill and they left, heading along the boardwalk toward the neighboring restaurant. "Sounds like a happening place."

"*Looks* like a happening place." The closer they got, the easier it was to make out the music, which was definitely country. Froggy's was packed with patrons of all legal drinking ages, and the dance floor was mobbed with lines of people moving in synchronicity.

Nick put his mouth closer to her ear to be heard over the music. "Do you know how to do any of those dances?"

She shook her head at the coordinated steps being executed on the dance floor. "Not a one."

"Fun to watch, though."

She nodded. Then a slower song came on and a lot of people in the dancing crowd split into couples and began to swirl around the floor in pairs.

Nick held out his hand. "Even I can slow-dance."

She smiled and took it.

He pulled her close and they mixed into the rotation. “This is nice,” he whispered into her ear.

She agreed as she leaned into him a little more, their hands together, their bodies moving in rhythm. It was more than nice. It was a rare thing to be so in sync with someone this way. Body, mind, and soul.

Maybe, if her firm didn’t approve her move... Maybe she should quit. Her mother had suggested as much. Jenny knew she could find other work. She was capable of doing all kinds of things.

Of course, that would leave Katie, Sophie, and Owen without the help they’d been expecting.

She sighed. It was all so complicated.

“Everything okay?” Nick asked.

She nodded, smiling. “Just too much in my own head.”

He snorted. “I do that, too.” He rested his check against her temple again, and they melted into the flow of the crowd.

They’d made it twice around the big dance floor when her purse vibrated against her hip. She ignored it. She’d check the message when the song was over. No way was she interrupting this magical moment for what was probably a useless notification.

When at last the song ended, and they’d returned the space to the dancers who knew every foot stomp and hip swivel that went with the upbeat tempo that had them rushing the floor, she dug into her purse.

With Nick patiently at her side, Jenny held up a finger to ask for a moment. He nodded as she looked to see what had caused her phone to vibrate.

She read the message. Then read it again. This was everything she'd hoped for. Vibrating with happiness, she looked up at Nick. "I can stay!"

# Chapter Nineteen

Grace insisted that they have dessert. She wanted the girls to taste the desserts Chantelle had created during her first shift as the pastry chef for The Palms' kitchen. "Come on," she said. "We're going to order one of each and all have a bite. There are only four desserts. Four bites aren't going to spoil anyone's diet. And I really want you all to chime in on Chantelle's first attempts to level up the resort's dessert game."

Olivia snorted. "Not like any of us are really on a diet anyway."

Leigh Ann smiled. "Ladies, I've been on a diet my entire life."

"Me, too," Amanda said. "And you know what? It's exhausting. Not saying I'm about to start eating carbs with wild abandon, but there are times when I just don't want to care as much as I do."

"Well, then," Grace said. "Dessert it is." She caught

their server's eye and waved him over. "Tell us about the new desserts for this evening."

Stephen smiled at her request. "I'd be happy to. Tonight we have four very special selections. To begin with, we have a chocolate blackout cake. This intensely chocolate cake is layered with black cocoa chiffon sponge, chocolate custard, chocolate ganache, mocha mousse, and finished with chocolate whipped cream."

"Wow," Leigh Ann whispered. "That might put me in a sugar coma, but it's a risk I'm willing to take."

He smiled. "Next, we have a tropical trifle. More layers, but this time there's no chocolate involved. Instead, there are layers of tropical fruits that include pineapple, papaya, kiwi, mango, and dragon fruit between more layers of vanilla pastry cream, coconut angel food cake, and guava whipped cream."

"Perfect," Amanda said. "It's practically a salad."

With a soft laugh, he continued. "We also have a duo of profiteroles, or cream puffs, filled with sharp passionfruit pastry cream, glazed with white chocolate and served with a scoop of crystalized ginger ice cream."

Katie let out a sigh of longing. "I have a serious weakness for profiteroles."

"She does," Sophie confirmed. "I don't think she'll be sharing those."

"In that case," their server said, "Maybe I could also

recommend our last dessert. A decadent tres leches cake with a salted Dulce de leche drizzle."

Olivia gave Grace a look. "You really think we're going to only have one bite of each of those?"

Grace laughed, happy the women were responding so well to the new desserts. She glanced at Stephen. "How about two orders of the profiteroles, and one each of the rest. Plus, some small plates for sharing."

Stephen nodded. "You got it. What about coffee for anyone?"

Olivia raised her hand. "I'll have a coffee."

Leigh Ann's hand went up, too. "I'd love a decaf."

"Same here," Sophie said.

Katie nodded. "They talked me into it."

"Okay," Stephen said. "One regular, three decafs. I'll be right back."

Olivia leaned in toward Grace. "Have you actually hired Chantelle?"

"Not yet," Grace answered. "But we've brought her on for a two-week trial period to see how she works out and how the desserts are received. But we're hopeful, obviously, that it's a win all the way around. David really wants to elevate the restaurant even further. Having an in-house pastry chef would be a great step in that direction."

A busboy dropped off condiments for the coffee, a dish of sweeteners and two small pitchers of creamer.

Leigh Ann nodded. "Honestly, I'm surprised that

this place doesn't already have a dedicated pastry chef."

Stephen returned with two carafes, another server coming ahead of him with cups, saucers, and spoons. Stephen directed him to place those in front of the women getting coffee, then Stephen filled the cups. "I'll be right back with those desserts."

The women fixed their coffee, making Grace wish she'd ordered one. It smelled good. But she didn't want anything else on her palate when she tasted these new desserts.

Stephen returned, again with a second server to help carry the plates. Stephen had the two orders of profiteroles on one plate. In his other hand, he had the trifle, which was beautifully presented in a small, footed glass dish which allowed all the colorful layers to be seen. It was topped with toasted meringue and a gorgeous purple dendrobium orchid, which was edible, but this one had also been sugared so that it glistened.

Nice touch, Grace thought. An extra step that a lot of restaurants wouldn't have done. Chantelle was killing it on presentation.

The server with him had the extra plates, along with chocolate blackout cake and the tres leches cake. Both of them were individual cakes as opposed to slices, which made for a much more appealing appearance. More points for Chantelle.

The chocolate blackout cake was garnished with a quenelle of whipped cream and an assortment of tropical fruits, while the tres leches had an impressive spun-sugar dome on top of it.

The women all oohed and ahhed, which made Grace happy. These desserts definitely looked like they'd come from a high-end kitchen.

"It's a shame we have to divide them up," Amanda said. "They're really beautiful."

"No one touch them," Sophie said as she whipped her phone out. "I need to get pictures of these. They are definitely social media worthy."

Everyone waited for Sophie to get her photos, but about halfway through, they got their phones out and started taking pictures, too.

"Hey," Grace said. "If you guys are posting those, use the hashtag Mother's Resort or The Palms so we get some notice, okay?"

"You got it," Leigh Ann said as she tapped her screen.

Grace picked up a spoon. "I hope you're all done, because I'm tired of waiting. Even if it is for a good cause."

Katie laughed and moved a profiterole to her small plate. "So am I. This one is mine. The rest of you can fend for yourselves."

She took a bite, causing a little of the pastry cream to ooze out of the sides. Her eyes closed. "Oh. My."

"Okay, share," Amanda said, reaching for the trifle that was closest to her. She dug deep to get all of the layers, then spooned it onto her plate and passed the trifle on to Leigh Ann.

Leigh Ann took the trifle and helped herself, but her eyes were on the chocolate cake. "I want that next. Someone slice it into six pieces."

"On it," Grace said. "I'll cut the tres leches, too."

In a few more minutes, everyone had a piece of everything on their plate.

Grace tried the tres leches first. It was creamy and laden with milk flavor, and yet somehow not overly dense or soggy. The salted dulce de leche drizzle was the perfect accompaniment. Cracking the spun sugar dome was fun, too. This was a dessert that would go amazingly well with coffee.

After that, she dug into the chocolate blackout cake. The chocolate could have been overpowering, but the variations in cake, mousse, ganache, and whipped cream kept it interesting. There was a note of something crunchy on one layer. Cocoa nibs maybe? Whatever it was, that change in texture helped as well. Overall, anyone who loved chocolate would be incredibly satisfied with this one.

The trifle came next. Grace thought it was perfect. Bright and tangy from the fruit, sweet and creamy from the pastry cream, with the added softness of the coconut angel cake and a little chew from the coconut shavings. The trifle tasted exactly like what a dessert on a tropical island should taste like. She had a momentary thought that this ought to be the restaurant's signature dessert.

Lastly, she tried her half of a cream puff. The choux pastry was golden brown on the outside and light as air on the inside, the filling was sharp, thanks to the passionfruit, but the sweetness of the white chocolate glaze on top balanced it out. And the ice cream added a little bite, thanks to the ginger.

She was biased, clearly, because Grace was Chantelle's number one fan and Grace had been the one who'd brought her to David's attention, so she held back and didn't say anything. She didn't want to influence the girls.

But she had nothing to worry about. The raves began shortly after the desserts were tasted.

Leigh Ann gestured at Grace with her spoon. "If you and David don't hire this young woman, you're nuts. These are the best things we've eaten so far. And we've eaten some outstanding desserts here."

Amanda's brows went up as she pulled her spoon from her mouth. "This is the same young woman who's making the wedding cake, right?"

Grace nodded. "Right."

"At least I won't have to worry about them liking the cake. She's really good."

Grace smiled.

Katie looked at the profiterole plate, now empty. "I should have taken two. That was one of the best cream puffs I've ever eaten. I'm kinda mad I only got one."

Sophie snorted. "Order another one."

"I might." Katie glanced up like she was looking for their server.

Olivia smiled at Grace. "Well done."

Grace laughed. "I didn't make them."

"No," Olivia said. "But you found Chantelle. And you gave her a chance to show us what she could do. And it seems to me that she's exactly what the resort needs."

Amanda nodded. "Having someone on-site who's capable of making a wedding cake is a big deal, especially as I'm hoping to bring in more weddings. There could be birthdays and anniversaries to think about, too. Great job, Grace."

"Thank you." Grace beamed at them, so happy with how they were reacting. It was such a good feeling to know she was helping to add value to this magical place. And helping out a talented young woman at the same time.

That cookbook might need a chapter on desserts.

# Chapter Twenty

"We should take these desserts to Iris," Katie said. "She should really taste these, but it would also be a great excuse for Leigh Ann and Olivia to see her new necklace."

"I love that idea," Grace said. "I'll text her right now and see if she's up for that."

Olivia was on her phone, too, but she'd only just picked it up. She sucked in a breath, staring at her phone like she'd just read interesting news. She looked at Katie and Sophie. "Jenny just heard from Irene, the woman who owns her firm. She's got the okay to move here!"

"Yes," Sophie said. "That's fantastic."

Katie nodded, smiling. "I agree. I'm so glad that worked out. I love having Jenny on my team."

Olivia texted a quick note back, then set her phone aside and put her hand over her heart. "Katie, thank you for helping Jenny make that happen. I know you and Owen played a big part in that. I need to tell him thank you as well."

"I'm so glad I could. And now she'll be getting the OM coin account. She's going to be plenty busy." Which made Katie want to tell the girls what she'd done in getting them all shares of Owen's new venture, but she didn't want to do it in the middle of this restaurant.

Grace waved at Stephen, then glanced around the table. "Iris said to come on over. I think that diamond has put her in a very good mood."

"Who can blame her?" Leigh Ann said. "It's a rare occasion in a woman's life that she gets a big rock that doesn't have a man attached." She grinned. "Although I know in Iris's case, she would have been thrilled if Arthur had been able to give her that stone himself."

"Trust me," Amanda said. "I knew exactly what you meant."

Stephen came over and Grace ordered the four desserts packaged to go, letting him know they were for Iris.

He nodded. "I'll get those together for you right away."

Good to his word, he was back in just under five minutes with a large bag containing four to-go containers.

Together, the girls got up and headed out, following the path past the bungalows toward Iris's.

At the fork in the road, Katie stopped and pointed toward the water. "Right about here is where the new dock would be. Just wanted to show you exactly where I was talking about."

"It would be convenient," Amanda said.

Leigh Ann nodded. "Especially if any of us eventually get a boat."

"I plan on it," Katie said. "It'll be small, probably the littlest pontoon they make. Sophie and I will share it. I want to have my own way to get to Owen and to access the mainland. I don't like having to rely on someone else. Especially not Eddie or Rico, not when they need to be looking after guests."

Olivia shifted position. "I wouldn't mind having my own boat, either, which is something I never thought in my life I'd say." She laughed. "But you make a really good point about not tying Eddie or Rico up."

"Does that mean you're signing off on the dock?" Katie asked.

Olivia shook her head. "Not yet. But nice try."

With a laugh, Katie started walking again. "You know, I wouldn't mind sharing my pontoon with any of you guys if Sophie and I aren't using it."

"That's kind of you," Grace said. "David and I talked about getting a small watercraft. But I think he's more interested in being able to fish."

They went up the ramp, hitting the front porch just

as Vera opened the door. "Good evening, ladies. Come on in."

"Thanks," Katie said.

Iris was sitting in her chair. The television was on, showing an old *Matlock* episode. She picked up the remote and hit Pause. "Hello, girls! I hear you brought me dessert."

Grace lifted the bag. "We did. We want you to try the desserts our potential new pastry chef made for her debut."

Iris rubbed her hands together. "I'm ready. I've had my dinner, which Vera will tell you was just what the doctor ordered. Dr. Nick, that is."

Katie took a seat on the couch while Grace and Vera got the desserts ready. "What did you have?"

"Vera fixed me a salmon filet with a Greek yogurt dill sauce. It was delicious. Nick said fish and yogurt both have good levels of B12, so I'm eating more of them."

"And more beef, too," Vera said as she came over with two of the dessert containers, tops removed.

Grace was right behind her with the other two containers.

But the desserts were momentarily forgotten as Leigh Ann, Olivia, and Sophie took in the glittering hunk of ice hanging around Iris's neck.

"Are you kidding me?" Leigh Ann said, eyes wide.

She shook her head. "We heard about Arthur's gift, but words don't do it justice.

Olivia sank into the chair beside Iris, who was grinning and lifting her chin so the pendant could be seen better. "Leigh Ann's right. The image in my head didn't come close to what it actually looks like."

Sophie just stared.

Katie laughed. "Pretty impressive, don't you think?"

"Impressive is an understatement," Leigh Ann said. "Iris, you must be blown away."

"I am," she said. "But to be honest, it could have been a piece of pretty sea glass and just knowing that it was from Arthur would have made it dear."

"Of course," Olivia said. "But having it be a diamond that could be swapped for a small country gives it a certain panache."

They all laughed. Iris clapped her hands. "Very true. Now, let me see those desserts."

Grace and Vera set the four desserts down on the coffee table and Grace explained what each one was. The cakes and profiteroles were just as beautiful as they had been in the restaurant, but the trifle, in its deep paper cup, lost some of its pizzazz without the layers being visible.

"They're all so lovely," Iris said. "They're fancier than our usual, aren't they? Looks-wise, I mean."

"They are," Grace confirmed. "The trifle was

presented in a glass dish so you could see all of the layers."

Katie pulled up the picture of the dessert on her phone and held it out for Iris to see. "It was stunning."

Iris put her glasses on. "Oh, that's gorgeous. I bet those got a lot of looks when they were carried through the dining room. Someone hand me a fork, please."

Vera came to the rescue.

Iris tried several bites of each one, proclaiming each one delicious.

She wasn't wrong, Katie thought. They were all winners. Although to her, the profiteroles were beyond good. She was biased, obviously, but if Chantelle continued to make those, or at least variations of those, Katie was going to have to find time to get into the fitness center.

Iris finished her last bite of the chocolate blackout cake and set the fork down. She shook her head as she stared at the containers on the table. "I don't know what to say. If you're asking me to pick my favorite that is."

Grace smiled. "You don't have to pick a favorite. I just wanted you to taste what Chantelle had created."

"Well, they're marvelous." Iris's gaze seemed to linger on the tres leches cake. "She's our new pastry chef?"

"Not yet," Grace explained. "We're trying her out on a two-week trial period."

“Pfft. Two-week trial period.” Iris shook her head. “Hire the woman. We can’t afford to lose her.”

Katie laughed and looked at Grace. “Whose idea was the trial period?”

“Mine,” Grace said, giving a little shrug. “Just in case.”

Katie lifted her hand. “I make a motion that we hire Chantelle full-time, effective immediately.”

Olivia raised her hand. “I second that motion.”

“Motion carries,” Leigh Ann said. “Chantelle is officially the resort’s new pastry chef.”

Iris clapped. “Good job, girls.”

Katie nodded at her. “Just wait. We’ve got all kinds of things planned. Like a new dock right out here so that employees and staff have a more convenient place to put their boats.”

“Maybe,” Olivia clarified.

But Iris reacted exactly how Katie expected her to, gasping and nodding. “I love that. You know, Arthur had plans to build a second marina area on this side of the island years ago, but he just never got to it.”

Olivia frowned at Katie, but there was amusement in her eyes. “You play dirty.”

Katie laughed. “Sorry.” She raised her hand. “There is something else I’d like to tell all of you.”

They all settled down, giving her their attention.

Katie took a breath. “Don’t be mad. But I purchased shares of Owen’s cryptocurrency for all of you.”

# Chapter Twenty-one

"What?" Leigh Ann shook her head. She was stunned by Katie's generosity, but a little taken aback, too. "You shouldn't have done that. It was terribly generous, but you know none of us can afford that right now."

"And as I've told all of you, I don't care. I'm not asking you to pay me back right now," Katie said. "In fact, I'm not asking you for anything. There was no way I was letting you guys miss out on this opportunity. None."

Amanda was frowning. "Katie, it's beyond generous. But you know that my financial situation is dire, at best."

"And soon," Katie said. "If this launch goes well, it won't be. Then you can pay me the initial investment out of the profits. Although there's a good chance this coin will continue to climb for quite a while, so my suggestion would be to only sell enough to pay me back, then let the rest of it ride."

Olivia crossed her arms. "You're not going to take no for an answer on this, are you?"

"Nope."

Grace rolled her eyes. "That kind of makes it hard for us to debate you."

"Good." Katie smiled. "Listen, don't be upset. This was my gift to all of you. Accept it for what it is. A gift. What's wrong with that?"

Leigh Ann laughed softly. "You make it very hard to argue."

"Again, good," Katie said.

Iris just smiled. "That was so generous of you, Katie."

"It was," Leigh Ann added. "It was a *very* generous gift. And you have to understand how unbalanced it feels to us." She didn't want to hurt Katie's feelings, just make her aware of how they all felt. Or at least how Leigh Ann thought they all felt. She glanced around, wondering if she was wrong.

Grace was smiling. "It's completely unbalanced, but I don't care. It's also very over the top and very Katie. Thank you."

Katie grinned. "You're welcome."

Leigh Ann realized she might have overreacted. Katie was a generous person. Leigh Ann didn't want to make her feel bad. "You're really okay with laying out that much money for us?"

Katie nodded. "For my sisters? Of course I am. Do you know how bad I'd feel if I only invested in his project for Sophie and myself and then we made all kinds of money from it? I'd feel awful. More than awful. I wouldn't be able to enjoy the windfall. I included you guys because it felt like the right thing to do. I wanted us all to be in this together. I needed us to be in this together."

"And I appreciate that." Olivia asked a question. "But what happens if the project doesn't succeed? I realize Owen has a very successful track record, but it's always a possibility with something like this."

"True," Katie said. "It is. And if the OM coin bombs, I absorb the loss. And before you argue that that's not fair, let me tell you that I can absolutely afford it and I will happily use those write-offs. I don't think you guys understand how much I pay in taxes. Write-offs are always useful."

"I understand," Olivia said. "Or at least I have an idea. Thank you, Katie."

Amanda's mouth curved in an emotional smile. "Yes, thank you, Katie. No one's done anything like this for me in a long time. Iris excluded, of course. And I'm not too proud to say that I could use a windfall right now. If you need us to be included in this, then who are we to tell you how to find your happiness?"

"Thank you." Katie looked around. "It wasn't my intention to make any of you feel bad. You have to understand that."

"I do," Leigh Ann said.

Olivia, Grace, and Amanda said the same.

"I think," Leigh Ann said. "That we've all forgotten how things used to be, back when Iris was our house mother and we operated more like a family." She made eye contact with the women around her. "Except maybe for Katie, who seems to have held on to that. From here on out, we need to remember that's what we are once again. A family."

Olivia nodded. "Well said."

Iris sniffed. "I love you girls."

They all got a little teary, too.

"No hard feelings?" Leigh Ann asked Katie.

"Of course not," Katie said. "I'm so glad you're not mad at *me*."

"Never." Leigh Ann stood. "Now, I hate to break this up, but tomorrow's a big day and sunrise yoga comes, well, at sunrise, so I'm going to turn in. Your necklace is amazing, Iris. As is your heart, Katie."

They all said their goodbyes, hugging and kissing each other and Iris, who'd pulled herself up to stand using her walker.

Leigh Ann got back to her bungalow a few minutes later. She couldn't stop thinking about Katie's amazing gift. She wasn't sure how soon the project would be live or launched or whatever the right term was, but with Marty still refusing to sign, maybe the OM coin would be the thing that helped her sell her studio.

She scowled at the air. Just thinking about that man irritated her. If he and Candi did show up at Grant's opening tomorrow night, Leigh Ann was going to have to be on her best behavior. She couldn't let Marty push her buttons. She couldn't react in a way that might tarnish Grant's night.

Poor Grant. He had no idea what she'd done.

She looked at her phone. She really owed it to him to tell him. She pulled up his contact info and called him.

"This is a pleasant surprise."

She laughed. "You're only saying that because you don't know why I called."

"Oh?" Grant's voice lost a little of its mirth.

"Nothing too terrible. Or maybe it is." Leigh Ann sighed. "I did a rash and probably stupid thing."

"Rash I'll buy. Stupid, I doubt it."

"I invited Candi and Marty to your gallery party."

Grant went silent for a moment. "Interesting choice of guests. But I can't say I blame you for wanting your ex-husband to see you as the Queen of the Eagle Rays. You look pretty amazing in that painting, if I do say so myself."

"So you're not mad?"

"Mad? His money is as green as anyone else's. Maybe he'll buy something."

She laughed. "Thanks for being so understanding."

"Leigh Ann, there's not much you could do that would upset me."

"You really mean that, don't you?"

"I do. Life is too short to get bent about the small stuff."

"Are you saying that this gallery party is a small thing?"

"Sure. In the scheme of life, it's a blip on the radar."

That surprised her. She'd been thinking about it very differently. "You have such an interesting take on things. I need to be more like you."

"Listen, I'm not saying the gallery party isn't important. It is. But am I going to lose sleep over it? No way. My life goes so much better when I keep my focus on the big things. And if I'm healthy, and have a roof over my head, food to eat, and a kind, beautiful woman at my side, my life is about as perfect as it can get."

She smiled, feeling so much more at ease than she had a few minutes ago. "You're really good for me, you know that? I needed that reminder that I am far more blessed than I acknowledge. All of this nonsense with Marty and the divorce has been taking its toll on me. It's made me lose sight of some of that big stuff. Thank you for that."

"You're welcome. I'm sure it's hard not to focus on the divorce, especially with Marty being at the resort, but there will come a time in your life when he's so far in your rear-view mirror that you go long stretches without thinking about him at all."

"I know you're right. I'm just eager to get to that point."

Grant laughed. "I'd be lying if I said I wasn't eager for that, too. For both our sakes."

She chuckled. "On a completely unrelated topic, would you teach me to drive a boat?"

"I can. You want to start Saturday? I'm a little busy tomorrow."

She laughed. "That would be fine. Although Saturday I might be a little busy helping Amanda get things ready for the wedding on Sunday."

"A wedding, huh? Who's getting married?"

"I can't tell you. Top-secret celebrity thing. But if you'd like to come over for breakfast on Monday, I'll tell you all about it. Then maybe we can have a boating lesson."

"It's a deal."

She yawned without meaning to. "Sorry. I guess I'm sleepier than I realized."

"No problem. See you tomorrow, beautiful."

"See you tomorrow, Grant." She hung up, all smiles as she went to clean her face and brush her teeth.

Whatever happened with Marty and Candi at the

gallery, she was going to stay cool and let it roll off her like water off of a duck's back.

At least, she thought, that was her new plan.

# Chapter Twenty-two

Olivia texted Eddie as soon as she walked up the steps to her bungalow. In fact, she did it while standing on her front porch, looking over at his. It still hadn't really sunk in that she was living next door to him. *Still up for the hot tub?*

*Sure. Meet you there?*

*Okay.* She smiled and got the key out from under the mat, then unlocked the door and went inside. She left her purse on the kitchen counter, then ran upstairs to change into her swimsuit.

A quick glance in the mirror made her glad she'd only had a few bites of dessert tonight. She really wanted to lose a couple of pounds. Maybe ten. Or twenty.

She put on sandals, grabbed a towel, and went downstairs. She took her phone out of her purse, but that was it. She thought about going back up to grab a coverup, but instead, just wrapped the towel around her waist like a sarong.

Starting Monday, she was going to the fitness center and working out. At least forty-five minutes three to four days a week. And she was absolutely cutting back on carbs. Dessert every day had to stop.

In fact, when she did her shopping tomorrow at the grocery store, she was only getting low-carb options. If Jenny wanted junk, she'd have to buy it herself. There would be no chips, ice cream, candy, or other unhealthy snacky stuff in the house.

She had to start taking better care of herself now that she lived here. There wasn't going to be a winter season where she could disappear into big cardigans.

Olivia locked the door, put the key back under the mat, then went out to the staff common area to meet Eddie.

He was already at the hot tub. He had a little cooler with him. "*Buenas noches.*"

She smiled. "*Buenas noches.*"

He lifted the cooler. "Would you like a root beer?"

"No. Thank you, though. I am officially off sugar. And carbs."

Eddie opened the top of the cooler and took out one of the brown glass bottles. "As it happens, I bought some diet, just for you."

She joined him. "You did?" He obviously listened.

"That was so sweet. Or not so sweet, since it's diet." She took the bottle. "Thank you."

"You're welcome." He grabbed a bottle for himself and set it near the edge of the hot tub, then kicked off his flipflops and pulled off his T-shirt.

Olivia put her towel on one of the lounge chairs, left her sandals next to it, then entered the hot tub, one step at a time. The water was very hot, but she was looking forward to the relaxation before she went to bed.

Of course, she was mostly looking forward to the time with Eddie. They'd been so busy lately she hadn't seen that much of him. And she loved spending time with him. He made her happy. She took a seat, sinking deeper into the water, then unscrewed the top from her root beer and took a sip. She supposed that's how their lives were going to be most of the time. Both of them busy.

"What's wrong?" Eddie asked as he came down the steps. "You look unhappy about something. Or is the root beer not good?"

"The root beer is great, and I'm fine. I was just thinking about how we haven't seen each other much because we've both been busy. And I was thinking about how that's probably the new normal. Us both being busy."

He sat beside her, then reached for his root beer and twisted off the top. "For me, it ebbs and flows.

Some days, like weekends when guests are coming in or leaving, are definitely busier for me. But my nights are almost always free. Once in a while, if a guest requests it, I do an evening fishing trip. But that's not often. And you don't work at night, right?"

"Not unless there are special reports to be done. Or taxes."

He held his bottle out toward her. "Then here's to evenings together. We can make that work."

She clinked her bottle against his. "To evenings together." That made her feel better, for sure. "Do you think that at least on one of those evenings you can give me more boat lessons?"

He nodded and set his root beer aside. "Of course. More than one night a week, if you want. I can definitely get you ready to take the test and get your license."

"Okay, great. Thank you." Olivia wasn't sure if she should mention Katie's idea about the second dock, but she really wanted to see what he thought of it. She eased her way in. "I'm probably going to get my own boat at some point. Way down the road, obviously, when I'm in a better place financially. But I would like to."

"Yeah?" He smiled. "I like that you're planning ahead."

"Well...Katie wants to build a second marina. A big

dock, really. With eight or ten slips, just for staff and employees."

He nodded. "I like that. Let me guess—on this side of the island?"

"Yes. You must have heard Arthur had those same plans once upon a time."

"I did hear that. From Arthur himself, actually. He always thought the staff should have their own area to keep their boats. He also thought it would make his and Iris's life a little easier, because they wouldn't have to walk through the resort every time they left the island."

Eddie took a drink of his root beer again. "As much as Arthur loved this place and loved people, he also loved his life with Iris and valued his private time with her. I think he liked the idea of being able to slip away with her, even if it was just to take the boat out for the evening and watch the sunset, without being interrupted by every guest that wanted to talk to them. Because, trust me, people loved to talk to them."

"I could see that," Olivia said. The privacy aspect was yet another angle she hadn't considered. It made sense.

"But you haven't given the project the financial stamp of approval yet, have you?"

She chuckled. "Am I that transparent?"

"No. But I know that since you've taken over the books, you must be more aware than ever of the resort's finances. I can't imagine there's enough money sitting around right now for a project of that size and scope. Or is the dock something that will happen if and when the embezzled funds are recovered?"

"Neither, actually. Katie has offered to pay for it. She's basically insisting. She got a settlement from *Star Watch* and she wants to use some of that money to build the dock."

"And you don't think that's a good idea? It's her money. I don't see why she shouldn't be allowed to invest in the property if that's what she wants to do."

"I agree. To a point. I need to see how much that new dock would add to our insurance payment."

"Ah." He nodded. "That makes sense. I hadn't even thought about that. But that's why you're the accountant and I'm just the boat captain." He winked at her. "You're awfully far away."

Smiling, she slid closer. "Better?"

"*Si.*" He wiggled his brows, making her laugh.

She was happy. Things were good. "Oh! Guess what."

"What?"

"Jenny is staying. Her firm okayed her opening a satellite office here. Which means, as you know, that she'll be living with me until she gets her own place."

"That's great news. You must be so happy."

"I am. It's all kinds of hard to believe, you know?

Not just her being here, but also that we have a good enough relationship to actually be sharing a house."

He nodded. "Your life has changed drastically in the last two weeks."

She laughed. "That might be an understatement." She sank a little deeper into the water. "Tomorrow is going to be crazy."

"It is. We have a lot to get done. And then there's the party. I'll be on call, in case guests need me, but Rico has agreed to cover the marina until we get back."

"I'm so glad." Glad didn't cover it. She was thrilled that he was going to be able to attend the party with her.

"So am I. Grant's a good guy and I'm happy to be able to support him. But I'm even happier that I get to be there with you." He closed the few inches between them to kiss her lightly on the lips.

She kissed him back. A soft, repetitive sound came to her over the bubbling water. It registered a few seconds later. Footsteps. They were no longer alone.

# Chapter Twenty-three

Amanda stood next to Duke, feeling very much like a peeping Tom. Or whatever the female version of that was. She clutched her lidded wine tumbler against her torso. "Sorry. We didn't know anyone else was in the hot tub."

Olivia and Eddie smiled up at them. Olivia's cheeks were a little pink, but Amanda thought that might have been from the steam. "It's okay," Olivia said. "It's a big hot tub. There's plenty of room. Get in."

Eddie nodded. "Join us."

"Thanks," Duke said. He tossed his towel on a free lounge chair and started for the steps. "Come on, babe."

*Babe*. Amanda smiled. "Coming."

They slipped into the water, but the heat made Amanda suck air through her teeth. "That is really warm."

Duke was already in up to his shoulders. "Yeah, it

is, but it feels great." He stretched out his arms along the edge of the spa and sighed.

Amanda worked her way into the water a little more slowly, but eventually eased down onto the seat beside him. She put her wine tumbler on the edge.

"Root beer?" Eddie asked.

She shook her head. "I'm good with my wine, thanks."

But Duke nodded. "Sounds good. Thanks."

Eddie handed him a bottle. "How was your day?"

Duke twisted the top off and a took a long drink. "Good. You?"

"Busy. You know."

"Yep." Duke set the bottle nearby. "Did you hear about Iris's new necklace?"

Eddie laughed. "Yeah. How about that?"

Olivia smiled. "I'm sure it'll be the talk of the resort soon."

Amanda had to agree. "How could people not talk about it? It's staggering."

"It's very Iris," Olivia said.

Amanda nodded. "That's a perfect way to put it."

Olivia nudged Eddie. "I think I'm cooked. I'm ready to go up."

"Okay," he said. "I'm right behind you." He looked at Duke and Amanda. "You guys have a good evening."

"Yes," Olivia said. "Have a great night. See you tomorrow." She stopped halfway up the steps. "I'll be busy most of the day tomorrow with a trip into town, but if there's anything I can do to help with the wedding stuff, please let me know."

Amanda nodded. "We're going into town tomorrow, too. I couldn't find a chalkboard, so Duke's going to make me one with stuff from the hardware store."

"Nice," Olivia said. "That's one of our stops, too. Plus, the thrift shop and the grocery store."

"Stocking up?" Amanda asked.

"Yep. The cupboards are bare." Olivia climbed out of the tub and wrapped her towel around her.

"Have fun. See you at the party, if I don't see you sooner."

"You got it." Olivia and Eddie walked off toward their bungalows.

Amanda hadn't minded the company, but she was happy to have some alone time with Duke. She snuggled in against him. "This is nice."

"It is." He bent his head so that his cheek touched the top of hers. "I'm going to sleep like a baby tonight."

"Me, too."

They sat in silence for a few minutes, listening to the water and watching the stars overhead. It was beautiful here, and even though Amanda was officially moved in and officially working at the resort, this moment still felt very much like a vacation.

"Penny for your thoughts?"

She smiled. "I was just thinking about how this still feels like a vacation."

"Yeah," he said. "It does sometimes. And this is one of those times."

A few more moments of silence passed before he spoke again. "Is Leigh Ann nervous about tomorrow night?"

"I don't think so," Amanda answered. "At least not that she's let on. Although she did invite her ex-husband and his new girlfriend to the party. Leigh Ann said it was a moment of weakness, but she really wants him to see that another man thinks enough of her to put her in his painting."

"After what you've told me about her ex, I can understand that. He didn't treat her with a whole lot of respect. Even without knowing the guy, I know Grant's a better man."

"I know he is, too. Just like you're a much better man than my late husband."

Duke shook his head. "Thank you, but I'm not going to comment. I don't want to speak ill of the dead."

"It's all right," Amanda reassured him. "Brian wasn't a good man. He was a thief and a criminal and he left me effectively destitute."

"I'm sorry you went through all of that."

"I am, too, except that I'm not as sorry as I used to

be. All of that led me here, so I'm trying to look at that time of my life like a learning experience now."

He nodded, smiling a little. "I like that. You've grown just in the short time you've been here."

"Your friendship has helped. A lot. You've opened my eyes to a lot of things."

He stared at her for a second, eyes narrowing. "Is that what this is? A friendship?"

All of her questions about this relationship filtered down into her thoughts. "I think so. Don't you?"

"I do. But I also think it's more than that. Although maybe I'm the only one who thinks that way."

She felt breathless and nervous and a little tongue-tied. The moment seemed make-or-break. She didn't want to say the wrong thing. She liked Duke a lot. She wanted him to stay in her life.

Maybe, she thought, she ought to just tell him that. So she did, twisting to face him and pulling her legs up under her. "I like you a lot. I like having you around. I like spending time with you. I want that to continue. But I don't want to push you toward something you're not interested in, either."

She laughed, her nerves coming out. "I'm not good at this. I spent too many years of my life married. My relationship skills are rusty."

"It's okay if they're rusty so long as you keep being honest with me about what you're feeling and what you want."

"I want you," she said. "What do you want?"

"You." He answered without hesitation. "I don't know what I've done to make you think otherwise, but I didn't start this because I was looking for fast fun. That's easy to come by. When I met you, I saw an opportunity to spend time with a woman who is as smart as she is beautiful. A woman who seems like she'd be worth the challenge of getting to know and getting past the wall she clearly had around herself."

She leaned back. "You think I had a wall around me?"

He nodded. "You still do a little. Not as much with me as you initially did, but I see it sometimes. It's not a big deal. After what you've been through, it's a pretty reasonable response. Natural human self-defense."

She took a deep breath. He read her so easily. Did that mean he knew what she was thinking right now? About how she was falling for him? "I think I like you more than you like me."

He laughed, a deep, hearty sound that made her smile. "No, you don't."

She flicked water at him. "You don't know that."

"Yes, I do. Because I'm crazy in love with you. And I don't think you're ready to say that."

His confession silenced her. Scared the words right out of her, if she was being honest. Her instinct was to shut down. That she wasn't ready for this.

But that wasn't true. She *was* ready for this. If there was ever a time in her life for a new love, this was it.

She took a breath and clung to the honesty that had seen her through so far. "That frightens me. But I don't care. Fear is one of those things that you just need to push through sometimes, right?"

He smiled. "You do if you want to get past that fear."

"I do," she whispered.

He cupped her face in his hands. "I promise I'm not going to hurt you."

She believed him. But she was more afraid that she might hurt him because she was so emotionally stunted from growing up with Militant Marge. "I'll do my best not to hurt you, either. But I worry about that."

He kissed her softly. "How about if I tell you if I sense that's about to happen? I don't think it will, but just in case, I'll give you fair warning."

She nodded, leaning into his embrace. "Okay. Thank you."

"Now come sit here next to me and let's look for a falling star. You could use some good celestial vibes right now."

She settled in closer beside him. "Thank you for being so understanding." She felt him nod. She remembered something he'd said. "You think I'm a challenge?"

He let out a short laugh. "I think all women are a

challenge. But you seemed worth it. Relationships in general are work. And if the person you're in a relationship with doesn't work as hard as you do, things get to feeling unbalanced. That's when things generally start to go south."

"You've really thought about this, huh?"

"I have." He glanced at her. "You've met my folks. They love to talk about this kind of stuff. It's their way of making sure Jamie and I understand the truths of life."

She nodded. "They're very smart people." She liked his parents very much. They were so different from the parents she'd grown up with. *So* different.

"They are. Which reminds me—they want me to bring you out for dinner again sometime soon."

"Let me get through this wedding, then we'll figure out a date. But I'd love to see them again. I like them a lot."

His arm tightened around her shoulders. "You'll get to see them tomorrow night."

"I will?"

"Sure. They'll be at the gallery party."

"Oh, that's great. I had no idea." She stared up at the stars. "That makes me happy."

"You make me happy."

She smiled and laced her fingers through his, sinking into the warm water and the sense of peace their talk had given her.

# Chapter Twenty-four

Iris sat in her chair on the side porch taking in the night air. Her three cats were all lounging nearby, and her new diamond dangled around her neck. Her fingers went to it constantly. She took comfort in touching it, knowing it had once been in Arthur's hands.

Probably the silly musings of an old woman, but she liked to think holding the diamond was like holding his hand. And in that way, it was very much an escape for her. She could imagine Arthur was still with her. In fact, he felt closer to her now than he had since he'd passed and with everything going on, that closeness gave her such solace.

The feeling settled over her with a warm glow that gave her a deep happiness she hadn't felt in a long time.

Vera came out onto the porch. "Need anything?"

"No," Iris said. "I'm good. I'm going to turn in soon."

"All right. I'm going to bed myself, then. Unless you want me to sit up with you?"

Iris shook her head. "Go on. You've done enough today."

Vera smiled. "Tomorrow will be quieter. Sleep tight."

"You, too."

Vera left. Mary Read came over and rubbed against Iris's legs. "You want a snack?"

Mary Read sat down, made big eyes at Iris, and let out a squeaky meow.

"Okay, just a minute." Iris reached over to the side table and picked up the little bag of cat treats. The crinkling of the bag caused two more furry heads to turn in her direction. She fished a handful of treats out and tossed a couple to each cat.

She was so glad she was staying. What a gift her girls had given her. And Duke, Grant, and Jack, too, because without that ramp, she'd never be able to navigate those stairs into her house.

Her house that she would now *not* be leaving.

Another reason to smile.

From her porch, through the thick spans of palms, live oaks, and other foliage, she could just detect the faint outlines of the closest staff bungalows.

She hoped her girls were settling in all right, and that they'd be happy here. That was what she desired most for them. Happy lives.

She certainly thought she was back on that path herself.

Her only regret was that she wouldn't be able to make Grant's gallery party. It would be the first one she'd missed since getting to know him. Arthur had loved Grant's work.

Iris grabbed hold of her walker and pulled herself to a standing position. She could go, she supposed, but it wouldn't be smart.

Being around so many people would raise the chance of someone bumping into her and, worse, possibly knocking her down. That would be disastrous. Grant would understand her absence. And, hopefully, her vanity at not wanting to be seen in a wheelchair.

She made her way toward her bedroom. She'd just have to content herself with staying home and reading a good book. Or maybe she'd watch a movie. It had been a while since she'd seen the Thin Man series. Might be time to revisit those. Nothing wrong with spending the evening with Myrna Loy and William Powell.

The cats ran ahead, knowing she was headed for bed and eager to take their spots. They beat her handily, which made her laugh and shake her head.

By the time she came out of the bathroom, teeth brushed, Calico Jack was curled up on Arthur's pillow, while Anne Bonny and Mary Read were at the foot of the bed.

Iris slipped under the covers, doing her best not to disturb the cats, then turned on the television to catch up on one of her favorite cooking shows. Ten minutes in, however, her lids were growing heavy. She turned the television off, then kissed her fingers and pressed them to Arthur's picture on her nightstand.

"Goodnight, my love. Thank you again for my necklace. I love it. And I love you."

In her mind, he answered her. But only in her mind. She no longer thought she heard his voice, like she once had. The B12 shots had fixed that.

It was the only thing about her ill health that she missed.

"You don't have to walk me to the door," Jenny told Nick as they cut around the staff common area.

"I want to," he said. "Besides, it's the right way to do things."

She smiled but said nothing.

"What?" He looked at her. "You think I'm old-fashioned?"

"You *are* old-fashioned, but in the best possible way." It was one of the things that made her so crazy about him. He was a gentleman. Such a rare quality in today's world. At least when it came to eligible guys her age.

His head turned and his voice lowered. "There are people in the hot tub."

She glanced over. From their position in the spa and the rising steam, it was hard to make out who it was. "I see that."

"We should sit in that hot tub sometime."

She grinned. "I'd be up for that. We could hang out by the pool, too. This one, I mean."

"That sounds really nice. I like the idea of spending time with you in a less crowded area."

She stopped at the steps that led up to her mom's place. "Are you saying you didn't enjoy Froggy's?"

He laughed. "Froggy's was fun. Slow-dancing with you was the highlight of my evening. No, that's not true." He pulled her into his arms. "Finding out you were going to stay was the highlight. But slow-dancing was a very close second."

She nodded. "It's too bad opportunities like that don't come up more often."

He held her close, letting her lean on him. "It's kind of surprising that a romantic place like this doesn't offer anything like that."

"I suppose so. But where would they do it? They don't have a nightclub."

"No, but they have that pavilion. Think about how

pretty that would be with strings of hanging lights. A great place for an evening of slow-dancing."

She stared up at him. "You know, you might be on to something. You mind if I tell my mom your idea?"

He shrugged. "Go ahead. I don't know if it's fully-formed enough to call it an idea, though. And you were the inspiration." He smiled. "You and Froggy's."

She laughed. He was so kind and handsome and amazing. "I had a great time tonight."

"Me, too. I'm so glad we did it. But the best part is, we can do it again." He kissed her, then finally let her go. "See you tomorrow."

She nodded, putting her hand on the railing that led up to the porch. "Tomorrow."

She jogged up the steps, gave him a little wave, then got the key out from under the mat, and went inside.

She closed the door and locked it before walking past the stairs to the second floor.

Her mom was in the kitchen, getting a glass of water. She glanced over. "You look happy."

"I am," Jenny said. She let out a contented sigh. "I think I'm in love."

Her mom smiled. "Is that so? With Nick, I assume."

Jenny laughed. "Yes, with Nick. He's amazing, Mom. I'm serious. He's so good, sometimes I think he's not real. He's like a Disney prince come to life."

Olivia sipped her water, eyes dancing with amusement. "Are you sure it's not just infatuation?"

Jenny sat in one of the two stools at the kitchen counter. "No, I'm not. Which is what's worrying me. How do I know?"

Olivia shrugged. "Sometimes you don't until you do."

Jenny rolled her eyes. "Oh, well, that clears it right up."

Olivia chuckled. "It's just one of those things, honey. It takes time. And after a while, that infatuation wears off and you know if it's more than that."

"How did you know with Dad?"

Her mother's amusement faded. "That's not a good example."

"But he wasn't an alcoholic when you first got together with him, was he?"

"No. But in retrospect, I'm not so sure what we had was love exactly. I mean, it was. I loved your dad. I'm just not sure I was *in* love with him. That's probably not helping you."

"I think I get it. I know there's a difference." She smiled. "I feel like I can see a future with Nick. I think about it, a lot. About being with him. About having a life with him. That must mean something, don't you think?"

Olivia nodded. "It's probably a good sign. You guys are going to the party tomorrow, right?"

"Yep."

"How was your evening tonight?"

Jenny let out a happy sigh. "So good, Mom. We had a beautiful dinner and then we went to a place called Froggy's and—oh, that reminds me. The resort should have a night for dancing. Let me explain." She laid it out for her mom, giving Nick credit.

Olivia tilted her head, eyes closing slightly like she was picturing it. "You know, that's a great idea."

"Yeah?"

"Yeah. I mean, really good." Olivia picked up her glass of water. "I'm going to talk to the girls about it tomorrow. Or as soon as I can. Tomorrow might be a little busy."

Jenny shrugged. "Whenever." She was happy to contribute.

But not as happy as she was to be staying.

# Chapter Twenty-five

Grace woke up with a new sense of purpose. One that didn't include sunrise yoga, but did involve snuggling closer to her still-sleeping husband and pretending she hadn't woken up as early as she had.

That lasted about twenty minutes and then she couldn't stay in bed any longer. There was a lot to do. And she really wanted coffee. She'd need it to get everything on her to-do list done. One of those things was to get them packed and moved into their new bungalow. That would be exciting.

She looked at her phone. J. Henry had approved a wedding menu, which Amanda had forwarded. Excellent.

She'd need to go over that menu with David to see if there was anything she could do to help with that. Another item on her list was making sure they had all the necessary linens for the wedding party. She knew they did, but double-checking wouldn't hurt and she wanted to set them aside so they wouldn't accidentally get used in the restaurant.

There was the question of the napkin fold to decide as well. A small thing, maybe, but it helped set the look of the table. Which was something else she needed to work on. Amanda wanted to use the gold chargers they had, easy enough, but she wanted shells and candles along with the flowers to really emphasize the tropical beach wedding theme.

Grace was going to do some more digging in the second storage room to see what she could find. Shells and candles seemed like an easy thing to come up with.

She slid out of bed quietly so that she didn't wake David up and got coffee going. It would be nice to be in their own, bigger place where she wouldn't have to worry about disturbing him.

With that done, she grabbed an easy outfit of shorts and a T-shirt, then went into the bathroom and took a quick shower. Her plan was to hit the storage room early so that if she couldn't find shells and candles, she could text either Amanda or Olivia to pick some up.

Both women were headed into town today, although Olivia's trip would take longer, as she had more to do.

Dressed but hair still damp, as she didn't want to

use the dryer, Grace came back out and considered what she was going to wear for the gallery party.

She was a little bummed that David wouldn't be able to join her, but with Chef Glenn's arrest, David couldn't take the evening off like he'd hoped.

He'd mentioned something to her last night about promoting one of the line cooks to sous-chef, an older man named Pascal who'd had some classical training.

Grace liked that idea. There was no reason David should have to do all of the heavy lifting. It was all part of getting the kitchen in better operating shape. Glenn had been a little slack, as they were coming to find out.

But she knew her husband would get the place whipped into tiptop form very soon.

She looked at the sundresses she'd brought. None of them were that dressy, but the blue one with the pink and yellow flowers was probably the nicest. It would do. Tonight wasn't about her anyway.

She fixed her coffee in a paper cup so she could take it with her, then left David a quick note to let him know where she was in case he forgot what she'd told him yesterday. She also asked him to order breakfast so they could eat together, then grabbed her key and phone and quietly left the bungalow.

The resort was so calm at this time of the morning. Some people were up, and probably at Leigh Ann's yoga class, but most of the people she passed on her way to the main building were workers. Housekeeping staff getting ready to clean rooms, groundskeepers sweeping sidewalks and grooming the landscape into perfection, more workers on the beach straightening lounge chairs and returning them all to the exact same position.

It took a surprising number of staff to keep Mother's in such great shape. She doubted any of the resort's guests knew just how many.

She walked through the quiet lobby and went straight to the second storage room, using her key to access it.

She flipped the lights on and had a look around. Unlike the other storage room, this one had tall metal shelves against both walls as well as a row down the middle. The shelves were packed with items, some in boxes, some not, but all smaller items. This room held no furniture or bulky things like the other one.

If there were shells and candles to be found, they'd be in here.

Sadly, this room was in no better shape than the other storage space. It was clear that any organization that had been present was long gone. Things were haphazardly shoved onto the shelves with no sense of putting similar items together.

There was nothing to do but start on the right-hand side and work her way around. She grabbed a small two-tier rolling cart that had been pushed into a corner. That would be useful for holding anything she found, but she wasn't going to worry about cleaning the room up and restoring order until she had an idea of what was here.

Hopefully, she'd find those shells and candles somewhere along the way.

She did, too, about fifteen minutes into her inspection. But two squat, pale blue candles and a mesh bag of random shells weren't going to cut it. They went on the cart anyway, because she wasn't counting anything out just yet. She'd show it all to Amanda and let her decide.

Two shelves down, she found an unopened box of twelve white tapers. Those could be useful but only if they had something to hold those candles.

She kept searching, uncovering more Christmas decorations, some for Fourth of July, two boxes of silverware that matched what was currently being used in The Palms, and six taper holders. Those were clear glass shells and definitely worth grabbing. She put them on the top shelf of the cart and the silverware on the bottom shelf to show to David.

She was only halfway around the room, so she had hope that she'd find a few more items they could use.

The bottom of the next shelving unit was full of boxes. Grace sat on the floor in front of the shelves, kicking out her booted foot to one side. She pulled out one of the boxes and opened it. The box held six pint-sized Mason jars. She opened a few more boxes and found More mason jars. The bigger boxes held quart-sized Mason jars. Amanda hadn't asked for them, but they seemed like something that could be useful. Grace put them on the cart.

A little sand, a couple of shells, maybe a little raffia tied around the top, and they'd make great beachy candleholders. Of course, Amanda might not think that was classy enough. Grace would let her decide.

She went back to work, scanning the shelves, and opening boxes whether or not they were labeled after finding a box marked "Calendars" that held small matchboxes imprinted with The Palms' logo.

A little more digging turned up five large white candles, three beautiful conch shells, an entire box of assorted shells in mesh bags that matched the first one she'd found, two boxes of silver chargers that held twelve each, a large box of white tea lights, and thirteen handled lanterns with white-washed metal frames.

She put it all on the cart, then checked the time. She wanted to get back to the bungalow before David left and she had an hour before that happened. She sent him a quick text. *Are you up?*

*Yep*, he responded. *I got your note. Ordered breakfast. Headed back soon?*

She smiled. *Yes, in about five minutes.*

She took pictures of everything she'd found that might be useful for the wedding, then sent those snaps to Amanda to let her make her decision. They were probably going to need more candles.

Grace locked up the storage room, then returned to her bungalow, happy with the work she'd gotten done.

Now she could eat breakfast with David, then get their stuff moved over to the new bungalow and get them unpacked. After that, she'd get back to work on whatever Amanda needed.

She brushed her clothes off, realizing she'd gotten a little dirty in the storage room. Ugh. They really needed to do laundry. And while she could borrow some soap from the girls, she was going to have to get her own soon.

Getting transitioned into one of the staff bungalows was going to take some work, but she would get it done. She didn't want David to have to worry about it. He had a lot on his shoulders already.

But the work would be worth it, no matter how hard.

She let herself into the bungalow.

David was dressed for work in his chef pants, jacket and clogs and sitting on the couch watching the news. He smiled when she came in. "You look like you've been busy."

She nodded. "I have been. I probably need another shower. Hey, I found two boxes of brand-new silverware in the storage room. Matches what's already in use. Do you want it for the dining room?"

"Sure. But all I really want right now is my wife." He held out his arms.

She smiled. "But my clothes are all dirty."

He shrugged and gave her a wink. "Then take your clothes off."

# Chapter Twenty-six

Katie and Sophie met Owen and Gage at the dock. Katie had worn the hat she'd bought last week in town and big sunglasses. Sophie was in a ball cap and shades, too. The boys were taking them into town to do some grocery shopping for the house. Food, mostly, but also Fabio needed cat food, treats, and litter.

It was going to be a quick trip. Owen had a conference call with some investors at one, and Katie was determined to get back to writing, starting today. Didn't matter if she only managed a few pages, she was starting her new book.

She had to get back to work and back into the rhythm of writing.

They got on the boat, not the speed boat this time but the more spacious pontoon. Gage was at the wheel. Owen helped Katie and Sophie on board. Sophie stood next to Gage.

"Morning," Katie said.

Owen smiled and kissed her cheek. "Morning. How are you? Settling in?"

She nodded as they sat in the shaded part of the boat. "A bit. Getting some groceries in the house will help. So will getting our stuff down here. But as soon as we get back today, and get the stuff put away, obviously, then I'm going to write."

"That's great."

She nodded as Gage motored the pontoon toward the mainland. "I have to. I need to get to work on my next book. It's my job, after all."

"I'm sure your readers are eagerly waiting for it."

"They are."

"So what's it about?" he asked.

She took a breath. "I think I'm going to start a new series. Based on this place."

His brows rose. "Yeah? That's a great idea."

"I hope my readers think so. It's a bit of a departure from what I usually write."

"You mean because the book won't be set in a big city?"

She nodded. She'd once freaked out that he'd read her books. Now she appreciated that he knew them well enough to talk about them. "Exactly. They've come to expect that kind of lifestyle, with the fast pace and flash. This place is anything but fast paced."

He laughed. "True. But it's still got a lot going on.

And your characters will be the same fully formed, interesting people with problems to solve and romance to fall into, right?"

"Right. I kind of think that the romance part will be more natural. It's hard not to fall in love when you're in paradise, you know?"

He smiled at her, looking deep into her eyes. "I know."

She smiled, full of happiness and amazement that this wonderful man was her guy.

The grocery store, a place called Publix, was new to her but apparently much loved by the locals.

She could see why as she took her sunglasses off and tucked them into her purse. The store was bright and clean, well-stocked, and the employees were friendly and helpful. "Is this your usual place?"

Owen nodded. "Yep. Although to be honest, Rika does most of the shopping. I think I've been here maybe three or four times in the last year. I like it, though, because they treat me like an ordinary shopper."

"Good to know."

Owen and Gage each got a cart. Katie and Sophie had already decided they'd divide and conquer, each taking a list of necessary items, which there were a lot of. Stocking a house that had nothing in it was a big job.

Sophie glanced over. "See you at the register."

Katie nodded. "Happy shopping."

Sophie and Gage headed toward the drinks and snacks aisles, then they were on to the meat and dairy sections.

Owen leaned on the cart. "Where are we going?"

"Produce, deli, bakery."

"Oooh…cake? Pie? Cookies?"

Katie laughed. "None of those things. But I was going to look for some kind of breakfast muffin. Something at least a little healthy."

"Spoilsport."

Still chuckling, she shook her head. "Drive."

The produce section was beautiful, full of colorful fresh fruits and vegetables. The urge to buy it all was hard to resist. She did her best to stick to the list, but some grapes and strawberries made it into the cart all the same.

Owen had taken a number and was waiting at the deli counter, so she gathered salad ingredients as well and brought them back to put in the cart.

A clear container of sugar cookies now sat underneath the container of blueberry muffins she'd put in there earlier. She looked at Owen.

He raised his brows and did a terrible job of suppressing his smile. "What?"

"Those don't look healthy." She really couldn't afford to have junk in the house or she'd eat it.

With a deep sigh and an eyeroll, he picked up the

cookies and took them back to the bakery.

Snickering, she checked her list to see what she needed from the deli. Turkey, ham, and sliced cheese.

Owen returned with a different bakery box in his hand. It held a single chocolate cupcake frosted with vanilla buttercream, which was covered in rainbow sprinkles. He held it up, smirking. "This is the cost of me giving you a ride into town."

She nodded, highly amused. "That seems fair."

Movement behind him caught her eye. A woman was not-so-subtly taking pictures of them. All happiness left Katie and she was filled with a mix of anger and panic.

"What's wrong?" Owen asked. He looked over his shoulder and frowned.

Katie wanted to leave. She couldn't stop staring at the woman. "We should go."

"Sweetheart, this is going to happen. Especially when you're out with me. Put your sunglasses back on and ignore her. That's all you can do."

Suddenly, a young man in a Publix shirt stepped in front of the woman to fix a display. The woman moved to be able to see Owen and Katie again. The young man also adjusted his position, putting himself in the way again.

Katie smiled as she understood what he was doing. She looked away to get her sunglasses out of her purse and slipped them on. "I'm okay."

Owen looked over his shoulder again, noticed what the young man was doing and joined Katie in her amusement. The LED sign over the deli changed to display a new number.

"Come on," Owen said. "That's us. Let's get our stuff and get moving."

Throughout the shopping trip, they were noticed several more times. But the Publix employee stayed with them, seemingly needing to straighten shelves or fix stock in the vicinity around them, conveniently blocking whoever was trying to take a photo.

"I want to tip him," Katie said quietly to Owen.

He shook his head. "You can't. The employees don't accept tips. But I will get his name and make sure management knows he went above and beyond."

"Thank you."

They finished up before Gage and Sophie, but only by a minute or two. They got in line, Katie paid, then the four of them pushed the carts full of bags out to Owen's car.

The men loaded the bags in, just barely getting them all to fit. The frozen and cold items went into three big coolers.

Gage slipped in behind the steering wheel. Sophie took the front passenger seat, while Owen and Katie got in the back.

Katie exhaled. "That was interesting."

Sophie twisted around to look at her. "Why?"

Owen answered. "We got noticed."

Sophie rolled her eyes. "I wondered if that would happen. Are you going to be all over social media again?"

Katie shrugged. "I have no idea. A very nice young man, an employee, took it upon himself to run interference."

"It wasn't paparazzi," Owen clarified. "Just regular people. They'll probably post it to their own social media accounts, but I doubt it'll go much farther than that. Grocery shopping isn't all that exciting, and *Star Watch* is probably still reeling from the settlement they had to pay out."

Katie looked at him. "Good point. This will be an interesting test of how much news we still are."

Owen nodded. "It will be, but I can guarantee you there will be a lot more press at the party tonight. There's no escaping that."

"I'm okay with that," Katie said. "In fact, if it helps bring Grant some publicity, I'm all for it. And I'll be prepared for it. But I wasn't today. I really thought the grocery store would be a safe space."

Owen put his arm around her. "Maybe Sophie will have to handle the shopping for a while."

Sophie looked at them through the mirror on her visor. "It's okay. It's always been one of my regular jobs anyway. I don't mind doing it." She glanced at Gage. "Although I will need a ride over here."

Gage smiled. "So long as my boss is okay with it, I'm happy to oblige."

Owen nudged Katie. "You definitely need to get your own boat."

She laughed. "Agreed. Otherwise, I see these shopping trips turning into long lunches."

"Hey," Sophie said. "I'm allowed to have lunch. With Gage."

Katie nodded. "Yes, you are." She snuggled in closer to Owen. "We really need that second dock. I hope it's not going to raise the insurance too much or Olivia will veto it."

"For good?" Owen asked.

"No, probably just until there's money in the budget to pay the increased premium."

"That's good," he said. "But you know what we need besides that dock?"

She looked at him. "What?"

"A walkway, like a boardwalk, that runs from Iris's house to my property."

"Oh, that would be cool," Katie said. "Then we could walk to each other's places."

He nodded. "Or bike. Probably wouldn't take more than a few minutes that way."

"I love that idea."

"Good," he said. "Because I just hired a contractor to build one."

# Chapter Twenty-seven

Leigh Ann walked into the spa expecting to find a place that was a little rundown and in need of an update, but that wasn't the case at all.

Maybe she was missing something, but it was a beautiful space that looked modern and clean and about as peaceful as you'd expect a spa to be.

Little glass mosaic tiles covered the walls with the opalescent sheen of mother of pearl. Filmy white curtains draped the doorways, and wide, polished teak planks on the floors gave the space a feeling of warmth and strength. Potted orchids bloomed in wall niches and a soft, natural scent filled the air.

A sandstone countertop dominated the reception desk. Behind it, water flowed down the entire rear wall, which was covered with more of the gleaming mosaic tiles in soft ocean-blue shades.

Soothing music played with just enough volume to be heard over the water feature.

Leigh Ann couldn't find any fault in it. In fact, it was lovely. Maybe the individual service rooms weren't in such good shape, though. She smiled at the girl behind the front desk. "Hi there."

"Hi. Welcome to Aqualina. Are you here for an appointment?"

"I am, although not for a spa appointment. I'm Leigh Ann. I'm supposed to meet with Manuela?" Leigh Ann had gotten the woman's email address from Vera. Since Iris's announcement had gone out to all the resort's employees about the five women taking over operations, Leigh Ann had sent Manuela, the acting spa and fitness center manager, a note yesterday afternoon about meeting.

They'd set things up for midday, since Manuela had some free time. Leigh Ann was a little apprehensive about the meeting. When she'd agreed to her new role here at the resort, she hadn't realized she'd be displacing someone else.

Now she had to explain to that woman that Leigh Ann was taking over her job.

The woman behind the counter nodded. "I'll let her know you're here."

"Thank you." Leigh Ann took a seat to wait, and the woman returned with another, older woman a few minutes later.

"Hi, Leigh Ann." The older woman stuck her hand out. She had shoulder-length black hair with a few strands of gray and a kind smile. "I'm Manuela."

Leigh Ann stood and shook the woman's hand. She seemed genuinely happy to see Leigh Ann, which wasn't what she'd been expecting. "Pleasure to meet you."

"The pleasure is all mine." Manuela tipped her head toward the hallway she'd just come through. "We can talk in the office."

Leigh Ann followed her back into a small, but well-furnished space. The office had one window, but the glass was frosted over. Still, it let a nice amount of light in. A desk sat in front of two bookcases with a long filing cabinet between them. A potted orchid sat on top of it. In front of the desk were two chairs.

Manuela shut the door, then took one of the chairs in front of the desk, gesturing for Leigh Ann to do the same. "I'm so glad you're here."

"You are?" Leigh Ann had been concerned that Manuela would be resentful of someone coming in from nowhere and taking over, so this response really surprised her.

Manuela nodded. "You bet. I'm an esthetician. I'm not a manager. But I've been doing my best. The thing is, I don't think my best as a manager is that great. We need help. And I know Iris hasn't been in a good place to do too much of that."

Manuela held her hands up suddenly. "I don't mean that as a dig against Iris. She's the best boss on this planet and I love working for her and working here. I just know her heart never fully recovered from losing Arthur."

Leigh Ann nodded. "So I understand. But I have to say the spa looks great. I expected it to look rundown or outdated but it doesn't seem that way to me at all."

Manuela smiled weakly. "We have two treatment rooms that are unusable because the beds are in rough shape and need to be replaced. The last faucet in the men's locker room hasn't had hot water in six months. And we really need to reevaluate our product line. There are better lines out there, but I didn't feel like it was my place to spend money on something like that."

Leigh Ann felt like she should be taking notes. "What else?"

"We turn down a lot of appointments because we don't have the staff. We could easily use two more massage therapists, another hair stylist, a nail technician, and a facialist." Manuela's voice lowered. "Between us, it would be great to get a nurse practitioner in here who could do Botox and fillers. We get a *lot* of requests for that."

"That doesn't surprise me." This was the right crowd for it. Could Nick do something like that? He was a doctor. It was worth talking to him about.

Although maybe that wouldn't appeal to him after his time spent doing humanitarian work overseas.

"Also," Manuela went on. "It would be great to send some of the spa and salon staff away for additional training, which is something we just haven't kept up with lately."

Leigh Ann glanced at the desk. "Do you have a notebook and pen I can have? I need to write all of this down."

"Sure, just a second." Manuela got up, rummaged in one of the drawers and came up with a large white pad of paper with the Aqualina name across the top. She handed it and a pen to Leigh Ann. "All yours."

"Thank you." Leigh Ann started writing, putting down everything that Manuela had told her. When she was done, she looked up. "What else?"

Manuela looked off to the side, like she was thinking. "For the spa, that's all I can think of right now. But the fitness center, which I've also been overseeing, needs work, too."

Leigh Ann kept her pen poised over the paper. "Go ahead. Tell me everything."

"One of the treadmills and two of the ellipticals don't work. Neither does one of the water fountains. The ceiling fan near the free weights only spins on high. The other option is to turn it off."

Leigh Ann sighed. "Has Duke been called about any of this stuff? Like the fan?"

Manuela nodded. "He replaced that fan two months ago, but there's a wiring issue. We need an electrician."

"Okay." Leigh Ann wrote that down.

"Some of the mirrors in the fitness room should be replaced and the whole space needs to be repainted."

Leigh Ann put that into another note, then clutched the pad to her chest. "I have a confession to make. I haven't been in the fitness center yet. Can we go have a look?"

"Absolutely." Manuela stood. "I'll give you the whole tour. The spa rooms, too."

"That would be great. Thank you."

An hour later, Manuela had shown Leigh Ann everything. And Leigh Ann had two more pages of notes and a slew of photos that she'd taken on her phone. They returned to the office.

Leigh Ann slumped into the chair she'd occupied earlier, a little daunted by how many things needed attention. "There's a lot of work to be done."

Manuela nodded, looking a little miserable. "I'm sorry. I did my best."

Leigh Ann smiled and put her hand on the woman's arm. "None of this is your fault. None of this. I can tell from that tour what a good job you've been doing, but I also know that you shouldn't have to handle all of this. And now you won't have to, because I'm here."

Manuela didn't seem as mollified by that as Leigh Ann had hoped. "Am I going to get fired?"

"What?" Leigh Ann leaned back. "Heck no. No one's getting fired. My plan is to fix all of this stuff and hire *more* people. I'm definitely not letting you go. My goal is for this spa to get rave reviews. To make it the kind of place people dream about coming to." If David could level up the restaurant, why couldn't she do the same with the spa? "I want us to be able to take care of all of the guests who want services. As far as I'm concerned, the resort is losing money every time someone can't get an appointment here."

Manuela nodded, looking much happier. "It's true. Plus, if we make all the fixes that need to be made, we could raise prices, too. That hasn't been done in a while." She leaned in. "Trust me, these people can afford to pay more."

Leigh Ann laughed. "I agree. I'd like you to become the managing esthetician. I want to know what new product lines you think we should be using, what additional services we should be offering, what classes are important and who should take them, and if you have any suggestions for new hires, I'm open to that, too. I'm open to anything you think I should know. Anything that you think would make this spa better. Can you do that for me?"

Manuela was grinning now. "Yes, I can."

"Fantastic. I think you and I are going to get along like peas and carrots."

Manuela laughed. "In my family, we say rice and beans."

"That, too." Leigh Ann smiled as she gestured toward the desk. "Why didn't you sit behind the desk when you brought me in here the first time?"

Manuela shrugged. "Didn't feel like my place. It never has."

Leigh Ann nodded. She really felt for the woman. She'd been carrying a lot on her shoulders without feeling as if she was capable. "Things are going to be different from here on out, okay?"

"Okay." Manuela smiled. "I'm so glad you're here."

"Me, too. Why don't you introduce me to some of the other staff, then I'm going to get to work." Leigh Ann didn't relish the conversation she would need to have with Olivia about the money that would have to be spent to fix everything, but there was no way around it.

Leigh Ann wasn't going to take on this job and not do it. That wasn't her way. And it wasn't why Iris had wanted her in this position.

# Chapter Twenty-eight

Olivia was in the middle of the Salvation Army, looking at a pair of white wicker barstools that would make great replacements for the chrome and vinyl ones currently in her bungalow. But did she really need to spend money on barstools when she already had some?

Granted, they looked more suited to a 1970s bachelor pad than a single woman's tropical bungalow, but they were functional.

And hideous.

"You want those?" Eddie asked. "They're really nice. Hardly look used at all."

Olivia sighed. "I do want them. I'm just trying to justify the money when I have barstools."

His eyes narrowed. "You do, yes, but aren't the seats on those ripped?"

"They are, but the duct tape is doing a fine job of—"

"No," Eddie said with a laugh. "It isn't. You need these."

She smiled. She liked shopping with him. "Okay."

He picked them up and set them on the long, low cart that already held two large paintings and one smaller one, a bunch of throw pillows — two of which were for Eddie — a small, rolled area rug, and big ceramic planter that looked like a shell. She didn't have a plant for it yet, but she wasn't worried about that.

In the back of the store, there was a Hold tag on a desk for her. Eddie had promised to come back and get it Monday morning with the resort's truck.

Her phone rang, the ringtone muted through her purse. She fished it out and answered even though the number wasn't familiar to her. "Hello?"

"Ms. Rhodes?"

"Yes?"

"This is Detective Murphy."

"Hi, Detective. How are you?" She almost held her breath. He sounded like he was in a good mood, but that didn't mean much.

"I'm well, thanks. I'm also happy to report that it looks like we'll be able to release the recovered funds to the resort in two weeks or so. I spoke with the district attorney and he's willing to make it happen. Arthur and Iris have been valued members of the community for a long time. Holding onto nine million dollars of their money until the end of this trial seemed cruel and unusual. The DA agreed with me."

Olivia exhaled. This was very good news indeed. "That's great. Thank you so much. The resort really needs that money for upkeep and repairs."

"I'm sure. Are you able to come by and sign some paperwork? You're listed as our main contact and since you're now an owner, your signature would be just fine. Unless you'd rather I ask Iris?"

"No, I can come by. That's not a problem."

Eddie looked at her, a question in his eyes.

"Great. I'll be here all day."

"Thank you. See you soon." She hung up and grinned. "After we finish up here, can you take me to the police station? Detective Murphy needs me to sign some paperwork."

"Of course. What paperwork?"

She shook her head. "I'm not sure but he told me he's pulled some strings and we're getting the stolen nine million back in about two weeks."

Eddie's mouth came open and his brows lifted. "That's incredible!"

She nodded. "It's *so* good. Iris will be thrilled."

"Does this mean you're giving the green light to the new dock?"

She laughed. "Probably. I still haven't heard back about what the new premium would be." She was waiting for the insurance company to answer that question.

He let out a little snort. “You’re going to keep a tight rein on the resort’s funds, aren’t you?”

Was that how she was coming off? “Maybe. When it’s necessary. Is that bad? I can’t help that I’m frugal.”

“I think it’s great. Arthur and Iris have always spent pretty freely, which was fine, as it was their money, but there are a lot more people involved now. You’re right to look out for them.”

“I’m looking out for all of us. You, me, all the girls, and Iris, too. It’s a lot of responsibility.”

“It is,” he said. “But I take great comfort knowing that you’re the one in charge of the accounts now. I know you’re only going to do what’s best for us and the resort.”

“Thank you.” She looked at her watch. “We’d better pay for this stuff and get moving if we’re going to the police station and the grocery store. By the time I get this all put away, I’ll have to get ready for the party tonight.”

“Yes, ma’am.” He grabbed the handle of the cart and started pulling it. “You sure you got everything you wanted?”

“No, but I got enough for now. We can always come back, right?”

“Right. You can come with me Monday to get the desk, if you want. Have another look around then.”

"Perfect."

On the way to the register, she ended up with a macrame plant holder that she decided she'd hang on the front porch, and a little square wood table that would be perfect out there, too, once she'd painted it.

With everything she'd gotten at the hardware store and was about to get here, she had a lot of work to do. She knew Jenny would help, but she didn't want to put too much on her daughter. After all, Jenny had her own job to consider.

And Olivia was looking forward to it. There was something really rewarding about putting effort into making your living space more to your taste. It was work that she wouldn't mind doing at all.

They checked out, got everything loaded into the truck, then Eddie drove them to the police station. Detective Murphy didn't keep them waiting long. She signed the paperwork he had for her, some releases, then they were off again, this time to the grocery store.

Her list was long, but Eddie helped.

By the time he was pushing the cart full of bags out to the car, Olivia was a little worn out. She was considering a nap. If there was time. It might be the only thing that got her through the evening. They still had to load the boat, get back to the island, then unload everything and cart it to her bungalow.

As they got into the truck to head back to Bluewater Marina, she glanced at Eddie. "How long do you think the party will go tonight?"

"Probably not later than ten. These things are pretty well controlled. It's not like a party that's at someone's house. It's got a clear end time."

Olivia nodded. "That's good. Because I don't think I'd last much longer than that. Even ten sounds like it might as well be three in the morning."

He laughed.

She smiled. "I'm really not an old woman, I swear."

"I know you're not. Today's been a long day and it's far from over. Plus, you get up early. So do I."

She knew he'd understand. "How about after I get the groceries put away, I make us some lunch? Nothing fancy. Just some wraps." She'd gotten some low carb wraps, along with lunch meat, cheese, lettuce, and tomatoes. She had pickles and carrot sticks, too, along with condiments.

"That would be great." He glanced at the groceries he'd just loaded. "But I didn't see any chips in there."

She rolled her eyes. "Because chips are neither low carb nor diet friendly."

He rolled his eyes right back at her. "And you don't need to be concerned with either of those things. There's nothing wrong with being curvy."

She grinned and looked straight ahead. "That's kind of you to say, but I'd just like to drop a few pounds. Living in a warmer climate like this, it seems to me I'd be more comfortable carrying a little less weight."

"Suit yourself. But I like how you look."

"Thanks." She gave him a smile. "I like how you look, too."

He laughed. "Good. Because I'm not about to go on a diet."

# Chapter Twenty-nine

Long did not begin to describe Amanda's day, but they'd gotten a lot done. She and Duke had run to the hardware store, gotten all of the supplies to make the chalkboard, which turned out to be more things than she'd imagined, and she'd picked up a bottle of window cleaner that she needed.

When they'd gotten back, she helped him unload and carry everything to his workshop, a small building just beyond the staff bungalows she hadn't even known existed. While he built the chalkboard, she'd gone back to her bungalow and made them lunch.

Nothing fancy, just sandwiches with a side of veggie pasta salad. She packed it up by putting the food on paper plates and covering them with foil. She carried the plates and some plastic forks in one plastic shopping bag, and two cans of soda in another.

She'd gotten back to the workshop to find he was

actually building two chalkboards, something he explained was about as easy as building one.

Having the second one made her happy. It would definitely come in handy, and it meant she wouldn't have to erase the one for the ceremony and quickly write the reception info on it.

After they'd eaten, they went back to work, him on the chalkboards, her on inspecting all the things Grace had found.

Somehow, as she walked back into her bungalow, it was now a few minutes after five. The day had sped by.

She turned on her shower and went back out to her closet to figure out what she was going to wear to the party. Duke was picking her up at six-twenty.

She had one dress she hadn't worn yet. She'd brought it thinking she might need something a little fancier than a sundress, but never really had. Until now. Tonight seemed like the perfect occasion.

It was a simple black dress in slinky rayon knit. Truth was, she hadn't worn it in a long, long time. Not since Brian had been alive, and certainly well before any of his crimes had come to light.

Black might be appropriate for mourning, but this dress was too form-fitting to pass off as widow's weeds. It was definitely not something she ever would have worn in front of her mother.

That alone made Amanda think it was just right for tonight.

Smiling, she showered and washed her hair. There was nothing wrong with wanting to look nice for Duke.

Which was exactly her plan.

She did her makeup with a slightly more dramatic hand than usual, adding some black eyeliner and an extra sweep or two of mascara, along with a berry-colored lip stain Militant Marge probably would have deemed scandalous. Then she dried her hair smooth and sleek, and pinned it back on one side with a small, sparkly clip she also hadn't worn in a long time.

Flat black sandals, hoop earrings, and a chain-link bracelet finished the look. A few spritzes of perfume made it perfect. A small, neutral clutch held her phone, her key, her lipstick, an ID, a fairly useless credit card, and a little cash. Her bare essentials.

She selected a colorful scarf to use as a wrap and went downstairs, wondering if she should go over to Duke's. A knock on her door answered that question.

She opened the door and smiled at him. Black had been a smart choice, as he was in tan linen pants and a short-sleeved black silk shirt with a little embroidered detailing.

He gaped at her. "That is...quite a dress. No, scratch that. It's not the dress that looks good. It's the woman in it."

She laughed. "Thanks. This is definitely not my usual style."

"It should be. At least when we go out. That dress

does amazing things for your figure." He whistled, winked at her, then offered her his arm.

He didn't drive the boat as fast as usual so that she wouldn't get too windblown, which she appreciated.

At the marina in town, they got into his truck, and he cranked on the air. It was a little warm, although the sun was setting, and the night would bring cooler temperatures.

"You okay?" he asked.

"I'm fine. Excited to see this painting."

"Me, too."

It took about fifteen minutes to get to Grant's gallery. Duke parked, then came around to get her door and, once again, offer her his arm.

They walked in together. People already milled about, so even though she and Duke were a few minutes early, they weren't the first to arrive. She didn't see Olivia, Grace, Katie, or Leigh Ann yet. Duke's parents weren't there, either.

The painting was in the center of the largest wall in the gallery, covered with a white cloth. She imagined there would be a dramatic unveiling when everyone was assembled.

As she looked around the gallery, there was no sign of Grant. He had to be here.

Servers with trays of drinks and appetizers began to mingle with the growing crowd. She took a glass of champagne from one.

Duke turned and smiled. "Hey, there's the man of the hour. And the woman, too."

Amanda faced the same direction he was and saw Grant and Leigh Ann walking out of the back room. Grant was immediately approached by a couple who seemed desperate to talk to him.

He waved Leigh Ann on, so she kept moving, headed for Amanda.

Leigh Ann looked drop-dead gorgeous in her new dress. It showed off her incredible body and the glowing tan she'd picked up while on the island. She looked ten years younger than her age and happier than Amanda had ever seen her.

Leigh Ann waved as she came over, and Amanda waved back, smiling.

"Hiya," Leigh Ann said. "You look beautiful."

"Please. I look like a box of frogs next to you."

Leigh Ann laughed. "I think not but thank you for the compliment." She glanced at Grant. "Doesn't he look good in a suit?"

Amanda looked at Grant. Duke had gone over to rescue him from the chatty couple. Grant was in a pale blue-gray summer suit with a white dress shirt, black belt and shoes. Crisp and modern and handsome. The two men standing together looked like they could have been modeling for a menswear catalog. "He looks great. You guys make a gorgeous couple."

Leigh Ann was still looking at Grant when she answered. "So do you two."

"Are you nervous?" Amanda asked.

Leigh Ann shook her head. "I was. And maybe I still am a tiny bit, but now I'm mostly just excited for tonight and for everyone to see Grant's work."

"What about you-know-who and his girlfriend showing up?"

Leigh Ann shrugged. "If they do, they do. I don't think they will. Marty's not an idiot. I'm sure he'll remember who Grant is when Candi tells him about the party."

"I guess we'll see, huh?"

"Yep." Leigh Ann's gaze lifted. "There's some more of the gang."

Amanda turned. Olivia, Eddie, Jenny, Nick, Vera, and Grace were all walking in. What a nice sight that was, to see friends. Something that had been missing from her life for so long. Then Jack and Dixie Shaw walked in behind them. Dixie saw Amanda, gave her a big wave, and smiled warmly. She tugged on Jack's shirt and pointed Amanda out to him. He, too, smiled and waved.

Their clear affection for her nearly choked her up. Her own parents had never reacted to seeing her that way. Especially not her mother.

Duke came over and slid his arm around her waist. "Hey, babe." Then he tipped his head. "You okay?"

She nodded and smiled. "Just appreciating my new community. My new life."

An understanding light shone in his eyes. "Now you know how I feel when I look at you."

# Chapter Thirty

Jenny held Nick's hand as they walked around the gallery and took in all of Grant's work. It was beautiful stuff. The kind of artwork that drew you in. The longer she looked at any one painting, the more she saw. A starfish hidden in a rock crevice. Two fish forming a heart. A pearl gleaming from a half-opened oyster.

And of all the emotions the art evoked in her, the one that surprised her the most was how his art made her happy that Compass Key was now her home.

It wasn't just the place, though. The feeling encompassed more than just living here. It included all of the new people that coming here had brought into her life, like Grant. And Katie. And Owen. And all of her mom's friends. She smiled. And Nick. Especially Nick.

"What's that look for?" Nick asked.

Jenny realized she was staring at him and smiling, which made her laugh. "Just thinking about how glad I am to be staying. This place has such a different vibe than Ohio. It's much...freer. Which isn't exactly what I mean, but it's close. People seem nicer. More concerned about those around them than themselves, too."

He nodded. "It's just a different way of life here. More about connecting with the world around you. Probably because the weather is so nice, and you can be outside so much it just makes you feel more tied to your environment and your neighbors."

"That's definitely true." She went back to the painting in front of them. "But when I look at something like this, it makes me feel proud to live here. Even though it's only been a little over a week. Weird, right?"

"I don't think it's weird." He stood shoulder to shoulder with her, studying the art. "But when you see something this cool, and you also happen to know the person who created it, it's human nature to feel proud that you're connected to someone that talented." He bumped his shoulder against hers. "I bet a lot of people feel that way about you."

She laughed and shook her head. "I don't do anything that equals this. This is art."

"Right, but you have valuable talents in other areas. Look at the way you helped Katie out."

She wasn't convinced it was an apples-to-apples situation. "I don't know."

"Well, I do. Your firm wouldn't be behind you moving here if they didn't know how brilliant and valuable you are. That makes *me* proud to know *you*."

"Come on. If anyone's going to be proud to know someone, it's me for knowing you." He was on a different level than her and if he didn't recognize that, he was being silly. "You're a doctor who's been working with a humanitarian concern for years."

"True, but I'm not the least bit artistic." He smiled at her, then at the painting. "I couldn't do something like this if my life depended on it."

"But you could save a life, so…" She shrugged. "Doesn't seem like much of a contest to me."

He waved over a server with a tray of champagne flutes and took two, handing one to Jenny. "Here's to us and whatever comes next."

She'd happily toast to that. "To us."

After a sip, he said, "Have I told you how beautiful you look tonight?"

She smiled. He had. And she was just wearing a black, flowered sundress with a little midriff cutout. Nothing all that special. "Yes, but I don't mind hearing it again."

"Good." He gestured at the painting with his glass. "Is that your favorite one?"

"I think so. It really speaks to me. Probably because of the sea turtles. I saw one the day my mom and I went snorkeling and it was about the coolest thing ever. So was seeing the dolphins. But the sea turtle just had this attitude." She laughed. "The dolphins seemed happy to see us. The sea turtle was more like a grumpy old man who wanted us off his lawn. Gotta respect that."

He laughed. "I love that." He looked at the painting again. "I'm going to buy that for you."

"Nick, you can't. It's too much."

He shook his head. "It's not an original. I saw a sign up front that explained that while they look just like paintings they're actually something called a giclée print, which is a fancy way of saying a really high-end, top-quality reproduction. And Grant adds some personal touches. Plus, he signs them all."

"It's still two hundred and fifty dollars."

He shrugged like it was no big deal. "It's an investment." He grinned at her. "Especially when I know, someday, it'll hang in the house we live in together."

* * *

Grace missed David, but she knew he was busy, and she understood. Being married to a chef meant a lifetime of sacrifices. Attending the party without him was just one of those, but it was a sacrifice for their future.

That didn't change the fact that looking around at her friends, all of them with a man at her side, caused Grace to feel a mix of jealousy and sadness.

Something inside her said it wasn't fair. The urge to drink was strong. It would be so easy to grab a glass of champagne and toss it back without anyone seeing her do it in this crowd. She exhaled, trying to get rid of the compulsion. She did *not* want to give in. She'd been doing so well.

If she couldn't get through a special event like this without slipping, how was she going to live at a resort where drinking was part and parcel with the vacation vibe?

Could she just have one? But she knew the answer to that before the question was fully formed. No. She couldn't have just one.

A server walked by with a tray of flutes, the golden liquid bubbling away inside them like a private party she was missing out on.

Grace slipped outside to get a little fresh air. She wasn't going to drink. She wasn't going to drink. *She wasn't.*

As she stood outside, Katie, Owen, Sophie, and Gage were walking in. They all smiled and waved and said hi.

"Hi." She smiled back, even though she didn't feel it.

They went inside. Then, two seconds later, Katie came back out. "You okay?"

Grace blew out a frustrated breath. She needed to

get past this. "Yeah, I'm fine. Just feeling sorry for myself because David isn't here."

"That sucks." Katie put her arm around Grace's shoulders. "I guess it's pretty hard for him to get out of the kitchen now that Chef Glenn is in the pokey."

Grace laughed. "No one says pokey."

Katie smiled. "Maybe not, but I made you laugh."

"You did," Grace agreed. "And it *is* hard. David's got a lot of responsibility on his shoulders now and after what happened with our restaurant, he's determined to prove himself. More than that, he wants to take The Palms to a new level."

"Seems like a lot of hard work. The Palms is already a good restaurant."

"It is. But there's room for growth and improvement."

Katie nodded. "Bringing Chantelle in proved that. Still sucks that he can't be here with you."

"Yeah." Grace exhaled. "It's okay. I'm used to it. Chefs don't get a lot of nights off. And it'll be a while before David feels comfortable enough to leave the kitchen under the command of the new sous-chef, I imagine."

"How do you feel, though?" Katie glanced back through the door. "I see a lot of drinking going on in there. Must be tempting."

"Which is why I'm out here." Grace frowned at the

parking lot. "I was feeling the urge. And I do *not* want to give in."

Katie turned toward the door. "How about I go in there and get you something you *can* drink? Might be easier if you have a safe drink in your hand, you know? Then we go back in and mingle and before you know it, you'll be in a better place. And I'm not just saying that because I see some very delicious-looking bites getting passed."

Grace smiled, grateful. "That would be awesome. Thank you."

"Be right back."

True to her word, Katie returned a few minutes later with two tall glasses of pink liquid decorated with fruit slices and a little umbrella. She handed one to Grace. "There you go."

Grace took the drink. "What is it?"

"The bartender called it a guava smash."

Grace made a face, skeptical. "You're sure it's alcohol-free?" It looked too good to be true.

Katie nodded. "I told him my friend was allergic to alcohol and the slightest trace would cause her to projectile vomit, and that I was a sympathetic vomiter, and it would get me going, too."

Laughter spilled out of Grace, her spirit lightening. She got her breath back and shook her head. She loved Katie. "You do have a way with words."

"Kinda my job." Katie pointed at herself with her

thumb. “Compass Key Communications Director, don’t forget. That’s what I’m getting the big bucks for.”

Grace sipped her drink. It was sweet and bubbly and fruity and exactly what she needed. So was Katie. Throughout her time on the island, her friends had been a great support. She had no doubt they would continue to play that role for her. “Thanks. This is really good. And I feel much better.”

“I’m glad,” Katie said. Then she grabbed Grace’s arm. “Now, let’s get back in there, because I saw some bacon-wrapped shrimp that I need to get to know better.”

# Chapter Thirty-one

Katie made a beeline for the bacon-wrapped shrimp, determined to get some food into Grace as well as into herself. As a server came by with a tray, Katie waved him over and nudged Grace. "Grab one of those."

Katie and Grace each took a cocktail napkin and a shrimp, which were conveniently skewered with bamboo picks so that their fingers stayed clean.

Katie ate hers right away. The shrimp was delicious, and the bacon seemed to be glazed with some kind of sauce. "What's on that, Grace? It's so good."

Grace chewed, eyes narrowed as if trying to analyze the taste. "Tastes like tamarind barbeque sauce to me. It's really good. I need to tell David about that. The tamarind adds a really interesting flavor profile."

Katie loved it when Grace went all foodie. "Let's try those things." Katie gestured at the server coming toward them.

"What is it?"

"No idea," Katie said. "But it's food on a skewer, so I'm in."

Grace snorted.

The server approached. "Five spice roasted pork belly?"

"Yes, please," Katie said. She helped herself to one of the small cubes and popped it in her mouth. Crunchy, meaty, fatty, and altogether delicious. She immediately wanted another one. "Wow. Get David to make some of that."

Grace was still chewing. She nodded. "No argument from me. I love pork belly, but I've never had it with Chinese five spice. That was so good." She sipped her drink. "Grant really knocked it out of the park with the catering, huh?"

"I'll say. Hey, there's Olivia and Eddie. Let's go say hi." She headed over, Grace beside her.

Olivia smiled as they joined her. "How are you guys doing? You both look beautiful."

"Thanks," Katie said. "So do you. Hi, Eddie."

He nodded at them. "Ladies. Nice to see you."

"You, too." Grace pointed at the little pie on the napkin in his hand. "What do you have there? Katie and I are trying to eat our way through the room."

"Chorizo empanada," he answered. "Really good."

Katie took a look at the small pastry. "Everything I've had so far has been really good."

"Same here," Olivia said. Then she glanced sideways as she spoke to them. "Did you see Leigh Ann in that dress? She looks like a movie star."

Katie smiled. "Maybe the paparazzi will get some shots of her."

Grace looked toward Leigh Ann. "She looks amazing. Kind of makes me hope that Marty does show up."

"I've been hoping that, too," Olivia said.

"Same here," Katie agreed. "I don't want there to be any kind of incident, just for him to see her and have some kind of epiphany that she's moved on and he needs to do the same."

Grace nodded. "And for him to finally sign those divorce papers."

"Yes," Olivia said. "By the way, Duke's mom and dad are here."

Katie found them standing by Duke and Amanda.

"Ladies," Eddie started. "Can I get anyone another drink?"

Katie lifted her guava smash. "I'd love another one of these. It's a guava smash."

"That sounds good," Eddie said. "Better than my Coke."

Olivia leaned in. "What is that now?"

"Guava smash," Grace said. "Mine's almost gone, too. I'd love another one, Eddie. Thanks."

"You got it." He looked at Olivia. "You want one?"

She nodded. "Yes, please."

"Be right back." He left them and went to get in line at the bar that had been set up near the back wall.

"Quite a turnout, huh?" Olivia looked around. "I'm happy for Grant. And Leigh Ann looks like the First Lady of art."

Katie nodded. "She looked radiant. And people are still coming in." The crowd had really grown in the last couple of minutes, meaning it was practically elbow to elbow in the gallery.

Near the door was a man with a camera around his neck, and another one in his hands. A woman stood next to him with her phone in hand. She was speaking into it, like it was a recorder. Probably an app designed to do just that.

"Don't look now," Katie said. "But I'm pretty sure the press is here. I wonder if I should tell Owen. I bet they're looking for him."

"They could just be here for the party," Grace said.

"True." But recent events had colored Katie's view of such things. She scanned the room and found Owen near the back, speaking to an older woman she didn't recognize.

Eddie returned with the drinks. Four guava smashes. He had them all together, using both hands to carry them. "Here you go."

They helped him, carefully taking the drinks. He lifted his. "*Salud*!"

They all clinked their glasses together, then took sips.

"Oooh," Olivia said. "That's tasty. You know, I never had guava until I came to Compass Key and now it's one of my favorite things."

"There are some guava trees around Iris's house," Eddie said.

"Really? I'd love to see those," Olivia said.

Grace nodded. "Me, too."

Katie sipped her smash. "Owen has some at his house, too. He grows all kinds of fruits and vegetables."

Eddie looked at his glass. "There is nothing like the smell of fresh guava. One of the greatest perfumes on Earth, if you ask me."

Olivia leaned in toward Eddie. "The press is here."

He nodded. "I saw them when I was coming back." He looked at Katie. "You okay?"

"I was prepared for them to be here, and to get some pictures taken," she said. "I just don't have a lot of love for them, you know?"

"I do." He went up on his toes to see over the crowd. "Ladies, why don't we move toward Owen. Might be better if Katie's in the vicinity of Gage, just in case."

"You think I'm going to need security?" Katie hadn't considered that.

"No," Eddie said. "But if that woman is a reporter who decides this is a good time to ask you questions you don't want to answer, better to let Gage do his job and intercede."

Katie nodded in understanding. "Good thinking."

Eddie lifted his drink. "Follow me. I'll make a path."

They made a train behind him as he cut through the crowd. Traversing the packed gallery, a grand total of maybe thirty feet, took nearly ten minutes.

When they joined Owen, Sophie, and Gage, Owen smiled and took Katie's hand. "There's my beautiful girlfriend." He pulled her close to him and addressed the woman he'd been speaking with. "Madam Mayor, this is Katie Walchech. Katie, this is Mayor Elaina Casteneda."

The mayor stuck her hand out. "It's always a pleasure to meet one of my new constituents, and in this case, one of my favorite authors."

Katie shook the mayor's hand and smiled. "Thank you. It's an honor to meet you." She made a mental note to send a signed book to the mayor. It never hurt to have friends in high places. Especially when you were part-owner of a place like Compass Key.

Owen introduced Grace, Olivia, and Eddie and more handshaking followed. Then the mayor excused herself, leaving them to chat.

Keeping a smile on her face, Katie asked Owen, "Did you see the press is here?"

He looked over her shoulder. "I do now. I don't

think they'll bother us too much. And a couple of publicity shots will be good for Grant."

"I'm fine with that. But I don't want to talk to anyone."

"Agreed. This isn't the time or place for questions about us." He leaned back and said something to Gage she couldn't quite make out, but Gage nodded.

Owen came back to her. "If anything happens, let Gage know."

"I will." She turned so she was beside him and could watch the crowd.

Grant and Leigh Ann were moving through the throng, headed for the still-shrouded painting.

"Looks like it's time for the reveal," Katie said.

The group repositioned itself to face that way. As they did, Amanda, Duke, and his parents joined them. Amanda smiled at the group. "Hi, guys."

"Hi," Katie said. "Having fun?"

Amanda nodded, glancing at Duke before looking at Katie again. "It's a lovely evening."

"Let's hope it stays that way," Katie said. While Grant stepped up onto a small dais so he could be seen, she searched for the reporter and cameraman.

She couldn't find them. But she did spot two other people. "How about that," she whispered.

Marty and Candi had shown up.

# Chapter Thirty-two

Leigh Ann stood near the dais, watching Grant and feeling like she was going to burst with pride and nerves, which were back now that he was about to unveil the painting. But mostly she was proud and grateful and feeling deeply blessed.

Cheyanne made her way through the crowd to hand Grant a cordless microphone.

He laughed as he lifted it to his mouth. "Do I need this? I've always thought I was loud enough."

The crowd settled a bit, laughing along with him.

"I see so many friendly faces and I'm honored. Thank you all for being here tonight and helping me celebrate this new work. It was, as all of my paintings are, a labor of love." He looked at Leigh Ann. "This painting more so than ever."

She smiled back, hoping he could see the admiration she felt for him in her gaze.

He looked out at the crowd again, his expression

turning more serious. "You see, somewhere along the way, I lost my muse."

Murmurs rose up, sounds of sympathy and disbelief.

He shook his head. "I had moments where I wasn't sure I'd ever complete this piece. Days would go by where all I did was stand in front of it and pray that inspiration would come. That some creative switch would get flipped and I'd be able to finish what I'd started."

He sighed. "That didn't happen."

He looked at Leigh Ann again. "Until one day, a woman walked into one of my watercolor classes and made the sun shine in my life again."

Her heart fluttered in her chest. There was no denying that she loved this man. How could she not?

He held his hand out toward her. "Ladies and gentlemen, my muse, my inspiration, a true living goddess, Leigh Ann Durham."

Her smile widened at his use of her maiden name and she laughed, her nerves showing as everyone looked at her. She took his hand.

He kissed her knuckles. "Thank you for giving my vision a reality." Still holding her hand, he glanced at the crowd again. "Ladies and gentlemen, I give you *The Queen of the Eagle Rays.*"

On the other side of the canvas, Cheyanne pulled a cord, releasing the fabric keeping the painting hidden.

As it fell, revealing the artwork, the crowd let out an audible gasp of appreciation and then began to cheer. They obviously liked the painting.

Grant dropped Leigh Ann's hand to press his palms together in front of his chest and bow to the crowd.

Without really knowing why, Leigh Ann's eyes welled up. They were happy tears, to be sure, but there were many more emotions flooding her.

Grant stepped down off the dais and was immediately swarmed by well-wishers. They showered him with praise and congratulations. But he put his hands up and forced a few people aside to get to her, taking her hand again and drawing her near.

He slipped his arm around her waist. "I think they like you."

"I think they like your painting, but either way, I'm so glad."

He kissed her cheek.

All around them, the adulation continued. Cell phones were up, snapping pictures of them in front of the painting. Leigh Ann was a little overwhelmed, but stayed at his side, following his cues.

After a few more moments, Grant raised his hand. "Please, enjoy the evening. If you'd like to order a print of *The Queen of the Eagle Rays*, please see Cheyanne and she'll take care of you. They'll be going into production this week, but tonight only, you'll be able to order a print that will be signed by myself and

Ms. Durham, so make sure you get on Cheyanne's list."

Leigh Ann looked at Grant. "Is that true? You're going to have me sign the prints, too?"

He nodded. "Of course. Why wouldn't I? I'm going to put you in a lot more paintings. It makes good business sense to involve my muse." He smiled. "I realize I run the risk of your star outshining mine, but I'm hoping you take pity on me when you become famous and remember who gave you your big break."

She rolled her eyes. Had the paint fumes gotten to him? "You're crazy, you know that?"

"Crazy about you."

She shook her head, trying not to cry again.

"Quite a show you put on there, Shoemaker."

Leigh Ann sucked in air at the sound of *that* voice, turned, and looked straight into her ex-husband's eyes. "Marty."

Candi was on his arm, all smiles in a low-cut blue bandage-style dress that left little to the imagination. "I think your painting is real nice."

Leigh Ann smiled at her. "Thank you, Candi."

Marty looked miffed. Like someone had peed in his Wheaties. "It's a little weird for my taste." He directed his attention to Leigh Ann. "Can we talk?"

"Here?" Leigh Ann's brows rose. "You've got to be kidding."

"Well, somewhere, then."

She shook her head. "There's nothing to talk about. Just sign the papers. What about that needs to be discussed?"

He sighed again, and Leigh Ann suddenly saw him with new eyes. He was pushing sixty and about to have a newborn and a much younger wife to deal with. He looked old and tired and a little bit like a dog who'd run out of leash.

To her own disbelief, she felt pity. Maybe she was asking too much. Or maybe she wasn't. He had the money. And he had cheated on her repeatedly.

And the fact that he was about to have a new wife and baby? That was fully on him. No one had forced him to sleep with Candi.

She steeled herself against whatever sympathy she'd felt. She had to protect herself and her kids. She wanted to put money away for both of them.

Marty shook his head. "I just thought maybe we could come to some kind of agreement."

"You know what I want. If you don't sign those papers before you leave the resort, I'll call my attorney and increase my demands. That's all the talking we need to do. Now, if you'll excuse me, I'd like to enjoy my party." She knew it wasn't her party, but she couldn't help but couch the evening in those terms to rub it into Marty's face a little more.

Candi tugged on his arm. "Come on. I want to order a print."

Marty scowled. “No.”

Candi pouted. “But you said—”

“This way,” Grant whispered in Leigh Ann’s ear. He took her arm and guided her through the crowd and away from Marty.

People clapped Grant on the back, told Leigh Ann she was beautiful, and took pictures as they made their way to the other side of the room.

When they came to a stop, they were standing with Olivia, Eddie, Amanda, Duke, Duke’s parents, Nick, Jenny, Katie, Owen, Grace, Sophie, and Gage. Leigh Ann knew from speaking with Vera earlier that the woman hadn’t planned to stay long, intending to get back to Iris as soon as the reveal was done.

Their friends gathered around them like a protective barrier, giving them a buffer from the crowd.

As the men congratulated Grant, Amanda put her hand on Leigh Ann’s arm. “You look gorgeous in that painting. Which is beyond beautiful.”

“Thank you.”

Olivia nodded. “She’s right. You do look gorgeous. Goddess is the perfect word.”

Leigh Ann shook her head. “You guys, it’s too much.”

“Enjoy it,” Grace said. “Tomorrow, it’s back to work.”

Leigh Ann laughed. “Good point. Are you guys having fun?”

They all nodded.

Katie leaned in. “Did I see Marty and Candi talking to you?”

Leigh Ann took a deep breath. “You did.”

“How’d that go?” Grace asked.

Leigh Ann glanced back to where Marty and Candi had been standing, but they weren’t there anymore. “He wanted to talk about the divorce papers, if you can believe that.”

“The nerve,” Olivia said. “What did you tell him?”

“That this was not the place and that if he doesn’t sign the papers soon, I’m going to call my attorney and increase my demands.” She laughed softly, remembering. “Then Candi told him she wanted to order a print of the painting.”

They all laughed. Grant put his hand on the small of her back. “I’ve promised a brief interview to the reporter from the *Keys Courier*, and she’d like to get a picture with both of us in front of the painting.”

“Okay.” She smiled at her friends. “Be right back.”

As she walked with him back to the painting, she noticed the crowd had thinned a bit. She scanned the room, hoping Marty and Candi were part of the group that had left.

Cheyanne was standing at the gallery counter, along with another young woman. Both seemed to be busy helping people with orders. Leigh Ann hoped this was Grant’s most successful showing ever.

The photographer positioned them in front of the painting and got everyone else out of the way, then took a rapid-fire series of snaps. She held her smile until he gave them the nod that he was done.

Then the reporter came in to interview Grant.

Leigh Ann gave her a smile and inched away so he could have his moment.

"Could you stay?" the reporter asked.

Leigh Ann put her hand to her chest. "Me?"

The reporter nodded. "Please."

Leigh Ann glanced at Grant, who gave her a subtle nod. "Okay."

"Thanks." The reporter held her phone up, the screen showing a recording app. "What was it like being painted by such a famous artist?"

Leigh Ann smiled at Grant. "Pretty amazing."

"Grant," the reporter said. "How did you know that Leigh Ann was your muse?"

He looked into Leigh Ann's eyes. "Because as soon as I saw her, my inspiration came back. All I could think about was getting back to my painting." He laughed. "That's not entirely true. I knew I had to get to know her better, too."

The reporter smiled. "So are you two a couple?"

Grant didn't answer, just keep looking at Leigh Ann.

Her smile grew. She nodded. "Yes, we are definitely a couple."

# Chapter Thirty-three

When Eddie took Olivia's hand, she just smiled and let him. She didn't care if Jenny or anyone else saw. They all knew she liked him. What was wrong with a little public display of the affection between them? It certainly wasn't going away.

After years of not having a man to keep company with, Olivia was ready to fully embrace this new chapter of her life.

"Grant does nice work, doesn't he?" Eddie looked up at the art in front of them.

"He does. I think his art is beautiful. I'm going to buy one of these prints someday," she told him. "I'd love to have one in my house."

"Can't go wrong with something like that," Eddie said. "But why not get it now?"

"It's too much." She shook her head. The prints were two hundred and fifty dollars. That was a lot of money for her and shelling out that much right now, even with the new salary she'd be making, felt like too big of a splurge. "I don't want to strap my budget. In a couple months, maybe."

"Which one, then? When the time is right?"

"I'm not sure." She glanced around the gallery. "I like a lot of them. But I really like this one with the gray-haired mermaid on the rocks. She looks strong and wise."

He smiled. "She looks a lot like you."

Olivia laughed. "Is that a subtle hint that I should do something about my gray?"

He shook his head. "Not at all. I was talking about the strong and wise part. And there's nothing wrong with gray hair, either. A woman's hair is her crowning glory. Nothing wrong with covering the gray, though, either. If that's what you want to do. A woman needs to do what she feels is right for her. But it's certainly not something to be ashamed of."

She could tell he was trying to cover his bases. She wasn't about to let him off so easily, though. She touched a strand of her hair. "So you don't think I should go blond?"

He shrugged. "It's your hair. Whatever makes you happy is fine by me."

She twisted the strand around her finger, enjoying the conversation immensely. "How about if I dye it pink?"

His eyes widened for a split second. "Pink?"

She grinned. "Just teasing."

He exhaled, instantly relieved.

She took on a much more serious expression. "Pink's not me. I'd do lavender if I was going to do a color."

"*Ay, Dios mío*! Purple?"

She laughed, mostly because of the face he was making but also because he'd believed her. "No, you silly man. I wouldn't dye my hair any color. I'm an accountant, not a rock-and-roller."

He snorted and shook his head. "You had me worried. Just for that I should make you drive us home."

She shrugged. "Okay, but if I crash the pontoon, it's your fault."

He was smiling now, obviously enjoying their little back and forth. "We'll do another boating lesson next week, I promise."

"Good. I'm excited to learn." Whoever would have thought that she'd end up with a boating license?

He let go of her hand to put his arm around her waist and get closer to her. He looked up at the mermaid print again. "You do kind of look like that mermaid. Strong and beautiful. Very sexy."

It was her turn to give him a skeptical look. "Were you drinking something besides the guava smash? Something alcoholic?"

He looked at her. “I know what I like, and I like you. And you are a strong, beautiful, *sexy* woman.”

She knew when to take a compliment, although it was something she was still learning. “Thank you. I don’t think anyone’s thought that about me in a long time.”

“The world is full of idiots.”

She laughed and kissed his cheek. “I love you.” She went stock-still, realizing what had just come out of her mouth. “I mean—” What had she meant?

He was smiling calmly. “I love you, too, *carina*. Don’t panic. It’s okay.”

She exhaled, having suddenly stopped breathing. She still couldn’t find her words.

He turned his gaze back to the painting and kept it there. “Are you afraid of how you feel?”

She stared at the painting, too. It was easier to talk that way. “Yes. A little.”

“Why?”

“Because…” She had to think about that. Why had that declaration filled her with such anxiety? “Things didn’t work out so well with the last man I gave my heart to.”

He nodded. “But I am not that man.”

“No, you’re not.” There was more to it than that. “There’s also the fear of rejection.”

“Which I have not done.”

Breathing got a little easier. "No, you haven't."

"In fact, I told you I loved you back."

"Isn't it too soon?"

She could see him smile out of the corner of her eye.

He shrugged. "Who says?"

"Most people?"

"Do you care?"

She smiled. "No." She really didn't.

"We can still keep it between us for a while, if you want. It's no one else's business but ours anyway." He gave her hip a little squeeze as if to say that they were in this together, no matter what.

She breathed out slowly. She really did love this man. He had so many wonderful qualities. Not the least of which was how he made her feel about herself.

She'd never had that before. That kind of unconditional affection, that rose-colored view that seemed unaffected by anything.

She glanced at him. "Thank you."

He gave her a small nod. "Anything for you."

Olivia took another breath as she made a new decision. "I'm going to buy this print right now. Tonight."

His brows lifted. "I thought you couldn't afford it."

"I can't. I mean, I can, but it's not the wisest thing to do with my money. But I'm going to do it anyway." She couldn't stand here, before this beautiful piece of artwork, and not take it home with her. Not after she and Eddie had shared such a special moment in front of it.

She'd never look at this painting and not think about that. And for that reason, it was going in her bedroom. Her sanctuary. She wanted to see it when she woke up in the morning. To be reminded of Eddie and how he made her feel.

It would be a great way to start her day.

Grant and Leigh Ann drifted over. Leigh Ann was all smiles. "How are you guys doing?"

"Good," Eddie said. "Great night, Grant."

"Thanks." He leaned forward. "Between us, I'm glad it's mostly over. I feel like I've been running for office."

Eddie and Olivia laughed. She understood. He'd been smiling and chatting and posing for photos all night. That seemed like it would wear a person out.

She pointed at the print on the wall. "I'm buying this one."

Grant blinked in surprise. "You are?"

Olivia nodded. "I love it."

He put his hand to his heart. "I'm honored. Thank you. Make sure you tell Cheyanne I said you get the friends-and-family discount."

"Thank you. You don't have to do that."

"For a friend who wants to support me? I absolutely do. You didn't have to give up your evening to spend it here, either, but you did and I am deeply appreciative. This was one of the best attended parties I've had." He smiled at Leigh Ann. "You have marvelous friends."

She smiled back at him. "They're your friends, too, now."

He nodded. "So they are. You are the gift that keeps on giving."

Olivia rolled her lips in to keep from laughing. Grant was something else. She tugged on Eddie's hand. "Let's go see Cheyanne so I can buy this, then we can gather everyone up and head back."

"You got it."

She looked at Grant and Leigh Ann again. "Thank you for a lovely evening. Leigh Ann, I'll see you tomorrow?"

Leigh Ann nodded, then her smile disappeared. "That reminds me. We need to talk."

Olivia was slightly taken aback by the sudden seriousness. "Okay. Want to give me a clue about the topic?"

"Sure," Leigh Ann said. "I took a tour of the spa and fitness center today. There's a *lot* that needs fixing. Which means money, I know, but I don't feel like it's something that can wait."

Olivia smiled. "No problem."

Leigh Ann looked confused. "Really?"

Olivia nodded. "With everything going on, I forgot

to let you all know. I didn't even tell Iris. Just too much going on. Anyway, I talked to Detective Murphy today at the station. We're getting almost all of the embezzled funds back. Nine million of it. Money isn't going to be a problem."

# Chapter Thirty-four

Amanda settled into the passenger seat of Duke's truck as she waited for him to come around and get behind the wheel. He smiled at her as he did just that. "Good night, huh?"

"Great evening," she agreed. "It was nice to see your parents."

"It was even nicer to hang out with the hottest woman there."

She laughed. "You're very smooth."

"Smooth enough to kiss?"

Her smile widened and she leaned over, meeting him halfway across the truck's console. The kiss was soft and sweet and lingered for a few delicious seconds.

When she sat back, she was warm and blissful. "Are you buttering me up for something?"

He shook his head and started the engine. "Just enjoying being with you."

She reached over and squeezed his arm. "I feel the

same way. You're very good company. You did a beautiful job on those chalkboards today, too."

"Thanks. I'll give them a second coat of paint tonight and by tomorrow afternoon they'll be ready to go."

"You're going to do that tonight?" She sat up a little. It was almost ten already.

He nodded and pulled out of the parking lot. "I have to if you want them usable for Sunday."

"I can help."

He glanced at her. "Not in that dress."

She shook her head. "I'll change. But I want to help. You wouldn't be making them if not for me."

"All right. You can help."

"Good." She sat back. "I'm ready to get out of this dress anyway."

He smiled but said nothing.

A few minutes later, they were at the Bluewater Marina and headed for his boat. He helped her aboard, got them untied and on their way home.

They spent the ride mostly in silence, just enjoying the evening.

At the resort's marina, he tied up, then got off first so he could assist her onto the dock. He held onto her hand for the walk back.

The night was beautiful, the air balmy, the sky full of stars. Amanda had the funniest feeling that she was on her way back from prom or some other similar event. Duke had that effect on her—he made her feel like a teenager.

The thought made her laugh.

He glanced over. "What's funny?"

She snorted air through her nostrils. "I just had this feeling like I was walking home from prom."

He smiled. "I remember those nights. I was a little more dressed up then."

"I bet you looked achingly handsome at that age."

He shook his head. "I was gangly and awkward and pimply. I didn't grow into this body until my early twenties."

"Remind me to ask your mother for visual proof of that the next time we're over there."

"Oh no," he said. "Those are not photos you need to see."

She grinned. "I think I do. Especially if this is going forward. I need to know everything there is to know about you."

He pulled her in close. "This is definitely going forward. If that means you have to see the most embarrassing photos of my life, then I guess I'll have to suck it up. Fair is fair, though. I should get to see pictures of you in high school."

"That's fair. I can arrange that."

His eyes narrowed. "You agreed to that awfully quick. You were hot in high school, weren't you?"

She smiled tightly and shrugged.

"You were. I can tell."

"I was a cheerleader in high school, so..."

He rolled his eyes. "I can't believe I'm dating the cheerleader." He winked at her. "If my high school friends could see me now, they'd be so jealous."

"I think one of your high school friends did see you recently."

His eyes narrowed like he wasn't sure what she meant.

"When we were at that restaurant? Free Willy's? Your friend Buddy?"

"Yep, you're right. That was a good moment. He was definitely jealous." Duke shook his head and snorted. "Buddy. That guy."

"I'd be happy to go to your next high school reunion with you."

"Yeah?"

They took the fork in the path that aimed them toward the staff bungalows.

"Absolutely," she said. "I'll even wear this dress."

"I wasn't planning to go, but you might have talked me into it." He walked her to her door, standing on the path as she went up the steps. "Meet you back here in five?"

She nodded. "Okay."

She went inside, took her shoes off, and ran upstairs with them in her hand. She shed the dress and quickly pulled on shorts and a T-shirt, leaving the dress on the bed. She took off her jewelry and put it on her dresser. She'd deal with that when she got back. Then she stuck her feet in flipflops, grabbed her phone and key, and ran back down.

Duke wasn't outside yet, so she locked her door and walked over to his bungalow. His door opened as she approached his stairs.

"Look at you," he said. "I thought I'd be waiting on you."

She put her hands on her hips. "I can change in five minutes."

"Obviously." He came down to meet her. "I figured it would take you longer to get out of that dress."

"Years of practice with formal wear."

"Your talents never cease to amaze me."

"Hold that thought until after you've seen me paint."

He took her hand and they started walking toward his workshop. "It's not hard. You'll see."

He was right, but then, he'd given her a small, narrow roller and showed her exactly what to do.

They got a second coat of paint on the chalkboards in about fifteen minutes, which wasn't too bad.

Duke set up a fan nearby to run overnight to help them dry. "All done."

"That was faster than I expected." She'd managed to keep most of the paint off of herself. She had a few smudges on her hands, but that was it.

"It helped that there were two of us." He tipped his head. "How about a walk on the beach?"

She nodded. "I'd like that."

They went back the way they'd come, passing the bungalows and going straight out to the beach from where the path diverged toward Iris's. Amanda had never been on this part of the beach. It was a little wilder.

Duke took her hand as they walked.

"I love the stars here," she said. "They seem closer somehow."

He nodded. "I don't travel that often, but when I do, I always think about how near the night sky seems here. Although I've been out to the Dakotas a couple times. The night sky is something out there. But, man, it gets cold."

She smiled. "I'm all right to give up cold weather. I was never a big fan of snow."

"Not a skier?"

"I have. Ice skated, too. But it's such a production getting into all of those layers." She wasn't going to miss anything about her old life.

After a few moments of silence, he spoke again. "Anything else you need help with for the wedding?"

"I'll probably need some help setting things up at the pavilion. Like the dance floor. Have you ever put that thing together?"

"Once. Years ago. I'm sure I can figure it out again."

"Good. Once you do that, I'll clean it a second time."

"I can help with that."

She shook her head. "You don't have to. I'm sure there will be other things I'll need you to do."

He shrugged. "Whatever you want. Just tell me, I'll get it done."

"Thanks."

They walked on a little further. Up ahead, Amanda saw something glint in the water. "There's something rolling in the waves. A bottle, I think."

The last small wave left it behind. It was a bottle. When they got to it, Amanda scooped it up. She turned it, trying to see inside. "I think there's something inside. A note."

"About a year ago, a class of local eighth graders did an experiment, sending out about a hundred bottles with notes in them. Every once in a while, one shows up. This might be one of them."

"That's pretty cool." She twisted at the top but it was stuck fast. She handed it to him. "I can't get it."

He took it and gave it a try, cranking on it hard. Finally, it loosened. He held onto the top but gave her the bottle back.

She fished the note out. It was ruled notepaper tied with yellow yarn. She slipped the yarn off and held the paper up to the light coming from the resort. She nodded. "That's exactly what it is. A note from one

Taylor Wynn, who says she likes ice cream, going out on her dad's boat, and playing with her cat, Linguine. There's also an email address to respond to if this note is found."

Duke grinned. "Are you going to?"

Amanda nodded, charmed by her find. "You bet I am."

"You should," Duke said. "Every time one of these shows up, it gets mentioned in the local paper."

"I'm really glad I found this." Amanda rolled the note back up and secured it with the yarn. "I've been trying to find an interesting thing to do for the wedding and I think this could be it. A message in a bottle is a pretty romantic thing. Might be fun for the newlyweds to send out a note themselves. What do you think?"

"I think if it's good enough for Nicholas Sparks, it's good enough for Mother's."

# Chapter Thirty-five

Iris knew she ought to be in bed, but she wasn't tired. The B12 shots Nick had been giving her had filled her with new energy. Tonight, she'd had the urge to watch *Arsenic and Old Lace* and she'd talked Vera into staying up with her. And making popcorn.

Vera had filled Iris in on the gallery party while she'd popped the corn. Iris thought the event sounded wonderful and while she was still sad she hadn't been able to make it, she was thrilled that Grant had gotten such a good turnout.

She was thankful, too, that Vera had remembered to order her a print of the new painting.

Now Vera sat in the chair next to her, her own bowl of popcorn nestled on her lap. The cats were sprawled out wherever they pleased, Calico Jack on the couch, Anne Bonny on the coffee table, and Mary Read on the back of Iris's chair.

Vera gestured at the screen with a handful of popcorn. "That Cary Grant was something else."

"Yes, he was," Iris agreed. "They don't make men like that anymore. Not many of them, anyway."

"Arthur was one of them," Vera said.

Iris smiled. "He sure was."

They went back to the movie and the popcorn but a few minutes later, someone knocked on the door. Iris hit Pause.

Vera set her popcorn aside. Calico Jack lifted his head, his little nose sniffing the air. "I'll get it. You keep the cats out of my popcorn."

"They like butter," Iris said.

Vera shot her a look. "Too bad. I don't like to share." She went over and opened the door. Eddie and Olivia stood there, all dressed up and looking smart.

"I hope it's okay to come by so late," Olivia said. "But the lights were on, and we saw the flickering of the TV, so we figured you were up."

Iris smiled, always happy for company. "We are. We're watching *Arsenic and Old Lace*. Come on in. You want some popcorn?"

Olivia shook her head as she and Eddie came over. "No, thanks. I had plenty to eat at the party. There was a lot of good food there."

"That's wonderful. You two look so nice." Iris pointed to the couch. "Have a seat. Calico Jack won't mind. Vera said there was a good crowd."

They sat beside the cat, who was still preoccupied with sniffing Vera's popcorn.

"There was," Eddie said. "It was elbow to elbow."

Iris was so glad to hear it. Vera returned and sat in her chair again, picking up her bowl and securing it on her lap.

Olivia smiled like she had a secret. "I bought a print for my bungalow."

"That's marvelous," Iris said. "Of the new painting?"

"No," Olivia said. "The one I got is a mermaid sitting on some rocks with flying fish jumping around her. I left it on the front porch. You want me to get it?"

"I'd love to see it." Iris also loved how happy Olivia looked.

Eddie stood up. "I'll get it." He went to the door, coming back a second later with the wrapped picture. He untied the twine and took off the brown paper covering it, then turned it around so Iris and Vera could see it. "There it is."

"I love it," Vera said.

"So do I," Iris agreed. "Good choice."

"Thanks." Olivia beamed with happiness.

"Do you think Grant sold a lot?" Iris asked.

Eddie nodded as he rewrapped the print. "I think he did all right. Everyone seemed to love the new painting."

Iris had, too. "Vera showed me a picture of it on her

phone. I can't wait to get my print. It's so beautiful and Leigh Ann looks so pretty in it."

"She does," Olivia said. "Did you see her in her new dress? She got it at the resort boutique. She looked stunning. I'm glad her ex showed up, although I don't know what the outcome of that will be."

Iris gasped. "Her ex came? Did he bring his girlfriend?" She would have cancelled that man's reservations at the resort if she'd known in time.

Eddie sat by Olivia again, leaning the print against the coffee table. Anne Bonny pawed at one of the dangling bits of twine without any serious intention.

Olivia nodded. "They were both there. Not sure how long they stayed. But they came because Leigh Ann invited Candi, the girlfriend. Leigh Ann wanted Marty to see where she is in her life right now. I'd say he got a pretty good glimpse of that tonight."

Iris groaned in disappointment. "I'm so sad I missed it. Sounds like an evening to remember. But that crowd wouldn't have been any kind of place to use a walker. I hope to be rid of this thing soon."

"That would be great," Olivia said.

"I hardly need it with that ramp. I can come right up and down that thing as easy as walking on the sidewalk." The ramp had changed her life. Getting to her home was no longer an issue. Although she had a feeling that in another month or two, stairs wouldn't be such a problem, either.

"I'm so glad to hear that," Olivia said. "That's great news." Her smile widened. "I have some more great news, which is why I stopped by. I wanted to tell you in person that Eddie and I were at the police station earlier today and spoke to Detective Murphy. I signed some release paperwork with him that will allow us to get almost all of the embezzled funds back in about two weeks. Nine million dollars."

Iris flattened her hand over her heart. "You're not teasing me, are you? That would be a terrible thing to tease about."

"No!" Olivia shook her head. "I promise, it's all true."

Iris looked at Vera, feeling a little like she might cry. "Vera. Did you hear that?"

Vera nodded, smiling. "I did."

Iris exhaled, her breath shuddering with emotion. "Thank you so much for giving me that news. I am so happy. Now you girls will have the funds you need to get this place back in tiptop shape."

Olivia nodded. "We will. I'm already working on a list of things to do and the order in which we'll do them."

"What about Katie's idea to build the second dock?" Iris noticed that Eddie gave Olivia a look then. She imagined he would very much like to have a dock on this side of Compass Key.

"Well, I still don't know what it'll do to our insurance premium but in light of the situation with the funds, I don't think I can say no. Besides that, I know it'll make things easier for those of us who live and work here. You included."

Iris clapped her hands. "I'm so glad. Arthur would be pleased." That knowledge gave her such a lightness of being.

Olivia scratched Calico Jack on the back, making him stretch out and roll over for tummy rubs, which she obliged him with. "We should go. Tomorrow's our last day of prep before the wedding and I'm sure there will be tons to do. Plus, I know you'd like to watch the rest of your movie."

"Thank you for coming by. I'm so happy to hear how everything is turning out." Iris felt a new peace knowing that her girls wouldn't have to struggle to make things work.

Olivia and Eddie got up. Olivia kissed Iris on the cheek. "Have a good night. You, too, Vera."

Iris squeezed Olivia's arm. "Sleep well, honey."

Vera got up and walked with them to the door, then locked up after them. She shook her head as she rejoined Iris. "How about that? I'm so glad that money isn't lost forever."

"Me, too. You know what else I'm glad about?"

"What's that?" Vera asked.

"That I get to be here to see how those girls put it to good use. They're going to do great things here, I just know it." She hadn't felt hope like this in a long time. "That dock is only the beginning."

Vera nodded. "I believe you're right."

"I know I am. I also know Arthur would be proud." Iris touched the diamond around her neck. "I hope he knows. I hope he sees all of this. And I hope he knows that even though I miss him terribly every day, I am also very happy."

Vera smiled. "I think he does."

# Chapter Thirty-six

Jenny was tired but energized, too. The evening had been fun, the print Nick had bought her an unexpected surprise, and she wasn't ready for the night to end.

She glanced over at him. He was carrying the print for her. "Thank you again for that. I can't say thanks enough. I love it. And I'll always think of you when I look at it."

He smiled. "You say that like I'm going somewhere."

She laughed. "You better not be. I just meant that you're a part of that painting now. Of my memory of it and this night."

"I like that."

They reached her mom's bungalow. She stopped at the bottom of the steps. "I'm not ready to turn in yet."

"What do you want to do?"

She shrugged. "I was thinking we could go for a swim, maybe? If you're up for it."

"Sure. The staff pool, the guest pool, or the ocean?"

She smiled. "So many options, but I'm going with the staff pool. As long as we're quiet, it should be all right, don't you think?"

He nodded. "Definitely. Or would you rather sit in the hot tub?"

"Oh, that does sound good. Fifteen minutes?"

"That'll work." He handed her the print and gave her a quick kiss. "I'll see you over there."

"Okay." She watched him go then went up the steps. The door was unlocked and her mom was in the kitchen, her back to Jenny. "Hey."

"Hey. Did you have a good time?"

"I had a great time." Jenny leaned the painting against the bar that separated the kitchen from the small dining area. "What are you up to?"

"Making a cup of decaf to take upstairs, then I'm going to do a little work before I turn in." Olivia finally turned around. "We found out today that we're going to get almost all of the embezzled money back, so I want to look over my list of things that need to be done around here and make sure that money will be put to the best possible use."

"Fantastic! Iris must be so happy."

"She is. Really happy. I am, too. Means a lot for the resort in terms of getting things up to date. Leigh Ann told me this evening there's a lot that needs doing at the spa and fitness center and now that won't be an issue."

"That's great. How was your night? Have a nice time with Eddie?"

Olivia smiled. "Yes."

The only time her mother smiled like that was when she was talking about Eddie. Or was with Eddie. "You're falling for him, aren't you?"

Olivia's cheeks went pink. "I might be. Is there anything wrong with that?"

"Not a thing." Jenny sat on one of the new barstools, which were far superior to the old ones that had originally been here. "I'm falling for Nick. You don't have a problem with that, do you?"

"Nope."

"Good, because I feel like things are about to get serious between us." Jenny reached down and picked up the print he'd bought her. "He got me this tonight."

"You got a print?"

She nodded. "The one with the sea turtles."

"I got one, too. The mermaid sitting on the rocks."

"With the flying fish?" Jenny asked.

"That's the one."

"How cool that we both got one. I'm putting it in my bedroom."

Olivia nodded. Behind her, the coffee maker sputtered. "That's where mine's going. I'll probably hang it tomorrow. If Amanda doesn't work us all to death getting ready for this wedding." She laughed and turned to get her coffee.

"If there's that much to do, I can help. I have some work of my own, but I can knock it out first thing."

Olivia added a few drops of some new sugar-free liquid sweetener she'd just started using. "We might need your help. I'll let you know as soon as I find out, okay?"

"Sounds good. I could even ask Nick to help after he's done with Iris's physical therapy. Oh! Nick!" Jenny slipped off the stool. "I'm supposed to be putting my suit on so I can meet him at the hot tub."

Olivia added a little half-and-half to her coffee, then gave it a stir. "Go on. I'm off to do a little work in bed anyway. Have fun."

"Thanks. Love you." Jenny headed for her room. "Is it okay if I leave the front door unlocked until I get back?"

"Yes. Love you, too."

She grabbed her black bikini and quickly changed, then helped herself to a beach towel and, with her flipflops on, went out to meet Nick.

He was there already, halfway down the steps into the water.

She'd obviously lost track of time a little. "Hey. Sorry I'm late. I got talking to my mom."

"It's okay." He grinned. "We're on island time now."

She laughed. "That might be true, but I don't think my firm would appreciate the sentiment."

"Probably not." He settled in, moving over to make room beside him for her.

She kicked her flipflops off and dropped her towel on a chaise, then grabbed the railing and stepped in. "Oooh, that's hot."

"Feels good."

"It does." She took another step down.

"Have I seen you in that suit before? Because I really feel like I would have remembered that."

She smiled. "I haven't worn it yet, because it's black and it gets hot really fast."

"You mean like as soon as you put it on?" He shook his head. "I'm definitely getting hot."

Her smile turned to pleased laughter. "You are sitting in a hundred and something degree water."

"What I'm feeling has nothing to do with this water.

She eased her way in and sat beside him. "Well, if you were hoping to make out, you picked the wrong pool."

He snorted. "You think your mom is watching?"

Jenny glanced at the back of her mom's bungalow. The light in the upstairs bedroom was on but the curtains were drawn. "No. She's working. But we are kind of surrounded here."

He shrugged and put his arm around her shoulders. "We'll keep the making out to a minimum then."

She leaned up and kissed him. "I'll be the judge of that."

"Yes, ma'am."

She sat back. "Do you think you'll be available tomorrow after Iris's physical therapy?"

He nodded. "Definitely. What did you have in mind?"

"Don't get too excited. I was going to ask if you'd help with doing setup for the wedding on Sunday. My mom thinks there's going to be a lot to do, so I told her I'd help, and I'd ask if you could, too."

"Yeah, happy to. My only other plans were to look at the resort's medical office."

She stared at him as his words sunk in. "Does that mean you're staying? I thought you weren't sure what you were going to do when Iris was fully recovered."

"I wasn't. She offered me a spot here at the resort as the doctor on duty, but I didn't commit." He smiled. "That was before I knew you were going to be here permanently. That changes things."

She bit her bottom lip. "I'm glad to hear that."

"I'd be a fool not to accept now." He laughed. "I don't even know what the salary is, but I don't really care."

She knew he was doing this for her. At least in part.

"I'm so glad." She couldn't imagine being away from him. Or trying to make things work long-distance.

"I am, too. Everything's coming together." He stared out at the bubbles for a moment. "The Zimbabweans have a saying. 'Passion is of greater consequence than facts.'"

She squinted. "Meaning…"

"I've always taken it to mean that it's better to listen to the heart than the head. And right now, I'm listening to my heart."

"I'm really glad about that. I guess you could say I've been listening to my heart, too. This is the start of a new path for me. For my life. You know, I think there's more for me in life than PR. I don't know what that is yet, but when I see the life you've lived and how you've helped people, it inspires me to do more."

"I think that's great. But you're so good at what you do. Why not combine the two things?"

She didn't quite understand. "How do you mean?"

"There are lots of charities that could use more press, more publicity. What about donating some hours to them and put your existing skills to work? Lawyers do pro bono. Why not you?"

She sat back, struck by the suggestion. "I never thought about that. I could absolutely do that. Thank you!"

"You're welcome."

She felt energized and ready to tackle this new

idea. She'd have to clear the pro bono work with her firm, but she couldn't imagine they'd say no. It would be good PR for *them*. She smiled and looked at Nick. "You're a keeper, you know that?"

He grinned. "Glad you've finally figured that out."

# Chapter Thirty-seven

Grace waited up for David. She really wanted to see him and talk to him before she went to bed.

He walked into the new bungalow around midnight.

She looked down from the loft balcony. "Welcome home." She'd texted him their new bungalow number earlier.

He smiled up at her. "So this is our new place, huh?"

"What do you think of it? I know it's not quite what we're used to but..."

He shook his head. "I'm okay with not quite what we're used to. Especially when it doesn't have a mortgage attached. It came furnished, I see."

"Mostly. The second bedroom doesn't have anything in it but a dresser." She came down the steps. "We'll need a table and chairs, too, unless we want to eat on the couch. Which has seen better days."

He glanced over and nodded. "Plus, there's no recliner. You know how I like my recliner."

She smiled. "Yes, I do. I think next week I should fly home and deal with our household stuff, get the cars sold, all of that."

His brows knit. "That's too much for you to do on your own."

"No, it's not. Besides, I could probably get Jeff to help me." Jeff was David's step-brother. They weren't super close, but he'd been around whenever they'd needed him, and they'd tried to do the same for him. He'd even helped them paint the restaurant when they bought it.

David nodded. "You know, if he's willing to help you with all that, we should probably just give Jeff my truck. It might not be brand new, but it's paid for and runs great. What do you think about that?"

She smiled. "I think that's a great idea. He could use a newer vehicle."

"Good. I'll call him in the morning and talk to him about it."

"Perfect."

He unbuttoned his chef coat. "I'm surprised you're still up."

She shrugged. "It was a late night anyway. I missed you at the party."

"How was it? I'm sorry I couldn't go."

"I know, and I understand. But I want to be honest and tell you that I struggled at first."

He went into the kitchen and opened the fridge. He took out a Gatorade and held it up. "Thanks for buying these."

She nodded and leaned against the kitchen counter from the dining room side. "I know what you like." He drank one every night when he got home. She'd done her best to stock the place with all of their usual things.

He twisted the top off and took a long drink. "Was the struggle because there was alcohol?"

She exhaled. "Yes. And because I was feeling sorry for myself that you weren't there, and all the other girls had partners with them." She stared at her hands. "I don't tell you that to make you feel guilty. I just want to be honest and up front about what I'm dealing with."

"No more secrets," he said. "We promised. And I want you to share, even if it's something like this that makes me feel bad."

She looked up at him. "I don't mean to do that."

"I know. I totally know. Sometimes this business that we're in sucks. I hate that part of it. It's why I've always wanted you to work with me. At least that way we were together. You're the reason I work as hard as I do, Gracie."

She smiled. "You're the hardest-working man I know."

"And you're the most amazing woman to put up with that schedule all of these years. You've been my rock for so many of them." He set his Gatorade down and came over to pull her into his arms. "I'm sorry you had a rough night."

"It's okay. Katie made me feel better and after about half an hour, I was completely fine."

He kissed the top of her head. "I'm glad. Getting through situations like that only makes you stronger. I'm proud of you for resisting. It would have been easy to give in, but you didn't. I love you."

It was so good to be in his arms. "I love you, too." She leaned back. "How was your night?"

"Not bad. Light crowd tonight. I think some of them must have gone to the gallery party, too."

"Maybe."

He smiled at her. "Tell me all about the food."

She laughed. "There were these bacon-wrapped shrimp glazed with tamarind barbeque sauce." She groaned. "So good. You need to work on something like that."

"That does sound interesting. What else?"

"Oh, this five spice roasted pork belly was amazing. Crispy on top, fatty and meaty underneath. I could have eaten a plateful of it."

"You know, pork belly might make a great special. It's not that expensive and people love it."

"*I* love it," she said. "Make some for me."

His eyes were sparkling, alive with new ideas. "I promise you'll get some. In fact, I might combine those two ideas and do a tamarind barbeque sauce glazed pork belly and run it as a special. If it's well received, it could go on the menu."

"Speaking of, I talked to Katie about the cookbook idea. She loved it. She's going to talk to her agent about it."

His brows went up. "Really? I thought we were just going to do a sort of local thing. Something to sell in the shop."

"Sure, but why not see if there's more interest? Can't hurt, right? Anyway, she knows people that can help you put it together and all of that. It could really happen."

"Wow." He picked up his Gatorade and took a big drink. "That's kind of staggering." He shook his head. "My own cookbook. Well, it would be for The Palms, but still. They'd be my recipes and it'd have my name on it."

She smiled and nodded. "Exciting, isn't it? I'm thinking we should give Chantelle the dessert chapter. You wouldn't mind, would you?"

"Mind? I think it's a great idea. The whole thing is dream-come-true stuff. It really is."

"I'm glad." She straightened up. "I'm going to turn in. Lots to do to get ready for the wedding tomorrow."

He nodded. "Same here, but not nearly as much as you have, I imagine. I just need to prep for those extra meals."

"See you upstairs. Which is where the bedroom is, by the way." She went over to give him a goodnight kiss.

He laughed. "Thanks for letting me know." He kissed her but held onto her. "I like the place. It needs a few things, but we'll get it fixed up. By which, I mean you'll get it fixed up and I'll help when I can."

She smiled. "I wouldn't have it any other way."

He looked up. "Is there a bathroom up there, too?"

"And a shower. Full service."

"Fantastic. Do we have towels?"

"And sheets and pillows and soap. We're living high."

"Great. I'm about to follow you up and take advantage of all that high living."

"I approve. You smell like a kitchen." Usually when he got home, he'd shower, then watch TV for an hour or so to unwind. The only TV in the bungalow was a small one she'd been able to borrow from the resort's replacement stock, thanks to Duke. As soon as they got one of their own, it would get returned.

"That reminds me—do I have clean stuff for tomorrow?"

She made a face and held out her hands. "No. But I can fix that. Take off your clothes."

He laughed and slipped out of his chef's coat. "You really do know the way to a man's heart."

"Yeah, yeah." She took the coat. "Pants, too. There's a second set of this stuff in the plastic laundry bag I brought over, so I'll get them both done and you'll be good for a couple days, but you're going to need a few more coats."

"I'll get them ordered tomorrow, I promise." He crossed his finger over his heart. "Do we have the budget for that, though?"

"Yes!" She grabbed the pants he handed her and went over to the pantry, where the washer and dryer were, to start a load. "As a matter of fact, Olivia sent out a text about an hour ago to tell us that almost all of the embezzled funds are being returned in about two weeks or so. We're going to be just fine."

"Wow. How did she swing that? I was sure they'd have to keep those funds as evidence. If they even found them."

Grace shook her head. "I don't know but that's an interesting question. I'll have to ask her tomorrow. How was Chantelle tonight?"

"Great. Her desserts are killing it. We actually ran out of two of them tonight."

"I knew she'd be a good addition." Grace added a

detergent pod. No wonder he was eager to include her in the cookbook.

"And you were right. She'll be in early tomorrow to finish the wedding cake."

"Did you see it?"

"No, she just told me that's why she was coming in early."

"I hope it's good. Not that I'm worried. Chantelle seems like she's got her business handled."

"She does. I could use a few more line cooks with that kind of attitude." He started for the stairs.

She followed him up to get the rest of the laundry. "You'll get there."

"I will, I know. Just ready for it to happen sooner rather than later."

"I understand that." But her mind was stuck on the cake. It would be good, wouldn't it? Because if it wasn't, they'd be out of time and options to get anything else made.

*It will be good.* She kept telling herself that. She was just a little stressed about this wedding. It was going to set a standard for what they could offer at the resort and if it didn't go well, they'd be unlikely to get more of that kind of business.

Even with the embezzled funds being returned, they still needed to bring in more revenue. They had more people to support. It was the kind of situation that would have pushed her to the bottle just a few short weeks ago.

Not anymore, though. She grabbed the laundry bag and went back downstairs. She heard David turn the shower on.

Everything would be fine. She just had to breathe and have faith. She threw the laundry in, set the timer to delay for an hour to give him a chance to get through his shower, then she closed the pantry doors and went over to look out the windows at the view beyond.

Even in the dark, Compass Key was beautiful. She didn't need a drink. She had all the mood lifters she needed right here.

# Chapter Thirty-eight

Katie woke up to her phone buzzing. *Really? On a Saturday morning?* Who could be calling her? Bleary-eyed, she picked up the phone off the nightstand and looked at the screen. She hit the button to accept the call and put the phone to her ear as she sat up a little higher. "Maxine?"

"Yes, sweetheart, it's me. I know it's Saturday morning and I should be letting my superstar sleep in, but I have things cooking and I need Daniel's number." She laughed. "Things cooking! I crack myself up."

Katie blinked to clear the sleep from her eyes. "Who's Daniel?"

"The chef! Your friend's husband?"

"David," Katie corrected her. She straightened more. "What kind of things?"

"Well, as it happens, I had dinner with Gayle Pennington last night and, would you believe it, her brother, Tom Sitwell, is the managing editor of *Tasters* magazine. They're, like, the number one food magazine in the world, honey. Anyway, I asked her if she knew how cookbooks were selling these days and she said she didn't know but that I'd reminded her of something Tom had just told her."

Katie was mostly awake now and trying to hold on to the story thread so Maxine didn't have to start again.

"It seems the magazine is doing this summer series on head chefs at famous resorts and one of the chefs Tom had lined up backed out for some reason and, of course, I immediately told her I knew of the most perfect replacement. Daniel."

"David."

"Right. But listen, if he does this interview, it raises his street cred, you see? And then I can get him a better deal on the cookbook, which I know I can make happen if he does this interview. It's a Catch-22. But in a good way. So I need his number."

Katie needed coffee. She could practically smell it, she wanted some so bad. "I don't have it, I only have his wife's number. But I can call Grace and get it for you."

"Fabulous. I owe you. How's the book coming?"

Katie exhaled, thankful she'd written yesterday so she didn't have to lie. "I'm really happy with the pages I did yesterday."

"Outstanding news. I have no doubt we'll be able to get a staggering advance for this next series. Your name has been everywhere lately."

"You might see it out there again today. I went to a gallery party last night with Owen. We had our photo taken for the local paper."

"Keep it up. It sells books. Gotta run. Get me that number."

"Will do. Have a good one."

"You, too." Maxine hung up.

Katie put her phone on the bed next to her and ran her hands over her face. She felt a little like she'd been woken up by a pack of excited puppies. But this was great news for Grace and David. Assuming David would do the interview. She couldn't imagine why he wouldn't.

She got up, picked up her phone, and went out to the kitchen. Sophie was sitting on the couch in the living room, laptop in front of her, working away, a cup of coffee steaming on the table. Fabio was sitting on his cat condo by the window, watching a bird on the porch railing and cackling at it.

"You're up?" Her eyes went back to the cup. "And you made coffee?"

Sophie nodded. "Yes and yes."

"You're my favorite sister."

"I'm also your only sister."

"Semantics." Katie shuffled to the pot, poured herself a cup, and doused it with sugar and cream, then carried it over to sit near Sophie.

"Did I hear you on the phone with Max?"

"You did." Katie sipped the hot liquid. It hugged her soul.

Sophie looked at her. "Anything I need to know about?"

Katie shook her head. "No. It was about David, actually. I had emailed Maxine about the possibility of getting a cookbook deal for him and, as it turns out, she may have gotten him an interview in *Tasters*."

"Really?" Sophie's brows lifted. "That's a pretty good get."

"It is," Katie said. "I'm sure she'll want him to sign with her before that gets confirmed, but she's pretty sure she can get him a cookbook deal if he does this interview."

"Cool. Gotta love that Maxine. She's a go-getter."

"That she is." Katie looked at her phone. It was barely eight a.m. She wasn't sure David and Grace would be up. Grace, maybe. Not that this wasn't worth being woken up for, but today and tomorrow were going to be busy. She hated to deprive anyone of their sleep.

She sent Grace a text. *Are you awake?*

Then she went back to her coffee. She was almost ready for a second cup. A shower would help, too. She certainly wasn't going to go back to bed now. Maybe she'd write for an hour or two, then see what she could help with for the wedding.

After a second cup of coffee.

Although she probably ought to check in with Amanda and make sure there wasn't something she needed Katie for. Katie wanted to be available to help. She knew what a big deal this wedding was.

She picked up her phone to text Amanda and it vibrated in her hand with Grace's answer.

*I'm up. Barely.*

*Same here.* Katie paused. She had too much to say to explain it all in text. *Okay if I call?*

*Give me ten minutes. Need coffee.*

Katie texted back a thumbs-up emoji. If there was anything she understood, it was Grace's last two words. She got up, looking at Sophie. "You want a refill?"

Sophie nodded. "More than you know. But I have to get up to get sugar and creamer anyway." She pushed to her feet.

Together they went into the kitchen and fixed themselves second cups, then each returned to their seats.

Katie drank a little from her cup before texting Amanda. *Just up. Do you need me immediately? If not, I'd like to write for a bit.*

*Go write*, Amanda answered. *I'll text when/if I need you.*

*TY.* Katie set her phone next to her on the chair and picked up her cup again. She'd shower after she talked to Grace. Then she'd get to work. She held her cup in both hands, looking over the rim at her sister. "What are you working on over there?"

"Jenny made all new headers and banners for your social media. I'm replacing them now. We're working on taking your branding up a notch."

"Yeah? I like the sound of that. Can I see?"

Sophie turned her laptop around. "What do you think?"

It was beautiful. The dark brocade background had an overhead shot of a woman on a velvet chaise reading Katie's last book. She was wearing a silk robe, and next to her was a small table holding a glass of wine, and a box of chocolates. Curled up by her feet was a beautiful long-haired cat. The tagline read, "Iris Deveraux – the ultimate indulgence."

"It's certainly different than anything I've had before." Her last banner had featured three of her book covers against a simple background with her name and website.

"That's the point," Sophie said. "We're selling you as a brand. A mood. We're trying to appeal to what readers want most right now. An escape from their everyday life. A way to leave their cares and worries behind and disappear into your world. We want them to think of you as a comfort read. We want to inhabit the same place in their brain where chocolate and wine live. When they would normally reach for a raspberry truffle or a glass of chardonnay, now they'll also think, 'Iris Devereaux novel.'"

Katie was impressed. "Wow. That's more than I ever would have thought of."

Sophie smiled. "Jenny is worth twice what you're paying her. I'm serious. You should have hired her years ago."

"Better late than never, right?"

"Right."

Still holding onto her coffee, Katie picked up her phone and stood. "I'm going to call Grace, then take a shower. After that I'm going to write for a bit."

"You want breakfast? I was going to make a frittata."

"Heck, yes, I want breakfast if it's frittata."

Sophie smiled. "I'll call you when it's ready."

"Thanks." Katie walked back to her room. Sophie only made frittata on the days she had time for that kind of thing. Hiring Jenny had been a smart move for all kinds of reasons.

Katie set her coffee on the dresser and dialed Grace. She answered right away. "Morning."

"Morning. Sorry to call so early but something's come up. Something good." Katie explained the whole Maxine and *Tasters* story.

Grace said nothing.

"You still there?"

"Yes, sorry. I'm just trying to process everything you just told me. Is this real?"

"A hundred percent. I'm sure Maxine will want to sign him as a client before any of this becomes official, otherwise she makes nothing off the cookbook deal, which she feels is a guarantee if he does this interview. So there's that."

"I don't think he'll care. I mean, none of this would be happening without her, so—"

"The cookbook we could still get done, but if she gets him a deal, there will be a lot less work on our part and he'll get an advance. No clue how much, but it'll be something. That's the big difference between traditional publishing and self-publishing. He may also get a little more press if he goes the traditional route."

"At this point, less work makes the traditional option a no-brainer," Grace said. "The last thing he needs is more work."

"I hear you. Then I have your blessing to give Maxine his number?"

"By all means. I'll text it to you right now. The only thing is, can she give him at least another hour to sleep?"

Katie laughed. "I'll make sure of it."

"Thanks. Are you coming to help with wedding prep?"

"Amanda said she didn't need me right away, so I'm going to shower and sit down at my computer for a bit." Katie was actually eager to get back to her story. "I'd like to knock out a couple thousand words today if possible, but I don't want to shortchange you guys, either. I'll tell you what I told Amanda. If you need me, just text."

"I'm sure we'll be all right. We can't have you missing a deadline because you were hanging party streamers."

Katie snorted. "I'll write as fast as I can."

"Thank you for everything you've done with the cookbook. I don't think David ever imagined he'd end up with a literary agent."

"You're welcome. Maxine's a little frenetic but she's good people. He'll be in good hands. Keep me posted."

"Will do. I hope you write all the words. Talk to you later."

"Thanks. Later." Katie hung up, still smiling. It was so nice to be able to help friends. And a cookbook based on The Palms restaurant would end up benefitting all of them if it did well. Katie picked up her coffee and headed for the shower, but when she got into the bathroom, she stared at the deep soaking tub.

Why not start her day with a bubble bath? She was a romance author. And a bubble bath seemed perfect for the woman whose books were the ultimate indulgence.

# Chapter Thirty-nine

Leigh Ann sat across from Olivia in Leigh Ann's new bungalow. There was a lot to be done to make the place feel like home, but nothing pressing. Once her things arrived, she'd make the space over in her own style and in her own time. "Thanks for coming over and bringing coffee."

Olivia smiled. "Thanks for having me. Jenny was just getting up when I was leaving, so this worked out."

"I figured it would be the easiest way to go over all the things that need attention at the spa and fitness center." Leigh Ann sipped her coffee.

"Agreed. I'm sure we'll be busy the rest of the day with wedding stuff."

"No doubt."

Olivia had her laptop set up and was looking at something on her screen. "I'm going to take notes on everything, but I won't really be able to budget the funds until we get bids in."

"Do we have to get bids? I talked to Duke about it a little bit last night at the party. He's going to help me with all of that. He and his dad can do a lot of it, he thinks. That should save some money."

"It should," Olivia said. "And I'm happy to give them the business. I'd prefer to keep it in-house anyway, although technically Jack isn't a resort employee."

Leigh Ann pondered that. "What if we made him one? At least for the duration of the repairs."

"Do you think Jack would be amenable to that? He is retired. He might not want to be employed again. Especially if he's already collecting social security. There are limits on what a person can earn."

"We could ask. It would make things simpler. Although maybe he'd make more as a contractor."

Olivia pursed her lips. "But he might have to increase his insurance for a bigger job like this. I don't know how that works. I'm happy to talk to him. Or Amanda could do it. She knows him better than any of us."

Leigh Ann nodded. "We can bring it up when we see her."

"All right," Olivia said. She poised her fingers over the keyboard. "Let's start with the spa. What's the first item?"

For the next twenty minutes, Leigh Ann went through her notes and detailed everything Manuela had told her about and what she'd seen with her own eyes.

Olivia looked shocked. "I had no idea things had been that neglected. Does the spa look bad?"

"Not really. Manuela's done a great job of keeping things hidden. She's done a great job in general, despite the lack of upkeep and staff."

Olivia blew out a breath. "We need to get those two beds replaced, along with everything else, obviously, but as soon as that gets done we can bring in more staff. Can you handle the price increases, or do you want help doing that?"

"Manuela and I can handle that. Along with Gina, who's the salon manager."

"Good. Make that a priority, because we'll need to get new spa menus printed up, too."

Leigh Ann jotted a note down about that. There was so much to do and remember, but it wasn't that much different from running her yoga studio. Just more options and different services. "I can handle that. Any idea who the resort uses to print their brochures?"

"No, but Carissa at the front desk might know."

"Good point." Leigh Ann's coffee was almost gone. She could have used a second cup, but she wasn't about to ask Olivia to run back to her place and make more. "Ready for the fitness center?"

"I am."

Giving Olivia all the information on the fitness

center didn't take nearly as long. But when Leigh Ann finished with the necessary repairs, she took a breath and started on the idea she'd had. "I think the fitness area could be consolidated a bit. There are some redundant machines. The free-weight area is huge. Bigger than it needs to be."

"Mm-hmm." Olivia was listening, but from the look in her eyes, Leigh Ann could tell she knew something was up.

"I'd love to create a separate room in the fitness center that could be used for yoga classes. The sunrise yoga on the beach is great, but if I had a studio room, I could give other classes. Even do private lessons, something that could bring in revenue. What do you think? We don't have to do it right away, but I figure if we're already working in there, it would be most convenient to do it now."

"That would make the most sense."

To Leigh Ann, Olivia didn't seem convinced. "The room could be used for other kinds of exercise classes, or as a space to stretch out, or even personal training. I was thinking that sometime in the future we could look into hiring a personal trainer, too. Just a thought."

Olivia nodded. "This is your area of expertise. If you think these are worthwhile changes to make, then I'm all for them."

"Really?" Leigh Ann had anticipated more of a fight from Olivia.

"Sure," Olivia said. "I think positioning ourselves as being more health and fitness focused is a good thing. The resort caters to a good number of celebrities and athletes. Those are people whose livelihoods often depend on their physical well-being."

Leigh Ann nodded, encouraged. "That's a great point. I was thinking, too, that if we have slower months, maybe we could offer some selfcare packages during that time. The kind of thing that might include a daily yoga lesson or session with a personal trainer, plus some additional spa treatments."

"This is all really good." Olivia smiled. "I like the way you're thinking. You've really taken this all to heart, haven't you?"

Leigh Ann shrugged, pleased with Olivia's assessment. "If I'm going to live here and do this job, I'm going to put all of my efforts into it. After all, whatever success I have, we all share in."

"I love that." Olivia drained her coffee cup. "Let's get moving on this as quickly as we can. We're losing money by not being able to operate at full capacity in the spa and salon. I don't think we're adequately selling those services to guests, either, so once we're fully up and running, that should become the new focus."

"What do you think about opening the spa to people who aren't guests of the resort?" Leigh Ann had mixed feelings about it herself, but she wanted Olivia's input.

"The same way I feel about opening the restaurant to non-guests. I'm not sure." Olivia let out a soft laugh. "I know that's not helpful."

"What if..." Leigh Ann was thinking as she spoke, hoping inspiration came that way. "It was something else we only did during the slower months?"

Olivia pointed at her. "Now that might work. At any rate, it would give us a chance to try it out, right? According to what the books have shown me, the summer months are the slowest because it's the hottest here. Too hot for some. But that doesn't mean we might not get locals who want to try out the spa and restaurant."

"And the spa could be ready for more bookings by then."

"So would the restaurant. I don't want to swamp David any more than he is right now. He's trying to do some additional hiring, too, from what Grace has told me." Olivia typed something into her notes. "Let's talk to everyone else about it, but I like that game plan. I think it's the perfect way to increase revenue when we need it the most."

Leigh Ann smiled. "Awesome. I couldn't be happier."

Olivia closed her laptop. "Can I ask how things went with Marty last night?"

Leigh Ann exhaled. "About the same as they always do. Except I think he got a full-frontal view of just how much I've moved on. I'm so tired of this divorce nonsense, Olivia. I can't even explain just how maddening it is."

"I can imagine. My divorce from Simon was nothing like this. He was ready to move on and so was I. Doesn't mean things weren't contentious or happened as quickly as I would have liked, but it now seems like a walk in the park compared to what you're going through."

Leigh Ann stared toward the windows and the bright blue sky and sunshine just beyond them. "It'll be over eventually. I cling to that."

"It will be. I just hope it happens sooner rather than later."

"Me, too." Leigh Ann looked at her friend. "I guess we should go find Amanda and see what needs doing."

"Sounds good." Olivia got up. "I'm going to take my laptop and the travel mugs back to my place, then head over. Do you know where she is?"

"No, but if you wait, I'll help you carry your stuff, then we can go together. I just need to grab my phone and key and put my shoes on."

"I can wait," Olivia said.

"Just be a sec." Leigh Ann went upstairs to get her things, her mind still on Marty.

Had last night made any difference to him and the

divorce? Or had she screwed up by inviting him? It was possible that seeing her happy without him could have caused him to dig his heels in further.

She put on a pair of slip-on sneakers. It was good she had the spa and fitness center to concentrate on, because dwelling on Marty and this wretched divorce would only make her lose her marbles.

# Chapter Forty

Olivia and Leigh Ann found Amanda in the pavilion with Grace and Duke, who was up on a stepladder, hanging lanterns from the beams. Amanda was conferring with Grace about something.

Olivia lifted her hands to announce their arrival with a wave. "Hi. Leigh Ann and I are here, ready to work. What needs to be done?"

Amanda gave Grace a nod before answering Olivia. "Morning. We need the beach set up for the ceremony. That means chairs, the arch, maybe some kind of path delineated for the bride to walk down. Mindy will be bringing the flowers over soon, but of course, they'll all be stored in the conference room until tomorrow. And we won't put flower petals down until right before the ceremony. Regardless, she'll need the chairs and arch in place. Can you guys handle that?"

"Sure." Leigh Ann nodded and looked at Olivia. "Right?"

"Right." How hard could it be for two people to set up chairs and an arch?

"Great, thank you." Amanda seemed relieved. "Everything is in the second storage room. Do you know where that is?"

Olivia shook her head. "Nope."

Grace gave them a nod. "I can show you. I have to go back to the kitchen to help David anyway. Come on."

Olivia and Leigh Ann followed Grace, who kept up a good pace despite the boot on her foot.

"The dance floor needs to be brought out here, too," Amanda called after them.

Olivia lifted her hand to acknowledge that they'd heard her. "Today's going to be a dirty, sweaty day, isn't it?"

Leigh Ann snorted. "Seems that way."

"There's a cart you can use to bring the pieces of the dance floor out," Grace said as she led them into the main building. "But seriously, after this wedding, we need to work on getting more organized. Both of these storage rooms are a mess of stuff. There's no reason this space couldn't be used better."

Even without seeing the rooms, Olivia agreed. "We need to start a master list of all the jobs we want to accomplish. Big or small. Doesn't matter. If we keep track of them, we won't forget anything."

"I'm all for that," Grace said. "But these rooms need

to go at the top." She pulled out her keys and unlocked the door, then pushed it wide open and flicked on the light. "See?"

Olivia made a face, and beside her, Leigh Ann let out a small groan. "This looks like a hoarding situation."

Grace nodded. "And that's after Amanda and I tried to straighten things up a bit. Basically, anything anyone wasn't sure about throwing away or saving got saved. In here. The room next door is about the same, but it's got a lot of shelving, so most of the stuff in there is smaller items and things in boxes."

Leigh Ann looked at Olivia. "Let's just work on dealing with what we need. We can worry about cleaning it up next week."

"Agreed," Olivia said. "Today has to be all about getting ready for the wedding. There will be plenty of time for the rest of it later."

Grace walked into the room and pointed out a few things. "Chairs are under this tarp. It's a small wedding party, so we don't need massive amounts. Ten will be plenty. Amanda suggested setting them up in a half-circle around the arch, leaving an aisle space in the center for the bride to come through."

"Okay," Olivia said. "So five on each side, half-circle, arch at the center. We can do that. Where's the arch?"

Grace moved a few feet back and touched another

tarped object. "Here. It's going to have to be opened up and then secured into the sand somehow. Once it gets the flowers put on it, it's going to be a little top heavy. We need to make sure it doesn't blow over."

"That would not be good." Olivia put her hands on her hips. "But we might need Duke for that."

Grace nodded. "He's here all day as much as we need him."

Leigh Ann glanced at Olivia. "Maybe we can talk to him at lunch about the spa and fitness center."

"Yes," Olivia said. "Let's do that."

Grace's brow furrowed. "What's going on with the spa and fitness center?"

"Lots of work to be done, repairs to be made, equipment to be updated, that kind of thing," Olivia said.

"Olivia and I sat down over coffee to go over it all this morning." Leigh Ann tucked a strand of hair behind her ear. "But the short story is the fitness center needs some work but the spa can't operate at full capacity because of the repairs that need to be done and the lack of staff."

Grace wrinkled her nose. "That must be costing us money."

"It is," Leigh Ann confirmed.

"Which is why," Olivia said, "fixing it is a priority. But don't worry, that doesn't mean your storage rooms won't be taken care of, too."

"Thanks." Grace smiled. "I'm happy to spearhead the reorganization project."

"I appreciate that," Olivia said. "Now, where do these chairs go? I know on the beach, but which section of it?"

"Right," Grace said. "I should show you that, too. Come on, let's all grab some chairs and make the trip worthwhile." She pulled back the tarp, uncovering the rack of gold bamboo folding chairs.

They each took two chairs, then let Grace lead the way again. Olivia and Leigh Ann would only have to make two more trips. One with the rest of the chairs, and a second with the arch, which she had a feeling would require both of them to carry it.

Grace took them through the building and out the front, then around the side and down a path lined with foliage and beautiful smooth-trunk palms. Beyond was a broad expanse of tranquil beach and serene blue water. In the distance, the mainland could be seen as a swipe of green. "This is it."

"It's perfect." Olivia leaned one chair against her leg so she could unfold the other one. "What a beautiful spot to get married in."

Leigh Ann nodded. "We need to social media the daylights out of this wedding. When we're allowed to, I mean. I know it's still a big secret. But pictures of this setup might go viral. It'll at least make it onto some wedding Pinterest boards. We could become a destination wedding spot."

"Amanda would love that." Grace was unfolding her second chair. "But do you really think that's possible with the kinds of prices Mother's charges?"

Leigh Ann smiled. "I do. People love exclusivity. And if you want a small, personal, unique wedding, what better place could there be than a luxury resort on a private island that also happens to resemble paradise?"

"She's got a point," Olivia said. "But if you want to make those photos mean something, they've got to go out with some kind of Mother's Resort watermark on them or that information will be lost in the sharing."

Leigh Ann shot Olivia a look. "When did you get so social media savvy?"

"When my very social media savvy daughter started working in the same space as me." Olivia laughed. "I pick up a lot of things just from listening to her do business."

Grace was nodding. "I need to do the same thing with the photos of the food I take. They should all have The Palms watermark on them. I want to set up an Instagram account for David, too, for him to share food pics and recipes and stuff like that. To help build his chef rep. Chantelle should probably do that, too. If she doesn't already." She grinned all of a sudden. "I haven't told you guys this yet, but Katie worked some magic on David's behalf."

Olivia moved her chair to about where she thought it ought to be in the sand. "What kind of magic?"

"Cookbook magic," Grace said. "Interview magic. Agent magic. I don't know what to call it but it's all of those things. Katie told her agent about David and the possibility of him doing a cookbook and somehow, as of about an hour ago, David has now signed with her agent, who is actively pursuing a cookbook deal for him. He's also going to be interviewed by *Tasters* magazine for a series they're doing about chefs at fancy resorts."

Leigh Ann gasped, "That's amazing."

"Oh, Grace, you must be thrilled." Olivia smiled. "And David must be beside himself."

Grace laughed. "He's a little busy with wedding food, but once he gets a free moment, I'm sure he's going to freak out. After he's done freaking out about the fact that he's cooking for J. Henry Parker."

Olivia pressed her hands together. There was so much fun, exciting stuff going on. It made all the work ahead of them less daunting. "You guys. We are so blessed to be here."

"We really are." Leigh Ann glanced out at the water. "Look at this place. It's unbelievable that this is our backyard."

Olivia nodded in wordless appreciation. She'd

been blessed with Jenny's presence, too, and blessed with the healing of that relationship.

A new thought came to her. Maybe it was all the wedding stuff going on, but she couldn't help but wonder. With Jenny and Nick spending so much time together, would Olivia soon be blessed with a son-in-law?

# Chapter Forty-one

Amanda collapsed into bed, the long, hard day of work behind her, and another long day of work ahead of her. Thankfully, tomorrow wouldn't be quite as hard. Although it would probably be a little frenzied at times.

The best weddings were like a duck in water. Smooth sailing on top, the frantic paddling under the water where no one could really see it.

She was happy to do the paddling if it meant the day went off without a hitch. All that mattered was giving the bride and groom the best wedding day ever and great memories to look back on.

That was her last thought before sleep took over.

Her eyes opened to a thin sliver of daylight streaming through her curtains. She'd left a tiny gap on purpose when she'd closed them just so the sun could slip through. It was a nice way to wake up.

She smiled. Today was Wedding Day.

She looked at the time, then jumped out of bed and got moving. Mindy, the florist, would be here in an hour to start arranging all the flowers she'd brought in yesterday. Her husband was coming with her, too. A retired photographer, he'd come out of retirement for this special occasion, something Amanda would be eternally grateful for.

Duke would be bringing Jamie over a little after that, so she could get set up as well. She was playing the music for both the ceremony and the reception.

Eddie was on duty and would be bringing J. Henry and his soon-to-be-bride in. They were scheduled to arrive by one. The wedding was supposed to take place at three – provided J. Henry's fiancée agreed to the surprise nuptials – with the reception to follow immediately.

She turned on the shower, ran downstairs, started some coffee, then came back up and opened her closet. She'd meant to pick out her outfit for the day sooner, but she'd been too tired last night.

As boring as it might be, she quickly decided on khaki capris and her new Mother's Resort turquoise polo shirt she'd recently gotten from Iris. Better to be easily spotted as a staff member on a day like this.

She got into the shower, her mind racing with everything that needed to be done.

At least the cake was taken care of. It had been one of the last things she'd checked on yesterday. Chantelle had done a masterful job. All the cake needed was the addition of fresh flowers, which would be arriving with Mindy.

Olivia was going along with Eddie on the boat to help with bringing the flowers back.

It was going to be a busy day for all of them.

She turned the shower off and got out, drying herself and her hair with a kind of nervous energy she hadn't felt since the last wedding she'd planned. But this was a little different. There was more riding on this. Not because the event was for two celebrities, but because the event was really for five women Amanda loved dearly.

Pulling this wedding off was all about forging a new path for them at the resort. Creating a new revenue stream but also increasing the resort's potential. And that meant a way to earn more for Leigh Ann, Grace, Olivia, Katie, Iris, and herself.

So what if Katie didn't need the money the way the rest of them did. They were all in this together and she'd already proven how generous she was.

Amanda did simple makeup, then got dressed and went back downstairs to the coffee that was now ready. She had her binder with all of her notes for the day, her purse, her key, her phone, and another bag she considered her wedding emergency kit.

It held everything from scissors to body tape. Bandages, clear nail polish, emery boards, antinausea medication, Aspirin, cold cream, a smaller bag full of makeup, hairspray, tweezers, tissues, breath spray, a travel toothbrush and toothpaste, superglue, phone chargers, a lint roller, bobby pins, and more.

There was nothing she hadn't thought of and, during her time as a wedding planner, nothing she hadn't used.

She poured a big cup of coffee and drank it while she made three eggs scrambled in butter and toasted an English muffin, which she spread with peanut butter. When she was almost done, she refilled her coffee and had a second cup. This was her power breakfast, the same one she ate before every wedding, because it stayed with her a long time.

It was doubtful she'd eat until well after the reception had begun. Although her wedding emergency kit did also contain granola bars, cheese and peanut butter crackers, and beef jerky, that wasn't her preferred meal.

She went back upstairs to brush her teeth, then she was out the door and off to make sure nothing had gone wrong overnight.

By the time Eddie was on his way back to Compass Key with J. Henry Parker, his fiancée, supermodel Miranda Campbell, and all of their accompanying friends and family, Amanda and the girls had accomplished everything that needed to get done. She knew with great confidence that the resort was one hundred percent ready for this surprise wedding.

The chalkboard at the pavilion's entrance read *Welcome to the Parker-Campbell reception!* Amanda had added a few hearts, flowers, and shells around the edges. Her calligraphy skills weren't so bad after all.

The pavilion looked like a romantic tropical wonderland, lit with glowing string lights, hanging lanterns, and a ton of the battery-operated candles she'd picked up on the mainland tucked into the arrangements. The long, family-style tabletop was scattered with shells, more lanterns, and Mason jars filled with sand, shells, and candles, and low, lush floral compositions that meant everyone would be able to see each other and converse without problems.

The bride and groom would be at the center of the table, their family and friends around them.

All of the pavilion's supporting pillars were wound with white tulle, garlands of fragrant flowers dotted with shells, and sprays of tropical greenery. The dance floor was ready to go, too, outlined with rope lighting to accentuate it even more. The tiki bar that Grace had found had been added at J. Henry's request. Amanda had arranged for a bartender from the resort's Parrot Lounge to provide service there.

Jamie had set up on one side but Duke had helped her hook into the pavilion's speaker system so her music would fill the space. After that, he'd gone to pick up the officiant.

Across from Jamie's spot was the cake table, although the cake itself wouldn't be brought out until right before they were ready for it.

Amanda had seen the finished version. It was three small tiers decorated in gum paste shells, real flowers, and Chantelle's pristine piping skills. Honestly, it was one of the prettiest cakes she'd laid eyes on in years.

The ceremony site on the beach, marked by the new chalkboard sign that read *Parker-Campbell Wedding*, looked every inch the fairy tale backdrop with its flowered arch and petal-strewn sand. She'd add more petals right before the ceremony, along with a white silk runner for the bride to walk down, something Mindy had thoughtfully provided. More battery-operated candles in glass lanterns decorated that area, too, even though the day was sunny and bright. Atmosphere was everything.

All that remained now was for J. Henry to actually ask the question. Not if Miranda would marry him—he'd already proposed—but he still needed to ask if she'd marry him on Compass Key *today*.

As Amanda had confirmed with him via many, many texts, he'd be doing that very soon after they arrived. Like, within minutes. She wasn't sure if that meant he was doing it at the marina or here in the lobby or when they arrived in their room, but as soon as Miranda said yes, the ceremony countdown began.

Amanda also knew, via texts, that Miranda's best friend, who was along on the trip, had packed three different wedding dresses for Miranda to choose from.

The resort's top stylist, a woman named Jazz, was at the ready to do Miranda's hair.

Amanda's phone buzzed. She checked the screen.

The message was from Duke. *I'm back with the officiant. Would have been here sooner but officiant lost his glasses. Found them in his suit.*

Amanda closed her eyes for a moment and gave thanks for that small crisis averted. *Thank you. Staging everyone in meeting room near lobby.*

*On our way.*

She headed for the meeting room herself, to await J. Henry's text that Miranda had said yes.

She walked in and saw Katie, Sophie, Jenny, Olivia, and Leigh Ann already in there, along with Mindy, the florist, and her photographer husband, Rob, and Jamie, Duke's sister. Grace, she knew, was in the kitchen with David, doing whatever needed doing to make the food side of things go as smoothly as possible. Chantelle would be bringing out the cake.

Leigh Ann looked up as Amanda entered. "Did she say yes?"

Amanda shook her head. "I'm not sure they're even on the island yet."

"They are," Olivia said. "Eddie just texted to say they were here."

Amanda took a breath, her nervous system fully awake and preparing for the next step. "Won't be long then."

"What if she doesn't say yes?" Jenny asked.

Amanda went completely still. "Never say those words again."

Katie snorted. "Yeah, you want to jinx everything? Of course she'll say yes. He's a famous Hollywood director and she's a supermodel. They're a match made in celebrity heaven. And I, for one, am thrilled that someone else is about to give the paparazzi something to talk about."

That caused a ripple of laughter to go through the small group.

Amanda's phone buzzed again, this time with a short, simple message that she immediately understood.

*SHE SAID YES!*

# Chapter Forty-two

The walk was long, but Iris wasn't about to be deterred. This was the first wedding that had taken place on Compass Key in a long, long time, and she was not about to miss it. Not when Amanda had gotten special permission for her to attend.

Iris had changed into one of her brightest and most festive caftans, a tropical blue floral number that she'd bought a few decades ago in Hawaii. It felt wedding appropriate to her and, indeed, she'd worn it to several weddings years back.

Besides her wedding ring, only one other accessory decorated her outfit. The only one she needed. The only one any woman would need. The Escape Diamond.

Her walker was still beside her chair back at the house. She'd felt strong enough to go out using just her cane. She'd be sitting soon enough. Amanda had promised there would be a chair for her at the ceremony.

Vera walked alongside Iris. She'd insisted. No surprise there, Iris thought. Her housekeeper had turned into a real watchdog since Iris had come home from the hospital. Even Nick wasn't as bad.

But Iris loved Vera, just like Vera loved Iris, so even though Iris pretended Vera's hovering was a bother, it wasn't. Not really. Iris secretly liked being fussed over. At least a little bit.

"How are you doing?" Vera asked.

"I'm fine. How are you doing?" Iris cut her eyes at Vera. "You look like you're falling behind."

Vera hmphed. "I am not. I just thought the weight of that diamond might be slowing you down."

Iris snorted, amused by the banter.

She knew where the ceremony would be, the exact section of beach. It was where all the weddings had always been held. It was the best section of beach for a gathering like that. Private and secluded, with no bungalows nearby.

She was so proud of Amanda for pulling this off. Proud of the rest of the girls for pitching in. She knew they'd helped. Amanda had told her.

These five women were something else. Strong and gutsy and, as they used to say, full of moxie. They weren't afraid of hard work or obstacles, either. They were exactly what this place needed.

Leigh Ann stood at the entrance to the ceremony's location. "Hi, Iris. You look beautiful. And very sparkly."

Iris grinned. "Am I too early or too late?"

"You're just on time. Only two other guests have arrived so far. The ceremony isn't supposed to start for another fifteen minutes."

"I'm happy to sit and wait."

Vera glanced down the path that led to the beach. "You want me to wait for you in the lobby?"

Leigh Ann shook her head. "You can go in, Vera. We made sure there was a seat for you too."

Vera's brows lifted ever so slightly. "You did?"

"Of course," Leigh Ann said.

Amanda came up to them, escorting a tall man with a mop of curly hair, round glasses, and a boyish smile. "Ladies, make way for the groom, please."

J. Henry waved at them, grinning like he'd won a prize at the county fair on his first try. Iris imagined that, in a way, he sort of had. Miranda Campbell seemed like a real catch. Good for him for being so happy about his wedding day, too. She gave him a nod. "Congratulations, young man."

"Thanks. You're Iris Cotton, aren't you?"

She nodded. "That's right."

He touched the center of his chest. "I've heard about you. I'm honored to have you as a guest."

"I'm honored you chose my home to get married in."

Amanda held her palm out, gesturing toward the beach. "We should really get you into position."

He nodded toward the path, then winked at Iris. "Wish me luck."

"You won't need it," she said. "This island is magic. Vows made here last a lifetime."

He grinned. "Very cool. Thanks." Then he headed down the path.

Amanda leaned in toward Iris. "I'm putting that in the wedding brochure." She went after J. Henry.

"Come on," Vera said. "Let's find our seats."

It was a small wedding, so the seats had been set up in a half-circle around the flowered arch where J. Henry and the officiant stood. Behind one of the little half-circles were two seats next to each other. Iris knew those had to be for them. How kind of Mr. Parker to include her and Vera.

The rest of the guests filtered in. The photographer moved about as inconspicuously as possible, taking lots of pictures.

Across from them, Duke's sister, Jamie, took a spot behind the other semi-circle of chairs and began to strum the wedding march on her guitar, playing it with a tropical flare that made Iris smile.

A few moments later, the bride, on her father's arm, walked toward her groom. Her dress was patterned with big, airy floral lace. The split short sleeves fluttered in the breeze and the hemline skimmed the sand. It was perfect, as were her glittery white flipflops and the way her hair had been twisted up but still had loose tendrils around her face.

On her head, she wore a crown of flowers that held a delicate veil.

Iris sniffed. Vera handed her a tissue. And before too long, the vows were said and the happy couple were kissing each other as man and wife.

"That was beautiful," Iris said as the couple walked down the aisle and off toward their reception, followed by their guests.

Vera nodded. "I've missed this. Having weddings on the island, I mean."

"So have I." Iris let out a happy sigh. "I suppose we should go."

Amanda suddenly appeared next to them. "Iris? The bride and groom would like you to join them for a photograph."

"Me?"

Amanda nodded. "They want one with you and with the five of us. Miranda is very impressed that we pulled this off on such short notice and she wants a picture with everyone who helped. She's even asked that I get Chef David to come out."

Iris nodded. "What a kind thing for her to do. We're on our way."

She joined the large group assembled in the pavilion, and was immediately placed in the very middle of the photograph with the bride and groom on either side of her. The honor of that spot was not lost on her.

If only Arthur could see her now. Maybe he could.

After a slew of photographs, Iris shook hands with all of them. The bride kissed her on the cheek and thanked her for making the day possible.

"Oh, it wasn't me," Iris said, leaning on her cane. "My girls did all of this."

She was proud to the point of bursting. She wished Miranda and J. Henry health and happiness, then slipped out of the pavilion with Vera and made her way home, her body tired, but her heart full.

The walk back was slower than the walk to the beach had been, but Vera didn't say a word about it.

"Those women did an amazing job," Vera said.

"Yes, they did. They must be exhausted."

"I'm sure." Vera took a few more steps without saying anything. "I don't know how you feel about it, but we ought to invite them for dinner. They probably won't have the energy to make anything for themselves. We won't do it too late, though. Maybe around six. Then they can get home and relax at a reasonable hour."

"That's a lovely idea. Do we have enough on hand? What would you make?"

"I was thinking that shrimp and pasta dish you like."

"With the peas and bacon?"

Vera nodded. "I could do a little green salad on the side. And there's time to make a coconut custard pie if I get to work on it right away."

"I love that idea. I'll help. I can peel the shrimp."

Vera laughed. "All right, you're on."

When they got back to the house, Vera went straight to the kitchen and began gathering ingredients for the pie. Iris went to her chair and sat so she could text the girls and invite them over. "Six o'clock, right?"

"Right," Vera said. "If these cats let me cook."

Iris smiled. She could hear the three beasts meowing at Vera for food. It was like they knew there was about to be shrimp on the counter.

She sent the girls a text. The responses were quick and thankful. She looked up at Vera. "They're coming."

Dinnertime arrived fast, but Vera had gotten everything done she'd needed to. Iris had peeled the shrimp, then set the big round table. She was still in her caftan, and still wearing her diamond, and still only using her cane.

The girls arrived promptly at six, all of them in their Mother's polo shirts and khaki pants.

Grace carried a large white box in with her. "J. Henry and Miranda wanted you to have some wedding cake, Iris. Although they sent enough for twenty people. Granted, Chantelle made probably enough for fifty, but then, I imagine making a wedding cake for nine would be rather limiting."

"That was very thoughtful of them," Iris said. "We'll definitely enjoy that."

As they settled around the table, Vera included, the talk was all about the wedding. Iris loved that. She wanted to hear every detail. The girls didn't let her down. They filled her in on everything. There was so much laughter and happiness her cheeks ached from smiling.

Leigh Ann's phone went off as they were finishing up. She looked at her screen, then pushed her chair back. "I need to run to the lobby. They have a package for me at the front desk."

"What is it?" Olivia asked.

"No idea." Leigh Ann got up. "Be right back."

"We'll have dessert when you return," Iris said.

Katie patted her stomach as Leigh Ann left. "I'm not sure I have room for dessert."

Vera carried a few plates to the kitchen. "I made coconut custard pie."

"You're a terrible person," Katie said, laughing. "Fine. You've talked me into it." She got to her feet and gathered a few more empty plates. "Let me see if I can burn off a few calories before that gets served."

Amanda, Grace, and Olivia all pitched in to help, too.

"Sit," Vera said. "You've all done enough today already."

Grace smiled. "You're not wrong about that, but I still have enough energy to help a little."

By the time Leigh Ann returned, the table had been cleaned, the dishes loaded into the dishwasher, and Vera was slicing the coconut custard pie.

Leigh Ann came in with a joyous look on her face. She held up the large manilla envelope in her hand. "He signed the papers! My divorce is final!"

Gasps and cheers and happy cries answered her.

Iris put her hand to her mouth, so amazed that Leigh Ann had finally gotten free. "What a perfect ending to a perfect day."

Leigh Ann nodded but looked a little sad suddenly. "One marriage begins while another ends. I suppose it's sort of poetic."

"Are you all right?" Amanda asked.

Leigh Ann smiled. "I'm good. I really am. This seems oddly final, which is what I wanted, but still... Hard to explain. It's just one of those things, you know?" She laughed. "Trust me, I am ready to celebrate this. Bring on the cake!"

Iris twisted to look at Vera. "Don't we have a nice bottle of champagne in the fridge?"

"We do," Vera said. She grinned. "I'll get it out."

Within minutes, they were sitting down to coconut

custard pie, wedding cake, and champagne. A more perfect evening, Iris couldn't imagine.

She lifted her glass. "I love you all. I am so proud of you for what you accomplished today. And that none of you harmed Amanda during the planning stages."

They all laughed.

"But I'm proud of you for more than just today. I'm proud of you for things you haven't even done yet. I know this place is in the best hands possible. Thank you for staying. And for making it possible for me to stay."

Teary gazes surrounded her. Then Calico Jack meowed loudly for attention, making them all laugh some more.

Iris reached down to scratch his head. "I'm proud of you, too, Calico Jack. For being such a good boy."

Katie lifted her glass. "To you, Iris. For making all of this possible."

Grace raised her water. "And to Arthur."

"To Arthur," Amanda said.

"May his memory be eternal," Vera offered.

Olivia put her flute in the air, too. "As long as we're here, I promise you, it will be."

Iris smiled as everyone brought their glasses into the middle to clink them together. Her home was safe. Her life full. Her family surrounding her.

There was nothing more she could want. The island's magic had done its work.

**Want to know when Maggie's next book comes out? Then don't forget to sign up for her newsletter at her website!**

**Also, if you enjoyed the book, please recommend it to a friend. Even better yet, leave a review and let others know.**

## Other Books by Maggie Miller

**The Blackbird Beach series:**

Gulf Coast Cottage

Gulf Coast Secrets

Gulf Coast Reunion

Gulf Coast Sunsets

Gulf Coast Moonlight

Gulf Coast Promises

Gulf Coast Wedding

Gulf Coast Christmas

**About Maggie:**

Maggie Miller thinks time off is time best spent at the beach, probably because the beach is her happy place. The sound of the waves is her favorite background music, and the sand between her toes is the best massage she can think of.

When she's not at the beach, she's writing or reading or cooking for her family. All of that stuff called life. She hopes her readers enjoy her books and welcomes them to drop her a line and let her know what they think!

**Maggie Online:**

www.maggiemillerauthor.com
www.facebook.com/MaggieMillerAuthor

Made in the USA
Middletown, DE
22 July 2025

11064334R00192